SUSAN
WITTIG ALBERT

THE LAST
CHANCE OLIVE
RANCH

BERKLEY PRIME CRIME
New York

BERKLEY PRIME CRIME
Published by Berkley
An imprint of Penguin Random House LLC
375 Hudson Street, New York, New York 10014

ISBN: 9780425280041

Berkley Prime Crime hardcover edition / April 2017
Berkley mass-market edition / March 2018

Printed in the United States of America
3   5   7   9   10   8   6   4

Cover art: *Illustration* © by Joe Burleson; *Olive wood background*
© R Szatkowski/Shutterstock;
Burned parchment © Ganovsky Vladislav/iStockphoto
Cover design by Judith Murello

For Bill, who demonstrates remarkable patience with my efforts to grow olives in the Texas Hill Country

The Legend of the Olive of Athens

To claim possession of the Greek region of Attica, the blustering, boastful god Poseidon struck the soil of the Acropolis with his trident, creating a well as a gift to the people and a symbol of his vast power. The people of the area flocked happily to the well, but to their dismay, they could not drink from it, for it was as salty as seawater. (Poseidon was, after all, the god of the sea.)

Then the beautiful and modest goddess Athena appeared, to dispute Poseidon's rule over the region. Quietly, she knelt down and planted a seed in the soil beside Poseidon's salty well. It grew with an almost magical swiftness into a magnificent olive tree. It flowered and bore fruit, bestowing on the people not only a healthful, nurturing food and medicine, but also wood for their homes and boats and tools, oil for their lamps, and fuel for cooking and heating.

Grateful for Athena's gift, the people chose her as their protector and patron deity. They called their city Athens and themselves Athenians. And for centuries, they revered the olive tree the goddess had planted as the symbol of their prosperous city.

Chapter One

More in the garden grows than the gardener knows.
                                                    Folk Saying

I hate it when the telephone rings at night.

Granted, it wasn't night, technically speaking. It was five a.m., according to the clock on my side of the bed. But the only light in the room was a dim nightlight and my husband and I had both been sound asleep. To me, that qualifies as night.

The phone is on McQuaid's side of the bed, so he was the one who groped for it, found it on the fourth ring, and growled, "Who the hell is this and whaddya want?"

My sentiments exactly, although I admit to lying very still, stiff with apprehension, conducting a mental inventory of the people I love while McQuaid listened to the voice on the other end of the line. Caitie, our daughter, was asleep down the hall, but our son, Brian, is a student at UT Austin. He's not the kind of kid who gets into trouble, but accidents do happen. Not to mention that my mother's husband, Sam, has a history of heart problems, and that my mother—Leatha—is no spring chicken. And Mom and Dad McQuaid are both nearly eighty and—

"Aw, *hell*," McQuaid said, drawing out the word, profoundly regretful. "He's dead?"

Dead. I pulled in a breath and held it, squeezing my eyes shut. "Who?" I whispered. *Who was he? Brian? Sam? Dad McQuaid?*

McQuaid pushed himself into a sitting position, pulling the pillow behind his head. "So where did this thing go down?" His voice was tense, urgent. "Yeah. Southwest Houston, right? Bellaire?"

Southwest Houston. I relaxed a little. Sam was at home at their ranch in South Texas—I'd talked to my mother just the night before. McQuaid's dad didn't drive, and anyway, he and Mom McQuaid were home, too, in Seguin, east of San Antonio. Which left Brian—but he was in Austin.

I caught my lower lip between my teeth. I *thought* Brian was in Austin. He was between terms, working part-time at The Natural Gardener, out on Bee Cave Road. He hadn't mentioned going out of town. But kids are kids. He and some friends might have decided to drive to Houston on a lark and he'd forgotten to let us know.

"Who?" I asked, louder now. I propped myself up on one elbow and put a hand on McQuaid's bare forearm. The room was dark, but the glow-in-the-dark clock cast a faint green shadow over his face. "*Who's* dead? What's going on, McQuaid?"

McQuaid looked down at me and shook his head with a brisk don't-interrupt-me-now frown—his cop frown. No, his *ex*-cop frown. I flopped back on my pillow. I didn't think he was talking about Brian. And if it wasn't about family, it must be about work. My husband is a part-time private eye, and PIs don't punch a clock. He's been known to work twenty-four-hour shifts, catch a couple of hours of sleep, and do it all over again. Still, he doesn't usually get calls at this hour of the night. I squinted at the clock again and groaned. Morning. At this hour of the morning.

McQuaid was shaking his head as if he didn't quite believe what he was hearing. "How in the hell did he manage that? Death Row is *tight*." He listened a moment more, then spat out, "Damn it, Jessie, if they can't keep a better handle on their prisoners, maybe they deserve to lose a few."

Ah. There had been a prison break. And Jessie had to be Jess Branson, one of McQuaid's cop buddies from his days as a detective in Houston Homicide. But that still left the question of why Jessie was calling our house at the unholy hour of five a.m. about a prison break. McQuaid no longer wore a badge. If a prisoner or two had escaped, tough titty. Somebody else was dealing with it. I closed my eyes. So go away, Jess. Get some coffee, get a doughnut, get off the phone.

"It doesn't sound good," McQuaid was saying grimly. "Okay, you guys work it at your end, and I'll get on it here." He leaned over to peer at the clock. "Hell, no, not *now*, Jess. It's not even six yet. Nothing's going to happen in the next hour, man. Max may be a freakin' genius, but he hasn't learned to fly. So far as I know, anyway."

Max. I frowned. He had to be talking about Max Mantel. Bad Max Mantel. McQuaid had been the lead detective on the team that tracked him down and arrested him. Mantel had been charged with killing two teenage girls who were trying to blow the whistle on his sex trafficking ring. McQuaid had once said that Bad Max was one of the smartest criminals he had ever put away, which was why the man had managed to keep his slimy slave trade hidden under the rocks for so long.

That had been ten or twelve years ago. McQuaid and I had been dating then, and I had listened to his take on the prosecution's case with a great deal of interest. While it is true that there is nothing in the law that I detest more than the death penalty, it is also true that every now and then there's a case—and a criminal—that causes me to think twice about my objections. Bad Max was one of them. I've never blamed McQuaid for saying—and only half joking—that it was too bad he hadn't pulled the trigger when he had Mantel in his gunsight and saved the state the cost of an execution.

Anyway, I was rooting for the prosecution, which had been deftly handled by smart-mouthed assistant district attorney Paul Watkins, whom I had also dated once upon a faraway time. Paul was a flamboyant showoff who loved being the center of attention. But he had the better case, hands down, and the jury did just what he asked them to do. They sent Bad Max to Huntsville. To Death Row.

My eyes popped open.

Max Mantel had *escaped?* But Huntsville was a maximum-security prison. Nobody had gotten out of there since 1998, when a Death Row inmate cut through a fence, scaled a roof, and went over the top of two security fences, clad in a clumsy suit of cardboard body armor to protect him from the razor wire. Finding the guy took a full week, five hundred officers, and a half-dozen tracking dogs, assisted by four cop choppers equipped with heat sensors. No doubt a similar team would be assembled and sent out to recapture Bad Max. But Mc-Quaid was no longer on the payroll. I didn't see what any of this had to do with him, especially at this hour.

I slid down and pulled the sheet over my head. Maybe I could manage a few more minutes of sleep before I had to get up and pack. Today was Friday, and Ruby and I were driving to the Last Chance Olive Ranch, where we were leading a workshop on Saturday afternoon. Ruby had been trying for months to get me out to the ranch, which is owned by her friend Maddie Haskell. She had even suggested that we tack on a couple of extra days—Sunday and Monday—for a little R and R. I was glad to agree. The month of May had been busy at the shops, and I was looking forward to the quiet pleasures of a long weekend. But I wasn't going to get any more shut-eye.

"Okay. I'll do that." McQuaid's voice was clipped. "In the meantime, you'd better call Carl Zumwalt. He's retired now, but he was the other lead on the Mantel investigation. He's still living in the Houston area—Pearland, I think. If Max is the one who took Watkins out, he might go for Carl next. Tell him to watch his back."

I flapped the sheet down and propped myself on my elbows. "Took Watkins out? Paul Watkins?" I sucked in a breath, hardly believing what I'd heard. "Mantel went after the *district attorney*?"

Because Paul Watkins, the larger-than-life prosecutor who had sent Mantel to Death Row, had gotten a career boost out of the case. He was now the Big Cheese he had always wanted to be: Harris County district attorney. I'd been hearing from people who knew him that he'd be the next candidate for Texas attorney general. After that, maybe governor.

McQuaid gave me a surprised look, as if he'd forgotten I was there. "Sure, Jessie," he said into the phone. "Listen, I can't get into it now. Thanks for the heads-up. I'll give you a call in a couple of hours." He hung up and switched on the small bedside light. "Mantel got out of Huntsville night before last. They're still trying to figure out how he did it—must've had inside help. The dogs went out, but they lost him at the highway. He probably had outside help, too. An accomplice waiting with a car. They're not sure where—"

"Wait a minute." I was still trying to get my mind around what I thought I'd heard. "Max Mantel *killed* Paul Watkins?" Paul—bigger than life and twice as vigorous—was *dead*?

McQuaid rubbed a hand across the dark morning stubble on his jaw. "They don't know for sure it was Mantel, China. But one of the Huntsville snitches reported that he'd been threatening to kill everybody associated with his conviction." He slanted me a quick look, and I knew he had said more than he intended. He cleared his throat and added hastily, "Somebody was waiting when Watkins and . . . When Watkins got home late last night from a party. Shot him. Jess says his team is still processing the scene."

I was still grappling with the terrible news about Paul, but I snatched at what McQuaid had just said. "Kill everybody associated with his conviction? That means—"

"Big talk," McQuaid said firmly. "You know how these cons are, China. They like to blow hot air. Mantel is probably in Mexico by now. And Watkins has put away more than his share of criminals since he's been in the DA's office. Any one of a couple of dozen would have been glad to pull that trigger."

He was right about that. Paul had been in the justice business for a long time. Anybody he'd ever prosecuted, any gang he'd gone after—they could all have him on their hit lists.

"Didn't have to be Mantel," McQuaid added firmly. "Probably wasn't, in fact."

As if that settled everything. As if I should just slide down under the covers and go back to sleep.

"But it *could* have been Mantel." The goose bumps were prickling across my shoulders and I could taste the sour fear at the back of my throat. I was remembering the awful night when McQuaid took a bullet in the neck and I thought he was going to die. Cops die, yes, every day. You never think it's going to happen to *your* cop, until it does, until he doesn't come home, never comes home again.

I swallowed hard. "Jess was calling to warn you, wasn't he? And you told him to warn Carl Zumwalt, too. You think Mantel is going to—"

I broke off, thinking that it really might have been better if McQuaid had taken Mantel out when he had the chance. Paul would still be alive right now, and McQuaid wouldn't be in danger.

"Hey." McQuaid swung toward me, his weight on one elbow, one eyebrow quirked. He touched my lips with his finger. "Don't sweat it, babe. I've been threatened by crooks who are a damn sight meaner than Mantel. I'm a big guy, you know. I can take care of myself." Eyes light, he bent over me, humorous, confident, macho. "Hey. I can take care of you, too."

I knew he was trying to reassure me. I also knew that he was about to use sex to distract me—which usually works because I am easily distracted by the prospect of sex with my husband. I pushed the fear down deep inside of me and brushed the dark hair off his forehead.

"Oh, yeah?" I was willing to go along, to play his game. It might make both of us feel better. It might make me forget that Paul—so full of life, with so much to live for—was dead and that the man who killed him might be coming to kill my husband. "You think so, do you, big fella?"

"I know so," he whispered, and put his hand on my breast. "Just watch me."

And for the next little while, we did what two people do when they're in bed and fully awake and it's not quite time to get up and face the world.

It was a lovely few moments. But I wasn't distracted.

And I could still taste the fear.

Chapter Two

Out of this nettle, danger, we pluck this flower, safety.
William Shakespeare
Henry IV, Part I

 The early-morning phone call prompted a change in the weekend plans.

Originally, we had planned that Caitie would stay home with McQuaid while Ruby and I spent Friday through Monday at the ranch. But Jess's unsettling call had given me some serious second thoughts. It would be a major inconvenience for Maddie Haskell—the ranch owner—if I canceled the Saturday workshop. It would be costly for her, too, since the workshop was sold out. She'd have to refund everybody's money and send them home, or reschedule, or try to find a replacement.

But as I got dressed and went downstairs to make breakfast—quietly, because Caitie was still asleep—I was remembering that Mantel, now on the loose, had been convicted of killing two teenage girls. I ought to cancel the workshop. I ought to stay home and keep an eye on Caitie, who owns a large chunk of my heart. And be close to my husband, in case . . . well, in case Mantel showed up. In case something happened.

In the kitchen, I was greeted by Winchester, the three-year-old basset we adopted at Basset Rescue a couple of months before. Winchester (like our beloved Howard Cosell, departed but fondly remembered) is lengthy and low-slung, with floppy brown ears, saggy jowls, a tendency to drool, and a remarkably doleful air. Clearly, his previous life brimmed with calamities and catastrophes, and he's not fully persuaded that his present life is an improvement—especially because he hasn't yet been allowed to spend the evening in McQuaid's leather recliner, or claim the entire foot of our bed, or get away with stealing bagels. But when I put his breakfast kibbles into his bowl, he clambered out of his basset basket and gave me a look of polite appreciation before he dug into it. Winchester may be a bagel thief, but he is a gentleman, through and through.

While I took our breakfast tacos out of the freezer, I was mentally going over the weekend schedule, figuring out how to handle it. I would cancel the workshop and stay in Pecan Springs. McQuaid would have to cancel his plans for the HOT Barbecue—the local Lions Club annual Heart of Texas barbecue at Pecan River Park. It started on Saturday at noon and ran until late in the evening. He was one of the two food coordinators this year. He'd be standing behind the barbecue table for hours on end, dishing out the food—a *very* visible target, if Mantel showed up and wanted to take a shot at him. Our friend Blackie Blackwell was the other coordinator. Blackie could handle the whole thing easily, I was sure.

But McQuaid had been thinking about the situation, too, and he'd been on the phone. By the time the tacos were out of the microwave, he had made up his mind. He wasn't taking any chances, at least with Caitie and me. He wanted us out of town. Both of us.

"So I won't have to worry about you," he said reasonably. I'm sure he didn't intend to sound as if he were speaking to a clueless first grader, but that's the way I heard it. "You go on out to the ranch with Ruby, do your workshop, and just kick back for a couple of days. I'll drive Caitie down to Seguin to spend the weekend with Dad and Mom. By the time you both get back home, all the excitement will be over." He waggled Winchester's ears. "Right, Winnie, old boy?"

I opened the refrigerator door and reached for the pitcher of orange juice. Excitement? What excitement? What I mostly hoped for at home these days was *no* excitement. For a nice, quiet, boring weekend in which nothing at all happened, except for maybe an afternoon rain shower or an unexpected visit from Brian. I wouldn't even complain if he brought his laundry.

McQuaid gave Winchester one last pat, helped himself to a taco, and stood at the counter, wolfing it down. "In fact, I've already called the folks," he said in an offhand tone. "They're thrilled at the idea of having Caitie for the weekend. So we're all set."

He had already called them? Without asking me first? I thumped the pitcher of orange juice on the table and turned to get the glasses, fighting a rising tide of annoyance. But after a moment, I took a deep breath. Maybe it *was* the best thing, after all. McQuaid's folks live in a very safe neighborhood, right next door to the Seguin chief of police. Caitie would be just fine with them. Safe. Out of sight, where Mantel couldn't get to her. I shivered. Out of the line of fire.

I poured the orange juice. "Okay," I said agreeably. "Caitie can go to Seguin, then. You're right. She'll like that. But I am staying here. With you. I'll call Maddie and tell her that something important has come up and we need to reschedule. She'll understand." I paused, thinking out loud. "Hey, wait. What am I thinking? Ruby can handle this workshop. She knows the material and we've got everything set up and ready to go. You just need to get Blackie to substitute for you at the barbecue food table and—"

"No."

"No what?" I stared at McQuaid. He fed Winchester the last bite of taco, then went to the sink to wash the sauce off his fingers. "No *what*?"

"Forget it, China." He reached for a paper towel and dried his hands. "*You* are going out to the ranch with Ruby and doing the workshop, just the way you planned. *I* am going to go to the park and do my job at the Lions Club barbecue, just the way I planned. Neither of us is doing a damned thing different just because of this."

There was a plaintive meow and Mr. P, Caitie's scruffy pumpkin-colored tabby, wound himself around my ankles, begging for breakfast. I frowned. "Really, McQuaid, I don't think—"

"Yes, you do." He gave me a tight smile and softened his tone, being reasonable—reasonable like a cop. It's a tone I have learned to actively dislike. "Look, babe. If Mantel is the one who offed the DA—which is not clear yet, by any means—he's already got his revenge. He's not going to waste time going after anybody else. He's hotfooting it for the border." He balled up the paper towel and launched it at the trash basket. "In fact, Border Patrol is watching for him, right now. Five gets you ten they'll nab him before lunch."

"Maybe." I opened the bin that holds Mr. P's dry cat food and filled his bowl. "But maybe not. Maybe he's on his way to Pecan Springs right now. Maybe—"

He went on as if I hadn't spoken. "But on the very, very slim chance that Mantel is crazy enough to show up here in Pecan Springs, I don't want you or Caitie here. I want Caitie with my folks, and I want you somewhere safe, like that olive ranch." He took a step toward me and put his hands on my shoulders. "You got that?" He put a finger under my chin and lifted my face so I had to look up at him. His voice was soft but his eyes were hard and steady. "Tell me you understand."

I understood all right. I understood that I could argue with McQuaid until the cows came home, but he wouldn't change his mind. While he and I share a very great deal, there are large pieces of his previous life—his marriage to his first wife, Sally; his years as a cop—that I'm not a part of. I get that, and it doesn't bother me. That's how it is with adults, especially two adults with years of tough, dirty experience on two different sides of the law: McQuaid's work as a cop, hunting down people charged with a crime and building the cases against them; my work as a criminal lawyer, defending people charged with a crime and tearing down the cases against them. This thing with Max Mantel had come out of his past, his cop-life, and he intended to keep it there. And keep me out of it.

So I wouldn't argue. I just . . . wouldn't argue.

"I understand," I said, adding in my good-housewifely tone what I knew he was expecting me to say. "But you've got to promise you won't run any dangerous risks." I summoned a smile. "You'll promise, won't you?"

"Of course," he said lightly, and kissed me.

Mr. P addressed himself diligently to his breakfast. Winchester gave us a long gloomy look over his shoulder, plodded to his basket, and settled down for his after-breakfast nap. As far as they were concerned, all was well. Which of course it wasn't.

An hour or so later, I was unlocking the front door of my herb shop, Thyme and Seasons, on Crockett Street a couple of blocks east of the town square. I bought the place—a one-hundred-and-fifty-year-old two-story limestone building—some years ago, after I left Houston and my fast-paced legal career, which paid me a pot of money but left me feeling empty inside, exhausted, wrung out. I found the gentler, slower life I was looking for in Pecan Springs, a friendly town at the eastern edge of the Texas Hill Country, halfway between Austin and San Antonio. I cashed in my savings and retirement and used the money to open Thyme and Seasons in half of the building and rented the other half to Ruby Wilcox, for a New Age shop she called the Crystal Cave.

Not long after, my friend Mike McQuaid left his law enforcement career and moved with his young son, Brian, to Pecan Springs, where he joined the faculty of the Criminal Justice department at Central Texas State University. Eventually, we got married and bought a big Victorian on Limekiln Road, several miles west of town. While McQuaid still teaches part-time at the university, he and Blackie Blackwell are now partners in their own PI firm: McQuaid, Blackwell, and Associates. I am *not* an associate, I tell him, and do my best to stay out of his business. My former life in criminal law was chockablock with criminals. I've had enough to last a lifetime. I do not need to go looking for more.

And if I had my druthers, McQuaid wouldn't be doing it, either. He swears it's not dangerous, and that the most serious threat to his health is being bored to death combing through property records in the county clerk's office. That's not true, though: witness his recent undercover investigation into a Mexican oil theft ring, which took him across the border and into dangerous territory. Personally, I wish he'd spend more of his time in the classroom. But he's driven by the love of the chase, the excitement of the foxhole. It's his life. He has to choose how to lead it. And bless him, he doesn't try to tell me how to lead mine—most of the time, anyway. Except today.

I was thinking of this as I unlocked the door and went in. I always love the first moment of a day in the shop, and a quick glance around the familiar space was especially comforting after that five a.m. phone call. I breathed in the sweetly pungent scent of blended herbs, with a citrusy undertone of dried orange and lemon, and smiled at the fall of golden morning light through the window in the east wall.

I locked the door behind me and turned. Thyme and Seasons' hand-cut limestone walls, oak floor, and beamed ceiling are a perfect setting for the antique hutches and wooden shelves that display bottles and jars and packages of herbal vinegars, oils, jellies, and teas. Personal care products—herbal shampoos, soaps, massage oils, fragrances, and bath herbs—fill the shelves of the old pine cupboard in the corner. In the middle of the room, there's a wooden rack filled with glass jars of dried culinary and medicinal herbs, along with extracts and tinctures and aromatherapy products. A four-tiered shelf displays books, stationery, and cards. Buckets of packaged potpourri fill the other corners, and baskets of artemisia, larkspur, yarrow, and tansy for dried arrangements are clustered under the windows. The stone walls are hung with seasonal wreaths and swags.

People sometimes ask me, "Why an herb shop, of all things?" I tell them it's because herbs have been people's friends since before anybody was taking notes, or because they are delightfully useful plants. But the real reason is that after spending more years than I care to count living a fast-paced city life, this is where I've found my peace. I love to work in this shop and in the surrounding gardens, and with the people who come here. I love this life. I wouldn't trade it for anything under the sun.

Just past the cash register counter, off to the left, is the door to the Crystal Cave, which stays open most of the time. In the beginning, there was just Ruby's shop and mine, with an empty cobwebby loft above and an apartment in the back of the building, where I lived until McQuaid and I moved in together. Now, the space behind our shops is occupied by Thyme for Tea, the tearoom that Ruby and I jointly own. Behind that, there is the well-equipped kitchen where Cass Wilde prepares food for the tearoom lunches; for our catering service, Party Thyme; and for the personal chef business, the Thymely Gourmet, which is owned by all three of us. Last spring, Ruby and I finally cleaned out and renovated the loft and rented the space to Lori Lowry, for her spinning and weaving classes—a good idea, for they bring extra traffic into the shops. Also for rent is Thyme Cottage (a remodeled stone stable) at the back of the garden. It's available as a B&B when Ruby and I aren't using the space as a classroom.

We consider ourselves lucky to be able to do what we love, but we also need to make a living from it. For that, it helps to have not just one or two but several different profit centers. When the shops don't do well, the tearoom picks up the slack. If the tearoom traffic falls off, the catering and personal chef businesses fill the gap. If we're still short, the rent from the loft and the B&B can help. And then of course there are the classes and the workshops and—more recently—the online retail sales from our websites. Being in business for ourselves is like keeping a dozen balls in the air at once. It's always a juggling act, always a challenge. But we love it.

As I went in, I heard strains of music—Ruby's favorite

CD of traditional Celtic harp and flute. I stood in the door between our shops.

"Hey, Ruby," I said. "Sorry to be late." Usually, I'm the early bird, getting to the shop before eight, while Ruby comes in at nine, when we both open our shops. "Something unexpected came up. Caitie is spending the weekend with her grandparents, and I had to get her packed and on her way."

I hesitated. There was more, but Ruby wasn't going to like it and I hadn't yet figured out the best way to tell her. She was the one who had set up the workshop at the ranch and nagged me until I agreed to spend the whole weekend. I'd resisted, because early June is a busy time in the garden, but she had been unusually urgent about it. Some ulterior motive, I suspected, maybe having to do with her friend Maddie. But she hadn't told me, and I hadn't asked.

Ruby had a feather duster in her hand and was bent over, dusting a shelf of crystals. She was wearing a summer costume so bright it made me blink: leggings splashed with a bold orange-and-green floral print; a floaty, flirty, thigh-length orange tunic and multistrand orange-and-green necklace; jeweled green sandals; and a green chiffon scarf tied around her wild frizz of carroty-red hair. I tend toward the modestly monochromatic, like the beige Thyme and Seasons T-shirt and khaki pants I was wearing this morning. But Ruby is a colorful soul. She is also six feet tall, and when she unfolds herself and straightens up, she is a jolting bolt of color that will make anybody smile. Even me. Even this morning.

"Actually, I came in early," she said cheerily. "I thought I'd better get things ready for Cass, to make it a little easier for her while we're away for the weekend. She's already in the kitchen, getting set up for lunch. Hazel is coming in at eleven for a couple of hours, and Lori says she's available

16

if she's needed—except for late afternoon. She has a weaving class upstairs from four to five today, so there'll be some extra traffic in the shops."

"Sounds like you've got everything under control." I gave her a crooked grin. "But something came up this morning. I'm afraid there's been a change in plans."

Ruby went behind the counter and hung her duster on a hook. Her forehead creased in a frown, and her glance flicked to my face and fastened there. Her eyes widened. "Something's wrong," she said. "Something's going on." Her voice flattened. "It's . . . McQuaid, isn't it? Is he okay?"

I understand why people often think that Ruby Wilcox is some kind of flake. At the Cave, she teaches classes on channeling spirits and using the Ouija board. She sells books on astrology and she'll draw your chart for you and explain the theory of the zodiac and help you explore the *I Ching*. She trades quite comfortably in the kind of thing that rational people laugh at and skeptics scorn, which means that people sometimes see her as . . . well, eccentric.

Now, I'm a skeptic by nature, and my legal experience has made me even more so. I'm verbal and analytic and I don't apologize for having done exceptionally well on the bar exam. I'm used to functioning from the left side of my brain, the rational side, and communing with the universe is not exactly my cup of tea. Ruby is very well organized, too, and a first-class businesswoman. But she is also a right-brained person with an intuitive streak that manifests itself every now and then, in a way that does not make a lick of sense to sensible people. She once received a startling message about a murder from a perfectly innocent Honda Civic, whose owner turned up dead in the boarded-up basement of an abandoned school. Another time, a Ouija board under her direction told us where to find Brian, who had been kidnapped by his mother. Laugh if you want to, but when Ruby Wilcox pulls one of those psychic rabbits out of her hat, she will make a believer out of you. Out of me, anyway.

"You're right, it's McQuaid," I said hesitantly, not sure how much I should tell her. But she was counting on our going out to the ranch together. I had to come up with a good reason to stay in Pecan Springs.

Ruby was staring at me with the kind of intent, *listening* look that suggested that she was decoding a message I couldn't hear. "The call, the situation that came up this morning," she said. "It's *bad*, isn't it?"

Bad. I sighed. Ruby tries not to poke around in her friends' thought processes, but it looked like this was going to be one of her psychic rabbits. It might be better if I spilled the whole story now, so she would understand why I couldn't go.

"Yes," I said. "Exactly. His name is Bad Max Mantel. When McQuaid was with Houston Homicide, he led the investigative team that sent him to Death Row. Bad Max told one of his prison mates that he intended to get revenge on everybody who convicted him. He broke out of Huntsville and apparently made good on part of his promise by killing the prosecutor last night. One of McQuaid's cop buddies phoned while we were still in bed this morning. Mantel could be on his way here."

Ruby's expression was grave. "It sounds . . . dangerous."

"It is," I said, wondering whether she knew something I didn't. That's one problem her friends have with her. Sometimes she knows more than we do, but (for what might be very good reasons) chooses not to let us in on it.

"Just to be on the safe side," I went on, "McQuaid is taking Caitie to Seguin. I'm feeling like I need to stay in

Pecan Springs, in case I'm needed. Instead of going out to the ranch, I mean. I thought of canceling, but there are about thirty people registered, and your friend Maddie will be disappointed. There's no reason you can't do the workshop, Ruby. Everything is loaded into the van and ready to go— supplies and handouts, all but the olive oil." I managed a small smile. "I understand that Maddie has barrels of that. Extra virgin, too."

I was hoping fervently that Ruby wouldn't snoop around in my not-so-subconscious and pick up on my guilt for mis- leading McQuaid. I had *not* agreed to go out to the ranch, as he had . . . well, ordered. I just hadn't argued with him. And when he had asked me if I understood why he wanted me to go, I'd said yes, I understood, which I did. I understood why he wanted to have it his way. I just hadn't agreed to *do* it his way.

Ruby was frowning. "I don't think that's going to work, China. McQuaid may have talked to Sheila and asked her to—"

She was interrupted by the bell over her shop door, and I turned to see our friend Sheila Dawson. She was suited up for her day as Pecan Springs' chief of police, wearing her official navy blue uniform, sharply creased; her tie, neatly tied; her cop cap, set at just the right angle; and her black duty belt loaded with a businesslike battery of cop-wise gear and weapons. I've always said that you have to wonder at somebody who looks like a homecoming queen and thinks like the regional director of the FBI, but that's Sheila, a beautiful blonde who is lovelier than your average Miss America and smarter than . . . Well, very, very smart. Tough, too. Her friends call her Smart Cookie (when the officers on her force are not listening), but we could just as easily call her Tough Cookie. You don't want to mess with Sheila when she is on the job. And from the sour look on her face, she had already been on the job for a while this morning, was expecting to be on the job for the whole day, and wasn't especially thrilled about any of it.

I looked from Sheila to Ruby and back again. Sheila wasn't here on a social call. McQuaid had asked her to drop in and Ruby had flashed onto it.

But I wasn't going to make it easy for her. "Good morning, Chief," I said. I didn't need to be psychic to know why Sheila was out of sorts, and it had nothing to do with Mc-Quaid. "How's your morning sickness?"

"Damn it, Bayles," Sheila muttered. She made a face. "Not too good, if you have to know."

Sheila is not only a very good friend, she is married to McQuaid's partner, Blackie Blackwell. There's a story behind that marriage, for Blackie was the Adams County sheriff for many years. He and Sheila wanted to get married, but they agreed that two law enforcement careers in one family were a disaster waiting to happen. After months of vigorous debate that didn't settle anything either way, they gave up talking and tossed a coin. Blackie liked to joke that he had lost the toss, lost a job, and won a wife. Sheila won the toss and kept her job as Pecan Springs' first female chief of police, now the first *pregnant* chief of police. She is four months along, expecting in November, although she hasn't yet announced that fact. This is her second pregnancy. The first one ended badly, so she's waiting to tell the world about this one—a smart plan from one point of view and not so smart from another. Sheila is slim, with a drop-dead-gorgeous figure that attracts attention, even when she's in uniform. Guys like to stare. Some guys have sharp eyes. It wouldn't be long before they would be drawing their own conclusions.

"I've got some ginger capsules I can give you," I offered helpfully. "And Cass is in the kitchen. I'm sure she'd be glad to brew up some lemon-and-ginger tea. Either one ought to help. Or both, if you like. Ginger is really good for morning sickness."

"Appreciate your concern but I'm good, thank you." Sheila squared her shoulders, letting me know that she aimed to tough it out. "I'm here because McQuaid asked me to be sure that you and Ruby got out of town without delay this morning."

Ruby gave me a tiny please-don't-shoot-the-messenger shrug, then dropped her eyes.

"Oh, really?" I asked pleasantly. "Well, gosh, Chief, that's a coincidence. I was telling Ruby that I've decided to stay in Pecan Springs this weekend. Ruby can do the workshop on her own. Everything is all set up and all she has to do is—"

"Actually, that's not such a good idea, China." Sheila's voice was casual but her eyes were very sharp. "This might turn into a thing, so it would be just as well if you went on out to the Last Chance Ranch with Ruby. Of course, you're a citizen and it's up to you. I can't give you an order but that's my advice. My *best* advice," she added emphatically.

The room got very still. Next to me, I could feel Ruby tensing.

"Might turn into a thing, huh?" I said. "What kind of a thing?" If this was really up to me (it probably wasn't), we'd better have everybody's cards on the table. All of them.

Sheila considered for a moment, then decided I would more likely be persuaded if I understood the full picture. "A thing involving a team of Houston officers, a crew from Huntsville, a squad of Pecan Springs cops, an escaped convict, and—"

"Ah," I said. "Quite a few players."

"Yeah," she said quietly. "That's in my job description, you know. Coordinate with law enforcement officers from other jurisdictions, as required. Cooperate with them when they come onto my turf to get a job done." She shifted her weight and gave me the rest of it. "McQuaid phoned after you left and asked me to see that you stayed with the original plan and got out of Dodge. This morning."

I sighed. "He doesn't trust me, does he?"

"Not so much, at least in this case." Sheila flicked me a quick smile. "Should he?"

"Actually, he shouldn't," Ruby put in helpfully. "As China said, she was asking me to do the workshop while *she* stayed here, in case she was needed. And I was telling her that it wasn't going to work because—"

"Because I'm not going to let it," Sheila said. She folded her arms and eyed me. "I appreciate your wanting to hang around, but we're not talking party games here, China. Mantel is extremely dangerous. We don't know where he is, but we know he's a killer. He's armed and has a vehicle. He had a pretty tight gang before he went up, so he may have other resources. He could be on his way to Pecan Springs right now. There are already two people dead and we don't want—"

"Two people? *Two?*" I broke in urgently. "So Mantel got Zumwalt?" I felt suddenly cold. McQuaid would be devastated. He and Carl had been partners for a decade. They'd had each other's backs in some very dangerous situations.

"Zumwalt?" She was puzzled.

I frowned. Not Zumwalt. But who? "So he killed a prison guard on his way out of the building," I hazarded. McQuaid hadn't told me that.

22

"No." She shifted again. Her face seemed to have a slightly greenish tint, and I guess that morning sickness was bothering her. "The DA's wife. She was in the car with her husband. Mantel was waiting by the garage. He shot them both."

"Ah, *hell*," I said. Jess, the detective who called McQuaid that morning, had been on the scene. He had undoubtedly reported that Paul's wife had been shot, too, but McQuaid had deliberately kept it to himself, not wanting me to be frightened. "McQuaid didn't tell me about Cindy. I'm sorry."

"You knew her?"

"I did. Her husband got where he was because she was behind him all the way." Cindy Watkins was a shy, pretty woman who had worked hard to put Paul through law school and pushed herself to give parties she didn't enjoy because she knew it would help her husband's career. I took a breath. Cindy had been with Paul when it happened. I didn't want to leave McQuaid to face this situation by himself. "Look, Sheila, I promise I'll be good. I'll stay out of the way. I—"

Sheila raised her hand palm out, like a cop directing traffic. "Sorry, China. Bottom line, we've got a job to do, and you're not going to be any help. In fact, you could create problems for us. McQuaid has agreed to let us use him as—" She thought better of whatever she'd been going to say. "As liaison," she finished lamely. "It's already a mob scene. You'd just be in the way."

"Liaison?" I stared at her. Some kind of arrangement had been made here, and I suspected that McQuaid had initiated it. Or at least had not resisted it. "My husband isn't a cop and he has no part in this," I said, thinking it through out loud. "But he's agreed to let you use him. He's going to put himself on display at the Lions Club barbecue tomorrow, with the idea of forcing Mantel to show his hand. That's it, isn't it? He'll be standing there behind the table, making sure that everybody sees him. He'll be a target. He'll be *bait*."

Sheila looked uncomfortable. "I don't think I'd use that word to describe—"

"I would," I growled. "It is exactly the word I would use. This is horsepucky, Sheila. If you want my opinion. Which you don't, obviously."

Sheila cast a silent appeal to Ruby. *Help me out here, Ruby. Get her moving. Get her out of town.*

"China." Ruby put a quieting hand on my arm. "Hey, come on, China. We can't stand around here all morning talking. I promised Maddie. We need to be on the road."

I shook her hand off roughly. "I'm not going."

Sheila folded her arms. "Yes, you are."

"There's nothing you can do here, China," Ruby said. She added urgently, "Everything is all set, and Maddie is expecting us for lunch. I don't want to disappoint her. She's planning to give us a tour of the olive groves and introduce us to her staff and—"

Clearly, Ruby had a private reason for going out to the ranch this weekend. But I wasn't done. I glared at Sheila. "You're using my husband as bait to catch an escaped convict and I'm supposed to just stay out of the damn way?"

"An escaped convict," Sheila retorted, "who held God only knows how many young girls as sex slaves, murdered two of them, and has now gunned down the Harris County DA and his wife." Her voice was thin and harder than I had ever heard it. "Deal with it, China. Mantel is a dangerous man, and your husband knows what he has to do. *I* know what *I* have to do. And you do, too. So let's put on our big girl panties and get the goddamn job done."

Ruby fixed a look at Sheila's duty belt, then dropped her

eyes to Sheila's feet and raised them to her cop cap. "Smart Cookie," she said, very quietly. "You already *have* your big girl panties on."

Sheila shot her a testy glance, but the effect was spoiled when she put a trembling hand to her mouth. "Excuse me," she said. "I think I'm going to be sick."

She was.

Chapter Three

Once someone tries a real extra virgin—an adult or a child, anybody with taste buds—they'll never go back to the fake kind. It's distinctive, complex, the freshest thing you've ever eaten. It makes you realize how rotten the other stuff is, literally rotten. But there has to be a first time. Somehow we have to get those first drops of real extra virgin oil into their mouths, to break them free from the habituation to bad oil, and from the brainwashing of advertising. There has to be some good oil left in the world for people to taste.

Tom Mueller
*Extra Virginity: The Sublime and
Scandalous World of Olive Oil*

I went, of course.

I resented being pushed around. I was angry about being sent out of town. But what was I going to do? Stand around and argue with the pregnant chief of police while she tossed her cookies? Hand her a cup of ginger-and-lemon tea and say sweetly, "Sorry, Sheila, I don't give a damn what McQuaid wants or what you want. I'm doing what *I* want, and I want to stay here, in case somebody shoots my husband."

I didn't do that, much as I wanted to. Nor did I call Mc-Quaid and give him a pointy piece of my mind for failing to tell me about Cindy's murder and for hooking up with Sheila to double-team me. But I did get Sheila to promise that she would call the ranch the minute Mantel was picked up so I would know that everything was copasetic and could relax and stop worrying that he had scored his third post-escape hit on McQuaid. Ruby gave her the number, which I jotted down on a slip of paper. I'd call McQuaid and give it to him.

I wasn't happy with this arrangement, of course, but I tried to comfort myself with the understanding that if I had been able to stay in town, there would have been nothing much I could do except worry. Which I could do out at the Last Chance, just as easily as here in Pecan Springs. The only difference was that if I were in town, I'd be on top of what was going on. Ruby had said that there was no reliable cell phone signal out at the ranch, which meant that I wouldn't be able to get the latest news. I would probably spend my time imagining the worst.

I made sure that there was plenty of change in the cash register and checked in with Cass in the kitchen. Then I joined Ruby out in the alley, where we park Big Red Mama.

Big Red Mama, who looks like a cross between a psychedelic milk truck and a Sweet Potato Queen float on the way to a Mardi Gras parade, is our shop van. Ruby and I bought her at the Hays County sheriff's auction a few years ago. We were attracted to her because she was cheap but also because of the swirling Art Deco designs of blue, green, and yellow that her former owner (a Wimberley hippie artist named Gerald) had painted all over her sides, perhaps under the influence of a certain hallucinatory herb. In fact, after we bought her, we had to give her a good cleaning and an even better airing. The odor of that hallucinatory herb still lingered—not the kind of scent you want wafting out of your vehicle window if the DPS pulls you over for a broken taillight.

But while Mama may attract curious glances as she ambles down the road, she is a serviceable van. I use her for hauling plants and gardening supplies, Ruby uses her to deliver stuff for our Party Thyme catering service, and Cass uses her for the Thymely Gourmet. This morning, Mama was loaded with supplies for the workshop at the Last Chance.

This would be my first visit to the ranch, but Ruby has been going out there since she was a girl, so she volunteered to do the driving. She negotiated the minor mid-morning traffic jam around the old Adams County courthouse and headed west on Limekiln Road toward my house. When I left that morning, I was planning to duck out of the workshop and let Ruby do it herself, so I hadn't packed. At my house, she waited while I snatched up my overnight things and folded an extra T-shirt and blouse and clean jeans and panties into a duffel bag. I left a note on the fridge for McQuaid—*I wish you'd let me stay but I love you anyway*—and said an affectionate good-bye to Winchester, who is always at his gloomiest when his people leave him alone for the day. A moment later, we were on our way.

We were headed west across the rugged Texas Hill Country, known for its upland string of man-made lakes cupped in rolling mesquite-and-cedar-clad hills. The sun was shining out of a cloudless blue sky and the fields along the narrow, winding road were brilliant with early summer wildflowers: orange and red and brown firewheels, bright yellow coreopsis, and coppery prickly pear blossoms. A little farther on, I saw pink pavonia spilling across the limestone rocks and purple coneflower beginning to bloom in the fence corners. Along the creeks and in the low-lying areas, pecans, oaks, and hackberry rose above a wild, dense understory of chokecherry and elbow bush, perfect cover for wild turkeys and possums and raccoons. May had been unusually rainy—the result of a lingering El Niño—and everything was green and lush. It was like driving through a park.

We were aiming for the western stretches of the Guadalupe River, some seventy miles away. The terrain was rugged, with only a few houses widely scattered along the road. When I took out my cell phone, I saw that I'd already lost the signal—not unusual in rural Texas—which meant that even if McQuaid wanted to call and ask me to come back and watch him get shot at, he couldn't. And I couldn't call and ask him whether he was still alive and healthy. The landscape outside the window wasn't quieting my irritation the way it usually did, and my mind kept leapfrogging back to the troublesome situation in Pecan Springs.

Why had I let McQuaid and Sheila bully me into leaving?

I might not have been able to help, but at least I'd know what was going on. I don't usually do what I'm told. I should have dug in my heels and refused.

But I hadn't. Instead, I was on my way to the edge of nowhere. So, to keep myself from chewing my nails up to my elbows, I asked Ruby to tell me about the Last Chance Ranch. Maybe she would say something that would give away her private reason—I was sure she had one—for setting up this weekend.

Ruby gave me the backstory first. Ruby's mother, Doris, had been a girlhood friend of Eliza Butler, the ranch's previous owner—dead now—and Ruby and Doris had visited the ranch often when Ruby was a kid. "I didn't know Eliza when she was young, of course, but Mom says that she was an adventurous young woman, headstrong, maybe a bit impulsive. Lots of chutzpah."

Eliza had grown up on the Butler ranch—a cowgirl down to the toes of her cowgirl boots—but left after high school to go to the University of Texas, where she majored in journalism. Still in her early twenties, she had landed a good job at a glitzy New York fashion magazine. Her work took her to Paris, where she met a handsome Spaniard ("Aren't they all?" Ruby asked parenthetically), fell madly in love, quit her job, and went to live with him in the south of Spain, where he managed an olive grove.

"Wow," I said. "For a ranch girl from the Texas back country, Eliza got around."

Ruby nodded. "Mom kept in touch with her through letters during those years," she said. "Unfortunately, the romance was one of those star-crossed affairs. The guy was married and his wife was a devout Catholic. She wouldn't give him a divorce."

"Kind of tough to plan a life together in that situation," I remarked dryly.

Ruby chuckled. "For ordinary people, maybe, but not for Eliza. I wish you could have known her, China. She didn't give a damn what people thought. Mom says she loved the trees as passionately as she loved her Spaniard, and she dedicated herself to learning all she could about olives." She sighed. "But then he was killed in an orchard accident. Eliza had no choice but to come back to the States. I'm sure she felt that she had lost everything—not just the man she loved but a way of life."

That made me catch my breath, made me think about McQuaid and what might be going on in Pecan Springs. Even when love goes right—when you love the right person, do the right things at the right time in the right way—it can all go horribly wrong, without any warning. Just look at what had happened to Paul and Cindy Watkins, both of them killed by an escaped convict bent on revenge. I shuddered. I had nearly lost McQuaid to a bullet once. It could happen again. It could happen *today*.

Ruby hadn't noticed my momentary disconnect and was going on with her story. At the point when Eliza came back to Texas from Spain, she had been gone for nearly ten years. She thought of returning to the ranch, but she and her father—Roy Butler was an irascible man who had cut a wide swath through the political and economic landscape of Kendall County—had never gotten along. She took a job with an ad agency in Houston and tried to get used to living in the city. But not long after her return, her father was diagnosed with terminal cancer. Howard—Eliza's younger brother—was an alcoholic ne'er-do-well who couldn't be relied on. So Eliza came back to the ranch to see her father through his last illness, not happily but out of a sense of duty.

Still, it was a good move. While she was nursing her father, Eliza began nurturing the seeds of an idea that was quite radical for its time and its place. She would establish an olive grove on the family ranch, grow the trees, and produce the fruit and the oil that she had loved in Spain. Olives are a Mediterranean fruit, and the calcareous soils and rainfall of Spain and Texas seemed similar enough to make the idea work.

"People laughed at her," Ruby said. "Everybody she talked to told her that olives couldn't be grown in the Hill Country. They're too susceptible to a hard winter freeze."

"That's right," I said. I know a little about olive trees because I've planted several at our place on Limekiln Road, with mixed success. "Once the trees are established, they tolerate cold pretty well. But you know how crazy Texas winters can be. The thermometer can hit sixty-five degrees in January and a hundred in February, then plunge into the twenties in March. In that kind of situation, olive trees will freeze back to the ground anywhere but far South Texas. And down there, the summers are too hot and humid for decent olive—"

"Hang on!" Ruby hit the brakes hard. We had come over the top of a hill. Thirty yards ahead, a large herd of twenty or so wild pigs was zigzagging across the road. I grabbed the panic bar above the door and braced my feet as Mama's tires screeched on the asphalt and she threatened to fishtail. Ruby braked again, fighting for control and just missing the last of the pigs.

I gulped. "That was a close call. Wonder what they're doing out here on the road in the middle of the day." Feral hogs—tusked brutes that can easily weigh up to five hundred pounds—are mostly nocturnal. But day or night, they're an ugly threat in Texas. Voracious omnivores introduced in the mid-1500s by Spanish conquistadors and now numbering over a million, they will eat chickens, fawns, lambs, kid goats, and the family cat. They'll also tear up the garden, as they had mine the previous spring. Worst of all, they have no predators. Except humans, that is. And we can't seem to get the job done.

Ruby's hands were clenched on the steering wheel. "We were lucky," she said, letting out her breath sharply. She shifted into a lower gear as the last of the pigs disappeared into the brush on the other side of the road. "Did you hear about the pickup that hit several hogs over on Route 130? It flipped. The driver was killed."

"Danger is everywhere, I guess." Here on the road, and

back in Pecan Springs. The world is a scary place. I put my hand on Ruby's arm and felt her trembling. "You're a good driver, Ruby. If you'd been going faster, or not paying attention, we could have plowed right into them."

I settled back into the seat. Then, because I was curious, I reminded her that we'd been talking about Eliza, who had gotten passionate about olive trees when she was introduced to them by her Spanish lover. "You were saying that people told her she couldn't grow olives in the Hill Country," I prompted.

"Yes." Ruby took a deep breath and pushed the accelerator down again. "It was like a red flag to a bull. When Eliza heard that it couldn't be done, she decided that *she* would be the one to do it. Mom and I began coming out to the ranch about the time she planted those first trees. Like everybody else, Mom thought Eliza was totally nuts. But even though I was pretty young—twelve or so—I was impressed with the woman's spirit. She was simply indomitable, China. When her father died and left her half of the ranch, she rolled up her sleeves and went to work. She worked like a demon, without stop. She drove herself and everybody else, from dawn to dark. But it wasn't about making money."

"Oh, really?" I asked skeptically. That would be unusual, to say the least. For most people, it's all about making money.

"Yes, really. Which was a good thing, I suppose, since the olive orchards have never made a lot of money. For Eliza, it was only about the land. And the olives. And her lover." Ruby sighed. "It was almost as if she thought that by planting the trees and raising them successfully, she could bring him back to life."

"Maybe that's just what she had in mind," I said. "Olives have been used to symbolize lots of things. Victory in war, peace after everybody puts their weapons down. Power and authority. Prosperity, wealth. Hope, and the possibility of new life. And yes, resurrection, especially in Greece. That's where that nasty Persian king, Xerxes, burned the city of Athens to the ground—including the olive grove at the Acropolis that was sacred to the goddess Athena. But when things cooled off and the Athenians went back home, they found that Athena's sacred olive tree, totally scorched, had already sprouted a green branch. Yes, resurrection. So maybe you're right. Maybe Eliza was trying to bring her lover back to life, in her mind, anyway."

Ruby nodded. "That's what Sofia said. And she knew Eliza better than anybody—even better than my mother."

"Sofia? Who's she?"

"Sofia Gonzales. She was born on the ranch. Her mother, Rena, was the cook-housekeeper. Her father was . . ." She stopped. "Rena was married to Emilio Gonzales, the ranch foreman. Anyway, Sofia and Eliza grew up together. But when Eliza left the ranch, Sofia stayed to work for Eliza's father as a cook and housekeeper. After he died, she stayed on to help Eliza. She's elderly now, but she still manages to do a full day's work in the kitchen or wherever she's needed. She has a cabin on the ranch, right next to the cabin where we'll be staying. She's very attached to Maddie, of course."

"So now we get to Maddie," I said. "Where exactly does she come into the picture? She's been running the ranch for a while now, hasn't she? Did she buy it from Eliza?"

"Oh, no," Ruby said. "She inherited it."

"Inherited!" I whistled. "No kidding? Eliza *gave* it to her?"

"That's right. Sofia brought Maddie to the ranch about the time that Eliza's father died. Maddie was just a toddler then, two, maybe three years old. She was orphaned when her parents—friends or relatives of Sofia's, I never understood which—were killed in an automobile accident in South Texas. She's not related to either Eliza or Sofia by blood, but she's always been like a daughter to both of them. They both loved her very much. When Eliza died, she left everything to Maddie—not just the ranch, but the Butler oil land out in West Texas. Pecos County, I think."

"Oil land?"

"At one time, it brought in a lot of money. But the oil has been pretty well depleted, I understand. It's under long-term lease. The leases are paying next to nothing and the land itself isn't worth much." Ruby glanced at me. "Anyway, there are some problems about Maddie's inheritance. I'm not sure where the lawsuit stands just now. We'll have to ask her to fill us in on the details."

There was an imperative honk, a whooshing roar, and a trio of long-haired, black-clad motorcyclists whipped around us. A woman riding on the back of the third Harley waved enthusiastically at Mama as they thundered past. The Hill Country is home to a great many different tribes. It looked like the female bike passenger thought our psychedelic Mama might belong to hers. Come to think of it, maybe she had, in her previous term of service with Gerald the hippie. Maybe Mama was a cousin to the Harley, once or twice removed.

"Lawsuit?" I returned Ruby's glance. "What kind of lawsuit? What are we talking about here?"

Ruby was evasive. "I don't know very much about it, China. All I know is that when all is said and done, Maddie may lose the ranch."

More questions. "Lose the ranch? Lose it how? Is it mortgaged? Is the bank threatening to take it away from her?"

"It's possible that Boyd—Eliza's nephew—is going to get it. That's what the lawsuit is about. As I say," she added hurriedly, "I don't know the details. But that's how I understand it."

Ah. So now I could guess why Ruby had been so insistent about getting me out to the ranch. She thought I might be able to tell Maddie how—legally—she could save her inheritance. Well, she was going to be disappointed. I'm a lawyer, yes. And yes, I keep my bar membership current, just in case (God forbid) everything goes south and I have to go back into practice. But my specialty is criminal law, not estate law. I wouldn't be much help in a dispute over land and wills.

"This guy Boyd," I said. "Tell me about him." Eliza, Sofia, Maddie, Boyd. I was beginning to think I needed a scorecard.

"Eliza's father divided the family ranch—the Last Chance—between Eliza and her brother, Howard."

"Right. The alcoholic who wasn't much help when it came to nursing."

One more motorcyclist roared around us, pushing hard to catch up to his tribe. He didn't wave.

"Yes," Ruby replied. "Each of them—Eliza and Howard—got two thousand acres, with the Guadalupe River flowing down the middle. Eliza had no children. Howard had just one, Boyd. When Howard died, Boyd inherited his father's half of the ranch—along with half of the Butler West Texas oil property. What there was of it," she added ruefully. "Howard drank a lot of it away. By the time Boyd inherited, there wasn't much left. That's why—"

I held up my hand. "Don't tell me, let me guess. Eliza was Boyd's aunt, so he expected—quite reasonably, I suppose—that her half of the property would one day belong to him. Instead, she left it to your friend. To Maddie, who isn't a blood relative. Which pissed Boyd off."

"That's right," Ruby said. "But there's another part of the story. Years back, when Howard saw the orchards his sister was planting, he thought he'd give olives a try. He wasn't nearly as diligent as she was, though, and never very successful. Boyd continued the effort, with a little more success. He's even selling some olive oil—not very good oil, as it turns out. But he was also keeping his eye on his aunt's orchards, thinking he was going to inherit."

"Because he assumed that the ranch would stay in the family."

Ruby nodded. "Exactly. And he had a good reason, Sofia says. He had a copy of a will that Eliza had made some twenty years ago. Maddie was just a kid then, and Eliza had no way of knowing that she would love the orchards and want to make them her life."

I could see it coming. "But when Maddie grew up and Eliza realized that this young woman was committed to the olive business, she made a new will. She left her nephew out. And she didn't tell him."

"There was another reason for leaving him out," Ruby said. "The olive oil he was selling. It was bad."

"Bad? What was wrong with it?"

"It was . . . what's the word? Adulterated? He was putting other stuff in it. Other kinds of oil, I mean."

"Ah." I'd read about that practice. A little bit of extra virgin olive oil is blended with a lot of low-grade olive oil or with canola or sunflower seed oil, then labeled and sold as pure olive oil, or even extra virgin. There are laws against this sort of thing, but it's hard to catch the violators. "So Eliza was afraid that if Boyd inherited, he might continue his evil ways and give her good olives a bad name."

"Yes." Ruby made a rueful face. "He didn't know about the new will. He was caught by surprise."

"That's unfortunate," I said. "The guy was her nephew. Eliza should have told him what she was doing, no matter how unpleasant it was. Or she should have instructed her lawyer to tell him."

"It's hard to tell Boyd Butler anything," Ruby said flatly. "He doesn't listen. And he *always* likes to get his way, especially with women. That's my personal opinion, anyway. It's not universally shared." She slid me a glance. "Have I mentioned that he is extremely good-looking? He can be a charmer, too. He can charm the socks off you." She chuckled ironically. "Well, not *you*, maybe. You're pretty charm-proof. But a lot of others."

"So?" I raised an eyebrow. "What does that have to do with anything?"

She hesitated. "I could tell you, but it would be just more of my opinion. And I've been known to be wrong." She laughed a little. "Occasionally."

"Wrong?" I grunted. "Where's your intuition, Ruby? Why don't you turn on your gift and see what's really going on?"

Ruby hesitated for a moment. "Because I have some pretty strong personal feelings that may be getting in the way of seeing what's happening," she said. Half under her breath, she added, "Boyd made a pass at me once. I was tempted. But I wasn't charmed."

I got it. Boyd was in the habit of charming women, and Ruby had no burning desire to be added to his list of conquests. Or maybe she did, and didn't want to admit it. She had some "pretty strong personal feelings," she'd said. Was *Boyd* the reason she was so intent on going out to the ranch this weekend?

"Anyway," she went on, "it would be better if you formed your own opinion, rather than listening to me."

I couldn't argue with that. But I like to gather other people's opinions, even if I don't accept them. "What about Maddie? What does she think?"

Ruby hesitated for a moment. "Maddie is a sweet, hard-working young woman who is focused on what needs to be done at the ranch, day in and day out. She hasn't been involved with very many men, and she's . . . well, inexperienced. Maybe even naïve. I'm not saying she's a pushover," she added hastily. "I'm just saying that it's sometimes hard for her to know when to push back. Especially now, when she's worried about losing the ranch." Another hesitation. "And especially where Boyd is concerned."

It sounded like Ruby thought Maddie might have been charmed by Boyd. Which muddled the matter even more. "And you've brought me along on this jaunt because you want me to—"

I broke off. At the corner up ahead, I could see a big orange-and-blue gas station sign. I wanted to hear how Ruby thought I could help in this mixed-up situation. But we were about to cross Route 281, and according to the map, we had only another twenty or so miles to drive.

"Before we get into that, let's take a break," I said. "I'd like something to drink."

"Works for me," Ruby said. "Mama needs gas, anyway. I'll fill her up. Get me a bottle of water, will you?"

I had an ulterior motive for wanting to stop. Route 281 carries a fair amount of traffic between Fort Worth and San Antonio, and there was bound to be cell phone service. The minute Ruby pulled up to the pump, I hopped out and took out my phone to call McQuaid and check up on what was happening. Sheila hadn't liked it when I said that my husband was being used as bait, but it was true. I didn't know how they were planning to use him, exactly, but I could guess that McQuaid would allow himself to be dangled out there in plain sight, tempting Mantel to make his move. At the barbecue, or at McQuaid's office. I shivered. Or even at our house. Which was why he had sent Caitie and me away. He knew Mantel might come to the house looking for him.

Four rings, no answer. My call went to voice mail and all I got was McQuaid's gruff, curt, "Sorry. I'm out of pocket right now. Leave a message and I'll get back to you when I can."

I closed my eyes, loving the sound of his voice, wishing I had just a little of Ruby's intuition and could make a guess about where he was, what he was doing, whether he was safe. "Hope all is well," I said into the phone. "Sheila told me that Mantel shot Cindy Watkins, too. Which of course makes me worry more." I paused, fishing around in my bag for the ranch's landline number that I'd jotted down. I found it and added it to my message, then put my heart into the last six words. "Be *careful*, McQuaid. I love you."

I dropped my phone into my shoulder bag, frowning. Be careful? Yes, of course. I worry about McQuaid when he's out doing what he does—an arson investigation, an undercover job in Mexico, baiting an escaped murderer. But Ruby hadn't been driving recklessly a few miles back, when we came over that hill and nearly ran into that pack of hogs. A few seconds earlier, a faster speed, a slower reaction time on the brakes, and both of us could have been killed. Even ordinary life is full of hazards. It is damn hard to be *careful*. And being careful may not save you anyway.

I bought two bottles of water and went back out to the pump, where Ruby was just finishing the fill-up. She had caught the attention of a burly, mustachioed truck driver, who was watching her with an unmistakable leer. He was about to hit on her when I walked up. I winked at him, then slid my arm around Ruby and gave her an affectionate nip on the ear.

"Hey, sweetheart," I said. "You ready to boogie?"

The truck driver gave us a disgusted look and climbed into his rig.

"I could have handled him." Ruby plugged the hose back into the pump and screwed Mama's gas cap on tight.

"I know." I grinned at her. "Just thought I'd have a little fun."

She took the receipt from the pump. "I guess you couldn't reach McQuaid." It wasn't a question.

I sobered. "I wish you wouldn't dial into me that way." I handed her the bottle of water. "But no. All I got was his voice mail." I gave her a quick look. "You don't know something I don't, do you?" I was halfway hoping that she might have picked something up that I needed to know—and halfway afraid that she had.

She shook her head. "I can read you, China, but McQuaid has always been sort of a blank page to me. Or a brick wall, to put it another way. It's hard to get through to him. Even if I wanted to," she added, climbing into the driver's seat. "Which I don't. Especially not today."

I got in and shut the door. "He's a brick wall to me, sometimes, too. That's the cop side of him, I guess. Cops like to cultivate the art of the impassive look and the flat voice. No expression, no emotion, no clue to what's going on inside."

"There's a lesson in there somewhere," Ruby said.

"Oh, yeah? What is it?"

"Never fall in love with a cop."

"Little late for that," I said. "You should have stopped me before I went over the cliff."

"Not much chance of that," Ruby said wryly. With a laugh, she cranked Mama's ignition and we started off.

41

We were in Kendall County now, on the western side of the Edwards Plateau, and the trees were a lot more sparse. This is ranching country, settled by the Germans in the 1840s. There are more sheep and goats than cattle, and the goats are Angoras, famous for their mohair, which still brings a decent return. The ranch buildings we could see from the road had a prosperous look.

I turned to Ruby. "Before we stopped, you were going to tell me why you brought me out here. The workshop is just a cover, isn't it? This visit is really about Boyd. And his lawsuit." I hadn't figured out which, so I included both.

"No, of course it's not a cover," Ruby said indignantly. "Maddie's advertised it to her mailing list and there are twenty-some people signed up. Your name is apparently quite a draw." She gave me a rueful, half-guilty look. "But yes, I admit it. I was also thinking about the lawsuit. And about Boyd. I know you don't want to get involved, legally speaking. But I was hoping . . ." Her voice trailed off. "I don't really know what I was hoping, I guess. Just that you could do *something*."

"I'm not sure what that would be," I said. By now, I was beginning to get curious about Boyd, who seemed to be in the middle of just about everything. But I needed to fill in some background first. "Let's go back to Maddie. I'd like to know more about her."

"I actually remember the day Sofia brought Maddie to the ranch," Ruby said. "I was twelve that summer, and my mother and sister and I were spending a week with Eliza. Little Maddie—she was just starting to talk—had survived the car wreck that killed her parents but she was pretty badly banged up. Her arm was broken, as I recall, and her face was badly cut. In fact, she still has the scar."

"Scar?"

"On her cheek and her neck. It's a pretty bad one. Maybe that's why . . ." Ruby sighed. "Why she's so shy around strangers. She's sensitive about how she looks. But Eliza fell in love with her immediately. My mother says she must have thought of her as the daughter she never had."

"Maybe Eliza needed somebody to love," I said, "after losing her lover. And I'm sure the little girl needed to be loved, after losing her parents. I paused. "Eliza never married? You said she didn't have children of her own."

"No, and neither did Sofia," Ruby replied. "So Maddie essentially had two moms. Sofia was the one who cuddled her and looked after her. Eliza made her do her homework and mind her p's and q's. After high school, Maddie went away to college, but not very far—just down to San Antonio, where she majored in horticulture at UTSA. She did very well, too. Graduated at the top of her class."

"That's a demanding program," I said. "She must be smart."

"She is. She could have gotten a really good job, but as I said, she's shy —definitely more confident with plants than with people. At the ranch, she lets the staff deal with visitors, while she works with the trees."

"Plant people are like that sometimes," I said. "You can talk to plants, but plants don't talk back. They're nice to be around." I certainly prefer plants to some of the people I met in my former incarnation as a criminal attorney.

Ruby nodded. "When she finished her degree, Maddie didn't even bother to send out her résumé. She came straight back to the ranch and settled in to help Eliza manage the olives. Which was good, because Eliza was getting older and having health problems."

"Was it good for her? For Maddie, I mean. It sounds like all work and no play. What about boyfriends?"

"Good for her?" Ruby repeated thoughtfully. "I'm not so sure. Maybe it would be better if she would get out more. But—well, you'll understand, when you see her. As far as guys are concerned, she was involved for a while with a man who owns a vineyard just across the river. He seemed pretty serious about her." She hesitated. "But if you ask me, it's the olives that matter most to Maddie. I doubt if she'll ever leave the Last Chance—unless she's forced to."

"You mean, if Boyd gets possession of the land."

"It's not just the land," Ruby said. "It's the business, too, and that's substantial. Eliza made the olive ranch work, right from the start, and in a very big way. She began with just a few varieties of olives—Spanish, mostly—and kept adding more and more, until she was growing a couple of dozen different kinds. Mom used to say that every time we went out to the ranch, Eliza had fallen in love with another olive. She was experimenting, you see, with the varieties that would grow best in the various microclimates around the ranch and in her soils. Some of the experiments were failures, and everybody learned to tiptoe around until Eliza got over her disappointment and started smiling again. But Eliza was simply dogged, and her persistence paid off."

We were driving past a flock of scruffy-looking Angora goats, scattered across a meadow. A couple of them were pushing their heads through the barbed-wire fence, getting after some tasty grass along the road. "I've read a little about the olive business," I said. "Raising olives is more complicated than, say, raising peaches or apples. Or ranching."

"It seems to be all very do-it-yourself," Ruby said. "First you have to figure out which are the best trees to grow where *you* are. And then you have to grow the trees and prune them and irrigate them and encourage them to produce. And when they do, there's the harvest. Do you pick the olives by hand, or with machines?" She laughed lightly. "Picking olives is serious work, I can tell you, China. I was out here at harvest time a few years ago, and I saw how difficult it is. And you can't let olives sit around for a few days, like watermelons or even tomatoes. If you're making oil, you want to press the fruit right away—the same day as the harvest, if you can. It's a huge challenge to produce an olive oil that is one-hundred percent grown, pressed, and bottled on the ranch. And then, to make it even harder, you have to find the right distributors so you can sell your oil. But Eliza did it. And now Maddie's doing it, too."

"Gosh," I said, impressed. "And Eliza invented everything from scratch?"

"Pretty much," Ruby replied. "Of course, she learned a lot when she was in Spain, but she had to make it work here in Texas. Maddie has been a partner in the business for quite a few years now. When she was in high school, she came up with the idea of developing an olive tree nursery—retail and wholesale—to increase the ranch's income. She worked with a couple of local soap crafters to develop olive oil skin care products that are sold at the ranch. And before Eliza got sick, they expanded the business to include several guest cabins, a café, and a wine-tasting room. The wines are produced by several local vineyards."

"Guest cabins and a café?" I shook my head. "I sometimes think you and Cass and I have bitten off more than we can chew, with our shops and the tearoom and the catering service and all. But olive groves and olive oil production, along with all that other stuff? That's a complicated business."

I considered the other issues for a moment—the kind of things I learned to think about in law school. Had Eliza and Maddie entered into a formal business partnership that protected Maddie's interests? If so, how was that partnership related to the land on which the orchards were growing? How would it play in the inheritance battle? Intriguing legal questions.

"How long has Eliza been dead?" I asked.

Ruby pulled around a slow-moving pickup pulling a cattle trailer loaded with cows. "Almost two years." She pulled down her mouth. "She drowned, actually."

"Drowned? Gosh. How did that happen?"

"She'd been in ill health, suffering from dementia."

"Dementia," I said. "That's sad. And it could complicate things, where the will is concerned."

"It did," Ruby replied, and went on. "Maddie and Sofia always kept an eye on Eliza, but she somehow managed to get out of the house one night and wandered down to the river. That's where Maddie found her the next morning. And that's when the trouble with Boyd really started."

"Ah, Boyd," I said wryly. "Back to him again. All I know is that he is charming, and that he was Eliza's nephew. And that he's sold bad olive oil and he's trying to steal the ranch. There must be a backstory here. Tell me more."

Ruby threw me a glance. "Maybe I should let Sofia do that, China. She has an opinion on the subject." That was mysterious enough, but Ruby didn't elaborate. She took a left, heading south down a narrow gravel lane. In a couple of miles, we drove through an open ranch gate. Olive orchards were laid out on either side of the road, the small pale green trees tidily pruned and growing in neat, weed-free rows. The orchards were irrigated, as I could see from the irrigation hoses—a drip system, it looked like—installed along the rows. A painted sign announced that we had arrived at the Last Chance Olive Ranch, and that the ranch house, guest cabins, nursery, and olive works were just ahead.

I let out my breath. "It's beautiful here," I said, looking around.

"It's the product of years of hard work," Ruby replied. She gave me a pointed look and added, "I hope Maddie will be able to keep it."

"I don't think there's much I can do that Maddie's lawyer can't." I was trying to be realistic.

With a confident smile, Ruby reached over and patted my arm. "I'm sure you'll think of something," she said.

Chapter Four

MCQUAID

Friday Morning

Mike McQuaid pulled into the parking lot of the strip center where his office was located and—as usual—parked his battered old blue Ford pickup truck in the shade of the large pecan tree at the west side of the lot.

Nothing different today, he reminded himself. *Act like this is just an ordinary day*, although of course it wasn't. Mantel was on the loose. The man had murdered two people, and old reflexes, old cautions, old habits, were already kicking in. For one thing, McQuaid was wearing his Glock 23 in a shoulder holster under his lightweight khaki blazer, which was not something he did every day. The reassuring weight of the gun was a physical reminder of the early-morning phone call, which had been a heavy load of bad news.

McQuaid sat for a moment, very still, doing a quick survey of the lot and the street beyond, scanning for anything unfamiliar, anything out of place. If it was there, he didn't see it. What he saw was the usual lineup of cars in front of the Laundromat at the east end of the strip, on Brazos Road. The yogurt shop next to the Laundromat wasn't open yet, since it was just—McQuaid checked his watch—9:17, and the Thai restaurant next door to the yogurt shop (a good place to pick up a quick lunch) didn't open until eleven. Their parking spaces were empty. But the copy shop had been open since seven, and a woman was just coming out and getting into a Honda Accord. Next door to the copy shop was a small, nondescript office. Its glass storefront window had been covered discreetly with textured plywood and the only clue to its occupants—McQuaid, Blackwell, and Associates—was a small brass plate beside the door.

Nothing different, McQuaid reminded himself again. *Same old same old, like every other day.* But he loosened his jacket as he got out of the truck. As he walked to his office door, he was watching the copy shop window, where he could see a reflection of the lot behind him and the passing cars on the street. Punching in the code that unlocked the keyless deadbolt, he stepped silently inside and shut the door. Hand poised over his Glock, he listened for movement. Hearing nothing, he flicked on the lights and glanced around, relieved to see that everything looked exactly as usual.

Only a little paranoid, he thought. But paranoia was good, necessary. Paranoia made you vigilant. Kept you alive.

McQuaid, Blackwell, and Associates occupied four small rooms, altogether about the size of a three-car garage, which was just fine, since it was only himself and Blackie most of the time. Their "associates" worked out of a car, mostly at night, and didn't need an office. The front room held a couple of upholstered chairs and a decent-looking receptionist's desk that featured a phone, a silk plant, a couple of framed photos, a notepad, and an open calendar book, all designed to make the desk look occupied. But there was no receptionist. He and Blackie had agreed they didn't need one, since they mostly worked on contract and didn't solicit walk-in business. The door to the left led to Blackie's office, the door to the right to McQuaid's, and the door in the middle to a conference room just large enough for a table and six chairs, with a sickly looking potted palm in one corner, obviously in need of some green-thumb attention. He should take it home and let China doctor it.

Charlie Lipman had been there for a meeting the afternoon before and the odor of his Rocky Patel cigar lingered on in the closed reception room. Charlie, a Pecan Springs lawyer, was an old friend and one of the firm's regular clients—a prompt pay, too, so McQuaid didn't mind the secondhand smoke. He didn't enjoy it as much on the second day, though, so he turned on the AC to clear some of the odor. Normally, he'd leave the front door ajar and open the window behind his desk to bring in some fresh air. But not today. No point in taking chances. Door locked, window closed, drapes closed.

First stop, the coffeemaker on the credenza in the conference room. A few minutes later, cup in hand, he had just stepped into his office when the phone on his desk buzzed. He picked it up fast to keep it from going to the answering machine on the receptionist's desk, where he hadn't yet cleared yesterday's messages. He was hoping it was Jess Branson, calling with the news that Mantel had been picked up. Or that Mantel was dead, which McQuaid thought was the way things would likely go down. The guy wasn't planning on being hauled back to Huntsville to wait his turn on Death Row.

He pulled out his chair and sat. "McQuaid," he said into the phone.

"I did your dirty work, Mike." The frost in the woman's voice might have chilled a lesser man. "You owe me."

"Yeah." He relaxed into a smile. "Oh, you bet, Sheila. Big time. Thanks."

Dealing with Sheila Dawson was always a little complicated, tricky even. She wasn't just a beautiful woman with a lot of years of solid police experience under her belt, or the first female chief of the Pecan Springs PD, or one of China's two best friends. She was also Blackie's wife, and Blackie Blackwell wasn't just his partner in the PI business but his fishing and poker buddy. He didn't want to get crosswise with the love of Blackie's life. He added carefully, "She take it okay, did she?"

"She wasn't any too happy about it." Sheila's tone was warmer, but still chilly. "I had other things to do, so I didn't hang around to see them off. But Ruby seemed to have the matter under control. So far as I know, they've left for the ranch."

McQuaid pulled out the bottom desk drawer and propped his cowboy boots on it, leaning back in the chair, coffee mug in one hand, phone in the other. "Sorry I had to get you involved, Sheila. But I thought it was a good idea if somebody made sure she got out of town—and I didn't think that somebody should be me. China doesn't like it when she thinks I'm ordering her around."

"I wonder why," Sheila said drily. There was a silence while he tried to think of an answer to that. After a moment, she went on. "What have you heard from Branson?"

McQuaid closed his eyes, feeling the weight of the morning's two deaths like a thirty-pound metal chain draped across his shoulders. If he had pulled the damn trigger when he had Mantel in his sights all those years ago, Watkins and his wife would be alive right now. Mantel had stood right in front of him, asking for it, all but begging for suicide by cop. But McQuaid—who believed that a cop did a cop's job, not the job of the judge or the juror—had refused the offer. And now he was regretting his refusal.

He took a sip of coffee, finding it flat and tasteless. "Nothing more since Branson's five a.m. call. He probably has his hands full with the investigation. He's got the press on his back, too. Must be a circus over there, with both the DA and his wife dead. It'll be breaking news on all the cable channels."

"You should have told China about the wife," Sheila said disapprovingly. "They were friends, apparently. Or at least acquaintances."

He sighed, agreeing. He should have told her. "I just . . . well, couldn't. Believe me, it would've made things worse. Thanks, Chief. I really do owe you."

"Uh-huh." Sheila sounded skeptical. "China has now come up with the notion that you might be thinking of putting yourself out there as a piece of bait. To catch Mantel. She let me know that she thinks the idea is horsepucky, quote unquote."

"Why am I not surprised?" McQuaid had to chuckle. "China is a smart gal, you know. She's been around. And it's not a bad idea," he added tentatively, testing Sheila's response. "Unless Houston can nail Mantel in the next couple of hours, somebody might need to draw him out."

"I didn't say that, *you* did," Sheila retorted. "If that's what you have in mind, don't tell China. I'm just letting you know because you're likely to get an urgent call from her, telling you that she wants you to stay out of it. All the way out."

McQuaid didn't think so. It was true that China preferred that he put his law enforcement experience to work in a CTSU classroom, where he taught a couple of criminal justice courses every year. She didn't like the idea that he might be out there on the front lines somewhere, doing what he used to do as a detective at Houston PD. But she never gave him a hard time about it.

He said, "You haven't heard anything from Houston?"

There was a commotion in the background and McQuaid heard the voice of Connie Page, Sheila's assistant. A murmured conversation, then Sheila said, "Take a message, Con. And get the door, will you? I need five more minutes." The sound of a door shutting.

"That's why I'm calling," Sheila said. "I just got off the phone with a Harris County assistant DA. Last name, Abbott. First name, Ian. I-A-N Abbott." She paused. "There was a witness in the Mantel case. A young woman named Martha Kennedy. Remember her?"

"I do." McQuaid remembered her clearly—a slight young woman, blond, with a wide-eyed innocence that belied the sordid life she'd been lured into. "She was one of Mantel's older girls. We located her down in Corpus and Watkins convinced her to testify for the prosecution." The DA had coerced her, really, with an arsenal of threats— charges of prostitution and conspiracy, even accessory to murder. "She wasn't too keen on the idea to start with, but she did a good job. Pretty compelling testimony, as I remember. The jury seemed to think so, anyway. She did a little time, but I heard that she straightened herself out, went to college, got an associate degree." He frowned. "What about her, Sheila? Why are you telling me—"

He understood then, with a gut-twisting wrench. "He got her."

"Right," Sheila said. "She's dead."

"Ah, *hell*." Not a surprise, though, not really. The only surprise was that Mantel had managed three killings already, the two Watkins and now the Kennedy woman. The weight on his shoulders—the weight of regret for not disposing of Mantel when he had the chance—suddenly got heavier. "Where did it happen? When? How?"

There was a pause, and then Sheila said, "That's the thing, Mike. It wasn't Mantel who killed her. Her body was found next to the Ship Channel late yesterday, not far from where that barge collision happened last year. She was dumped out of a vehicle, looks like. She'd been dead since Sunday night or Monday—multiple gunshot wounds." Another pause. "Mantel didn't get out of Huntsville until Wednesday. So maybe it's unrelated. A coincidence."

"Or he's teamed up with somebody," McQuaid said, not quite thinking, not wanting to think, just going through possibilities out loud. "Maybe the person who picked him up in Huntsville after the escape. Maybe others. Maybe he's calling in favors." Which would give Mantel more options, extend his reach, make him more dangerous.

A long moment. "Sounds right," Sheila said finally. "But at this point, we're guessing. Just wanted you to be aware of the situation."

McQuaid put down his coffee mug, sat forward, and took a yellow pad out of a top drawer. "Well, I hope this guy you're talking to in the DA's office has notified the people who helped to make the case against Mantel. Watkins had a couple of assistants who questioned witnesses at trial. Mantel might be nuts enough to make a run at them, too." He picked up a pencil. "Witnesses—maybe a half dozen, counting the Kennedy woman. They'll have a list in the DA's office. Not sure they'll have the names of my team, though. Branson, Carl Zumwalt, a young cop named Bradley, Jack Phillips, Jim Lash, a couple of others." He was writing the names down as he said them.

"Here's the number you should call," Sheila said, and gave it to him. "Ask to talk to Ian Abbott. At this point, nobody's saying publically that Mantel is behind the Watkins' murders. The DA accumulated plenty of enemies over the years, so it could be pretty much anybody. The press doesn't seem to have made the connection, either—not yet. But Abbott is the one who spotted the Mantel-Kennedy link. He's the one you'll want to talk to. Maybe you can get him to put out a heads-up to the guys who were on your team."

McQuaid drew a circle around Abbott's phone number. "Who's coordinating the search for Mantel?"

"The Texas Rangers are already on it. It's complicated. Huntsville wants a piece, since they're the ones who lost him. Houston, too, because of the Watkins' murders."

"And you," McQuaid said. Blackie's wife might look like a fashion model, but at heart she was a shark. An ambitious shark.

Sheila sounded grim. "If he shows up over here, of course I'd want us to catch him—before he kills anybody else." Both of them reflected on that for a moment, then Sheila said, "I have no idea how much firepower the Rangers will put behind the search. Do you have a guess?"

She was asking because, a few years back, McQuaid had done some work for the Texas Rangers, the elite investigative division of the Department of Public Safety. He still carried a souvenir of one investigation—a bullet fragment lodged near his upper spine—and memories of long, painful months in rehab. He'd also collected some useful connections— Harry Royce, for instance, who was in charge of the SRTs, the Rangers' regional Special Response Teams. He wrote Royce's name, circled it, and drew a line to the circle around Abbott's name.

"The Rangers will pull a team together," he said. "Chances are they'll concentrate on Harris County, though. We're two hundred miles west. Mantel's not very likely to make it over here." But as he said the words, the skin prick-led on his shoulders. Mantel wasn't dumb. He'd figure where they'd likely be looking for him, and where they wouldn't. That's where he'd strike—especially if somebody threw out a piece of bait. He frowned. That was the word China had used. He didn't like it, but—

"Want me to see what I can find out from the Rangers?" he asked. "Maybe they'd let us join the team. Give them a hand."

Us. Meaning PSPD. And himself. With the Rangers. Back in the game, with skin.

"I'd be glad to help, if we're invited." Sheila hesitated. "You're sure you want to deal yourself in, though? It's not your job, Mike. It's risky."

"Breathing is risky," McQuaid said.

Sheila chuckled. "Yeah, but with breathing, we don't have a choice. There's nothing that says you have to lay it on the line in this case."

He thought about that, and thought about the night he'd had Mantel in his sights and had chosen not to fire. There was choice, and there was *choice*. And choices had consequences.

"I know the guy who runs the Rangers' SRTs," he said. "I'll talk to him and get back to you."

He hung up the phone and sat for a moment, thinking. He checked his watch: 9:40. He made another trip to the coffeemaker, where he poured a second cup. He took his mug and the yellow tablet to the receptionist's desk and sat down to clear yesterday's calls on the answering machine. Once he got that quick chore out of the way, he'd phone Harry Royce.

There were five messages on the machine. A late-afternoon call from Charlie Lipman with the name and address of a woman a suspicious husband wanted surveilled—not the kind of work McQuaid liked to do, so he'd line up one of the associates, Meredith Curtis, if she was available. The second was a quick, breathy "Oops, sorry, must've dialed the wrong number." The third was an early-evening call from a client down in the Valley, where Blackie had been working a case of industrial espionage. McQuaid filled out a pink slip and stuck it on Blackie's spindle. The fourth, at nine twenty, was a call from—

With a surge of irritation, McQuaid recognized the number. "Hellfire and blazes," he muttered, and threw his pencil down.

It was Sally, his ex-wife, Brian's mother, and the raw reminder of a very bad time in his life. Sally, who turned up like a bad penny when she wanted a favor or needed money or had to hide out for a few days from whatever threat was menacing her untidy life. How long had it been since he'd heard from her? Six months, seven? She was supposed to be picking up half of Brian's University of Texas tuition, the part that the boy's scholarship didn't cover. But she hadn't been able to come up with the money, and McQuaid—and China, too, of course—were carrying the full load themselves. China was philosophical about the situation, but McQuaid saw red whenever he thought of it. It was just like Sally to promise the boy she'd help with his college expenses, and then duck out. A promise meant nothing to her.

He hit the *Play* button and Sally's voice came on again, thin and reedy, plaintive. "Mike, listen, Mike, honey, I'm not calling the house because I know how China feels about me asking for favors and I don't want to risk her picking up the phone. But I really, *really* need to talk to you. So could you call me just as quick as you can? Pretty please. I'm in trouble, and I've exhausted every other option. You're my

last chance, Mike. My absolutely, positively *last* chance."
She rattled off her number and hung up.

Her last chance? It sounded like she was short of money
again. McQuaid had heard that song—same verse, same
chorus—so many times he couldn't begin to count the re-
peats. Sally had a lot of problems, the most challenging of
which was a split personality. Some days she was Sally.
Other days, she was a vagrant, profligate character named
Juanita whose favorite hobby was spending somebody else's
money. When he and Sally were married, of course, it had
been *his* money Juanita liked to spend, and she had gone
through quite a lot of it before he understood what was
happening.

He distrusted psychobabble, so when he first learned
about the diagnosis—that multiple-personality business,
something called dissociative identity disorder—he'd been
skeptical. But he had to admit that in Sally's case, it made a
certain kind of sense. She had always said she wanted to be
an actress, and when Juanita had first showed up, he'd
thought maybe Sally was trying on some sort of role, complete with makeup and hair and costume changes: expensive
costumes from Neiman Marcus and rings and bracelets from
Deutsch & Deutsch. Actually, acting would be a good career
choice for Sally. She was a chameleon who could move from
one persona to another with the flick of an eyelash.

Of course, Sally blamed Juanita for the cataclysmic meltdown of their marriage. China said this was an evasion, like
blaming another woman when Sally should have accepted
her own share of the responsibility. But even now, years into
a happy second marriage, McQuaid had trouble disconnect-
ing emotionally from Sally, for he felt that much of the
blame for their failure was his. She had been very young
when they got married. She had no idea how hard it would

be to be a cop's wife, what it would be like to spend night after night alone, imagining one dangerous scenario after another, dreading the knock on the door and the announcement that her husband had been shot or knifed or run down by a vehicle. That was when Juanita had put in her first appearance. And no wonder, really, given Sally's inability to cope with the stresses, which got worse, not better, after Brian was born and she had the full care of a baby.

But after the divorce and detox and rehab, after McQuaid had gotten custody of Brian and paid off most of the debts his ex-wife had left him, Juanita still continued to show up and make messes. When he could, McQuaid had tried to help Sally get her life back on track, because he still felt partly responsible for Juanita's arrival in the first place. And because Sally/Juanita was, after all, Brian's mother. The boy tried to pretend that he wasn't disappointed when she failed to remember his birthday or didn't call to congratulate him when his science project won first place in the district. But McQuaid knew that Brian cared, and that he worried about his mom.

And now there was something going on with her. Again. He sighed. He'd better check and see what her trouble was. Sometimes all it took was a phone call, a few soothing words. Maybe he'd even get lucky and she'd tell him her problem was solved. But when he punched in her number, he was shunted off to voice mail. So he left a message and clicked off.

Then back to the answering machine for that last call, at 6:10 this morning. He pushed the *Play* button. There was a silence, then a low, grating voice, like somebody crunching a mouthful of gravel.

"Hey, McQuaid. If you've heard about Kennedy and the DA and his wife, you'll know who this is. If you haven't, well, you'll hear pretty soon. Either way, just want you to know that I'm coming for you. Thought you might want to know, so you won't go to the trouble of coming for me." Then that laugh. The crazy, unmistakable laugh, like fingernails on a chalkboard, that sent a cold shudder down McQuaid's spine. "I'll be over there, my friend, as soon as I take care of a few others first."

McQuaid glanced quickly at the caller display, but it said *Unknown Number*. Mantel must be using one of those untraceable prepaid phones. He sat back for a few moments, feeling the cold settling in the pit of his stomach and thinking about choices and the number of people who were dead today because he had chosen not to shoot when he could have. When he *should* have, damn it.

Then he got up and went to the desk in his office, where he took out his Rolodex, looked up the number for the Rangers' headquarters in Austin, and punched it into his cell phone, glancing at the clock. It was 10:05. A couple of minutes later, he was back at the receptionist's desk and Harry Royce was on the line.

"Yo, McQuaid," Royce rumbled. "Good to hear from you, buddy. Got something on your mind?"

"Matter of fact, I have. His name is Mantel. Max Mantel. I had the lead on the investigative team that put him away a few years ago."

There was a silence. Then a flat, guarded, "I guess you heard he let himself out of Huntsville."

"And took out Paul Watkins and his wife. One of the investigators called me. Five a.m. this morning." He paused. "I also heard about the Kennedy woman. The witness. You know about that one?"

"Yep." Royce was laconic. "No clear connection with Mantel, though. Not that I've heard, anyway."

"I have," McQuaid said. "Sit back and listen." He hit *Play* again and held his cell phone a few inches from the speaker.

"Well, that clears up the Kennedy mystery," Royce said when the message ended. "I'll pass the word up the line. If you don't mind leaving it on the machine, I'll send somebody to make a copy."

"I can do that." McQuaid didn't offer to make the copy himself. The law enforcement officer who copied the tape and took possession of it would be at one end of the custody chain that could end in court. "I had something else in mind, though," he added, and laid out what he'd been thinking.

Royce listened to the whole thing without comment. When McQuaid was finished, he said, "I dunno, fella. It's a stunt. And it won't work if you don't line up some media, quick." He sounded doubtful. "You think you can do that?"

"It's meant to be a stunt," McQuaid said. "It's meant to attract attention." Thinking of his friend Hark Hibler, the editor, publisher, and owner of the *Pecan Springs Enterprise*, he added, "And yes, I can line up the media."

"It would spread us pretty thin," Royce said, still dubious. "I don't have an army, you know. I've got to cover the bases over in the Houston area, also down in Corpus, where Mantel's family lives. My guys are all strung out, and there's no good way to narrow the search. All I can send you is one, maybe two. Maybe not even that."

McQuaid was ready for that. "No sweat, Harry. We can handle it here. I just talked to Chief Dawson—Sheila Dawson, Pecan Springs PD. She's willing to assign some of her uniforms, if you're willing. Want me to ask her to call you?"

Royce chuckled with a cynical good humor. "Sounds like the two of you have got this plan already worked out. Yeah, sure, have her call me. We can probably put something together." His voice hardened. "And you, you watch your back,

McQuaid. You hear? If you get good media, this stunt of yours might just work too well. We don't need to be giving this bastard the satisfaction of killing another ex-cop."

McQuaid sucked in a breath. It was like pulling ice into his lungs. "*Another* ex-cop?"

Royce was regretful. "You didn't mention Zumwalt in your list of the takedowns. Reckon you haven't heard about him."

"No. I haven't." *Carl*. McQuaid felt frozen. *Four. Now there were four.* "How did it happen?"

"Drive-by. Mowing his grass out front early this morning, in Pearland. His wife heard the shots, ran out, found him facedown on the lawn. No witnesses." He cleared his throat. "We might not have made the connection so quick if his wife hadn't told the investigator that Jessie Branson phoned early this morning to tell Zumwalt about the Watkins' murders. She said Branson warned him to watch himself, to be especially careful, but he didn't take it seriously." There was a pause. "You sure you still want to go through with this stunt?"

"Yes," McQuaid said softly. *Four people, dead.* He was remembering the gun in his hand and Mantel, standing there in front of him, asking for it. Asking for suicide by cop. "Yes, I want to, Harry. I do. I really do."

"Okay, then," Royce said. "Get back to me when you've got it set up." He hung up.

McQuaid sat for a moment, trying to think of nothing, nothing at all. Then he checked his cell. Another call had come in while he was talking to Royce. He went to voice mail and heard China's voice, letting him know that she knew that Cindy Watkins had been shot, giving him the landline number at the ranch, telling him to be careful. *Be careful, McQuaid*, she said. *I love you.*

He clicked off and sat tapping his pencil on the yellow pad, a sick feeling in the pit of his stomach. *Be careful. Be careful.* He was thinking of Carl Zumwalt, who had been his partner for the better part of a decade. The two of them had always watched out for each other. They'd been careful, as careful as they could be, given their risky profession. And now Carl was dead. He had died mowing his grass. Mowing his damn grass in the goddamn front yard.

McQuaid looked down at the yellow tablet on the desk in front of him, the guilty regret weighing on his shoulders, on his conscience, the pain gnawing like a live thing in his belly. He drew a heavy line through Carl's name.

And then, in a sudden blaze of anger, he snapped the pencil in two.

Chapter Five

An ancient Roman proverb says it: *Partes humani cultus necessariae vinum atque oleum olivarum*. The necessary ingredients of civilization are wine and olive oil. But the historian Pliny put his finger on the crucial difference: "It is not with olive oil as it is with wine, for by age the oil acquires a bad flavor, and at the end of a year it is already old."

That's true, but like lots of other things in life, it depends. Your olive oil's shelf life might be as short as three or four months for an unfiltered late-harvest oil in a clear glass bottle with the cap loosened that you've stored on a sunny kitchen windowsill. It might be as long as three or four years for a filtered early-harvest, high-polyphenol oil sealed in a tin or dark bottle and stored on a dark, cool shelf in the supermarket and in your kitchen.

China Bayles
"Virgin Territory"
Pecan Springs Enterprise

"There it is," Ruby said with satisfaction as we pulled up the drive. "Not fancy or elegant, but it's comfortable."

The ranch house looked like most old Texas ranch houses, long and low, built for utility, not beauty, with a narrow porch across the front and a rusty metal roof. But it somehow managed to be beautiful anyway. The weathered gray siding could have used a fresh coat of paint, but the house seemed to settle back comfortably among the surrounding pecan and sycamore trees, easy with its age and not at all worried about being photographed for *House Beautiful*. It had been built on a slope a hundred yards from the Guadalupe River. As Ruby parked Mama on the gravel strip beside the house and we climbed out, I could see the sunshine glinting off the water between the tall cypress trees that lined the banks.

The river looked cool and inviting, especially since the June sun was already making the day feel like July and my Thyme and Seasons T-shirt was sticking to my shoulders. I glanced around. Somewhere close by, a redbird was singing— *Cheer cheer cheer!*—and the light breeze carried the pungent scent of sun-warmed cedar. The place seemed to have an almost tangible air of serenity. I could see why Ruby liked to come here.

The house was old and so was the barn behind it. But as I walked around the van I saw that there were a half dozen other buildings clustered around the barn, several of them quite large and all of them looking as if they'd been built in the last ten years—the ranch's olive oil production and storage facilities, I guessed. Off to the right, I caught a glimpse of a vegetable garden and what looked like the plant nursery Ruby had mentioned, with young trees in pots arranged in neat rows under a shade-cloth canopy.

But there wasn't time to look around, for a young woman had come to the end of the porch and was waiting to welcome us. A chunky black Lab was standing close to her knee, his tail wagging.

"Maddie!" Ruby cried, running up the three steps onto the porch. "We're so glad to be here!" She gave the woman a quick hug and bent over the dog. "Hello, Bronco. Remember me?"

"He remembers," Maddie said. The dog—obviously Ruby's friend—sat down on his haunches and held up his paw for Ruby to shake.

Maddie turned to me as I came up on the porch. "And you must be China Bayles." Her smile was shy but warm. "Hey, I just got off the phone—a couple more people from San Antonio wanting to RSVP for your workshop tomorrow. Which brings us to twenty-four registrations." She put out her hand. "Thank you for agreeing to do it, China. It's very nice of you."

"You're welcome, Maddie." I took her hand, noticing the work-hardened skin. "Glad I could make it."

I didn't say that I would have canceled if I hadn't been rudely instructed to get out of town by both my husband and the local police chief, but the thought came into my mind. And then, just as quickly, I pushed it away. Whatever was going to happen in Pecan Springs was going to happen *there*, and I couldn't do a damn thing about it. I was *here*, and the Last Chance Ranch seemed a pretty nice place to be, at first sight, anyway. If I could have known what lay ahead in the next twenty-four hours, I might have felt differently. But for now, I was just going to relax and enjoy myself.

Maddie was almost as tall as Ruby, her skin darkly tanned and her hair black, parted in the middle and worn in two thick, glossy braids—more to keep it out of her way,

I thought, than to make a style statement. It was hard to guess her age, but from what Ruby had said about her, I thought she must be in her early thirties. Her features were striking: a broad forehead, high cheekbones, aquiline nose.

But what caught and held the attention was the bold scar that slashed across her right cheek, her jaw, and down her neck—the signature of the accident that had killed her parents. If it was the cause of the wariness I read in her expression, I could understand why. Some women would have considered that scar disfiguring and headed straight for cosmetic surgery. But Maddie was slender and athletic, and her worn jeans, plaid cotton blouse, and sneakers gave her the look of a woman who cared more about getting the job done than impressing people with her appearance. The scar belonged to her. She owned it—not the other way around.

"I was admiring your olive grove as we drove in," I said. "The trees look really good."

Maddie's eyes lit up. "Thank you. The last couple of years have been hard on them, with the drought. But the weather was kind to us in the spring, and it looks like we'll have a good harvest."

"I noticed that you're irrigating," I said.

She nodded. "We pump water from the Guadalupe. Plus, we have a sixteen-hundred-gallon tanker trailer that we can tow where we need it. Good for brush fires, too." She waved her hand at a large white tank on a two-axle trailer, parked under a tree. "As you could see, the large orchards along the lane—the ones that we harvest mechanically—are irrigated. But there are smaller plantings around the ranch, dryland olives. No irrigation. That may be the future, here at Last Chance." She turned to Ruby. "Are you guys ready to eat? The men have been out working all morning. They'll be here in a few minutes, and they'll be hungry. After lunch, I'll show you your cabin and the room where you'll be doing your workshop. I can take China for a tour of the ranch, too."

Ruby raised an eyebrow. "Just China? Bronco and I can't come along?"

That drew a quick smile from Maddie. "Sure, if you want. There are a few things that are new since you were out here last." She turned back to me. "I suppose Ruby told you that she's not really a visitor. She first came to the ranch as a girl, long before I arrived on the scene."

"Hey, stop," Ruby protested. "You're making me feel *ancient.*"

I had to laugh at that. "Yes, Ruby told me. She said she remembers you as a toddler."

"That's right." Maddie's smile became a laugh. "I was one of those curious little kids who sticks her nose into everything on the ranch. When Ruby was here, she always looked out for me. She can tell you how many lessons I had to learn the hard way. And I'm still getting knocked on my butt twice a day, at least." She flung a tanned arm at the surrounding landscape in a gesture that was part demonstration, part possession—and part determination. "Eliza . . ." She paused. "Ruby told you about her?"

"A little, and about Sofia, too," I said.

She nodded and went on. "Eliza always said that the olive trees were her children. To me, growing up here on the ranch, they were my brothers and sisters. I'll do anything I have to, *anything*, to keep them growing." Another laugh, this one with a little edge. "Some people call me a tree hugger, you know."

I wondered who had called her that. "Tree huggers are my kind of people," I said warmly.

Ruby wrinkled her nose. "I knew you'd like her," she said, in a stage whisper that Maddie was meant to overhear.

From somewhere behind the house, I heard a bell clanging loudly, like an old-time dinner bell. "That's the ranch bell," Maddie said. "Come on."

I followed Maddie into the house. "It's lovely," I said as we walked through the long, dim central hall, Ruby and Bronco behind us. The hallway walls were painted a deep muted saffron, a strong contrast to the dark woodwork. The living room opened out to the right through a wide archway that revealed an expanse of polished wooden floor, a fireplace, and several comfortable overstuffed chairs covered with brightly colored Mexican weavings. The doors to the left were closed—bedrooms, I thought.

"Eliza's father built this place almost a hundred years ago," Maddie said. "The Last Chance was a working sheep ranch back then. Four thousand acres. Mr. Butler had just two children—Eliza and her brother, Howard—but he had to feed a couple of dozen ranch hands. That's why the dining room and kitchen are so large. The men ate at least two meals a day here, every day." She opened a door on the right to give me a quick glimpse of a large modern kitchen. "Sofia's kitchen," she said.

"Nice," I said appreciatively, glancing at the layout and the industrial-sized appliances. "I became a connoisseur of working kitchens when we installed the kitchen at our tearoom and had to make sure it was up to code. It was a big job."

Maddie nodded. "Big job here, too. Eliza was planning to hire a professional chef, expand to a restaurant menu, and open on weekend evenings and for special events—a pretty ambitious agenda. Still, we're less than an hour's drive from San Antonio, and with the right kind of advertising, Eliza thought we could do it." She shut the door. "But that was then," she added matter-of-factly. "Under the circumstances,

I've put the plan on hold, along with several other parts of the business. The café is open with a soup-and-sandwich menu on tour and workshop weekends—like tomorrow. Sofia and her helper Abby do the cooking, and Abby's sisters do the serving."

I guessed that the "circumstances" had to do with the fact that Maddie's inheritance was on hold. I was about to ask but she was already moving briskly, leading me into a large, light room some twenty feet wide. It spanned the entire length of the house, perhaps sixty feet.

"We set up ten small tables here when the café is open," Maddie said as we went in. "We can seat up to forty. As a dining room, it works very well. And it's really very nice."

It was. On the far wall, there were four sliding glass patio doors that opened onto a sunny flagstone patio bordered by rosemary and artemisia and with small islands of olive trees underplanted with blooming lavender. The room's other three walls, rough-plastered, were painted a pale ochre and hung with an interesting collection of folk art—weavings, paintings, wooden objects. The floor was made of terracotta tiles, the warm color contrasting with the pale walls. A long Spanish-style oak table in the middle of the room was set for ten with brightly colored placemats, wineglasses at each place, and several pottery pitchers filled with olive branches and wildflowers. It looked like there'd be a crowd for lunch. I wondered who would be joining us.

An old woman, bent and frail-looking, came in from the kitchen. She wore a dark cotton dress with an olive-green apron embroidered with the words *Last Chance Olive Ranch*, and a half-dozen strands of wooden and bright ceramic beads around her neck. She was pushing a tiered cart loaded with a tray of cheese and cold cuts, a wooden bowl of crisp salad greens and a half dozen smaller bowls of cut raw veggies, and a dishpan-sized glass bowl of chunky gazpacho. A young woman followed her with a basket of sliced bread. She put the bread down and went back into the kitchen.

Ruby took my arm. "China, I'd like you to meet Sofia. When I was a kid, she always made tamales when I visited—tamales with olives, of course."

"And how else would a tamale be made?" Sofia asked in a cracked voice. "Tamales *must* have olives. That is a Last Chance rule."

I found myself holding the old woman's thin, wrinkled hand, which gripped mine with a surprising firmness. It was hard to guess her age—late seventies, perhaps older. Her hair, braided and coiled into a crown around her head, was a silvery contrast to the dark skin of her face. Her eyes were very dark under heavy dark brows, but they were not the eyes of an old woman. They were alert and inquiring, and I felt as if she could see through me somehow. It was a slightly uncomfortable feeling.

After a moment, the old woman nodded, as if she had found what she was looking for and was satisfied. "I am glad to meet Ruby's friend," she said, letting go of my hand. "She has spoken often of you. You are a lawyer." Her smile was oddly calculating. "It is interesting to be a lawyer, is it not?"

I was about to say that I was no longer in practice, but Ruby was beginning to move the dishes from the cart to the oak buffet that stood against the wall nearby. "I'll help you with this, Sofia," she said. "The guys are here."

I looked around. Several men dressed in jeans, work shirts, and boots had come in from the patio and were talking to Maddie. I noticed that she didn't seem shy with them—she was friendly and laughing. But Sofia had put a hand on my arm and was drawing me aside, with a quick glance over her shoulder.

71

"I would like to talk," she said in a low voice. "Perhaps after you get back from your tour of the ranch this afternoon? I will be finished with the kitchen work then, and in my cabin, resting." She tilted her head, birdlike, but those eyes betrayed a canny intelligence. "An old woman enjoys her rest, you know."

"I'd like to do that," I said, wondering what she wanted.

But I didn't have time to think about it. The men were heading toward the buffet, and Maddie was leading me through a quick round of introductions. Then I found myself standing behind Ruby and several others in the buffet line, making small talk with the guy behind me as I picked up my sandwich makings and put them on my tray, along with silverware and an olive-green napkin.

"Maddie says you drove over from Pecan Springs this morning," he said. "You and Ruby are staying for the weekend?"

The man who had asked the question was tall and well built, with broad shoulders, thinning gingery hair, pale eyebrows, and very blue eyes in a sunburned face—a man with the look of a cowboy. He'd been introduced to me as Pete Lawrence, the manager of the ranch's olive groves. Behind him, the smaller, younger man in T-shirt and jeans, wearing a Last Chance olive-green gimme cap with the bill turned backwards, was Jerry Kinkaid. He was in charge of the plant nursery, which (as he quickly told me) involved propagating and growing young trees and potting them up from one-to three-to five-gallon pots, ready for sale to retail and wholesale customers.

"Jerry also manages the olive press during the harvest," Pete said. "That's when he gets a real workout. It's a round-the-clock job, for as long as it takes."

"I'd love to come and watch when you're pressing the

oil," I said, adding salad greens and some raw broccoli, green peppers, and cauliflower to my plate.

Pete picked up two pieces of bread, some cheese, and two thick slices of ham. "Get Maddie to show you the video we made of Jerry doing the pressing last year. That's as good as a visit." He grinned. "Although of course you're welcome to come and watch."

"Yeah," Jerry said. "If you come, you can take home a bottle of fresh olive oil. Fresh, very fresh, *unbelievably* fresh. Not that two- or three-year-old oil you find on the supermarket shelves." He leaned around Pete to frown at me. "Which I hope you are not buying. It's better to go without than use that stuff. Most of it, anyway."

"I know," I said, a little smugly. "I always check for a date on the bottle."

I had been doing research on the subject of olives and had learned that olive "oil" isn't an oil at all. It's actually a fruit *juice*, the juice of ripe olives, pressed, filtered, and bottled. Like any fruit juice, the fresher the better, which is why local olive oil may be preferable, all things considered. Even if it *is* truly extra virgin (that is, the cold-pressed juice from the first pressing of the olives), imported olive oil has been on the move for months: shipped from place to place, stored and bottled and perhaps even rebottled, nobody knows how many times. By the time it gets to your kitchen, it may be two or three years old. Even if the oil doesn't smell or taste rancid, many of the heart-healthy compounds—the all-important polyphenols—have degraded to the point where they won't do you a dime's worth of good.

"Good that you check for the date," Jerry said approvingly. "But even that doesn't always help. For instance, if it's a use-by date, you have no idea how it was calculated. A specific harvest date is better. But there's a new wrinkle, too. California, which produces most of the olives in the U.S., allows this year's olives to bear next year's date—making them look fresher than they are."

"No kidding?" Pete had finished constructing his sandwich and was adding some luscious-looking marinated olives to his plate. "I hadn't heard. How are they getting by with that?"

"They harvest the olives in the fall, same as we do here in Texas," Jerry said. "The oil is pressed at the time of harvest, of course. But it's stored and bottled in the spring. The date on the label is really the bottling date. Which may push other states—and European producers as well—to adopt the same practice. In the name of competition, you know. It's a really competitive business," he added, to me. "Cutthroat."

"Deceptive," Pete growled. "Some growers will do anything to get ahead. Cut any corner. Screw standards. To hell with quality." The words *some growers* had a special emphasis.

"Damn right," Jerry said, as if he knew who Pete was talking about.

I didn't. To cover the awkward gap in the conversation, I chirped brightly, "So the next time I buy California oil, I just need to remember to subtract a year from the date on the label. Right?"

"Nah," Pete said, as we moved forward in the line, toward the bowl of gazpacho. "You don't have to do that. In fact, you don't need to buy any oil at all. We'll send you home with a liter of our estate oil, produced from the most recent harvest. And the next time you're here, we'll give you another one."

"Best in Texas," Jerry said, nodding to a pair of carafes. One was labeled *Lemon and Olive Oil*, the other *Balsamic*

Vinegar and Olive Oil. "Sofia uses it to make her dressings," he added. "And in her gazpacho."

"Estate oil?" I gave my salad greens a liberal dressing of the lemon and olive oil. "What's that?"

"A blend of oils from several different kinds of olives," Pete said. "We produce both a Spanish and an Italian estate oil, blended in small lots, carefully. And I do mean carefully. We can trace every single olive back to the tree that produced it."

Jerry laughed. "Well, not quite. But almost. Anyway, we'll make sure that you get a nice sample of each."

Ahead of us in the buffet line, Ruby was filling her bowl with gazpacho. With a laugh, she asked, "Didn't I say you'd love it here, China?" She filled another bowl and set it on the buffet for me. "Didn't I, huh? Bet you're sorry now that you didn't come out with me sooner."

"Yes, I am," I said truthfully, as Ruby left the buffet and headed for the table. "But I'm glad I finally managed to get here." I picked up the bowl she had filled for me, sniffing appreciatively, and put it on my tray. I looked up and noticed that there were several bottles of wine at the end of the buffet.

"Wow," I said over my shoulder to Pete. "Wine with lunch. Now I'm *really* glad. Do you guys do this all the time, or is it a special occasion?" But Pete wasn't there. He was following Ruby to the table.

"A *very* special occasion," a deep voice said behind me— a familiar voice that I recognized at once. I turned quickly, so fast that I lost my balance, and my napkin. A strong arm steadied me, and a man bent over and picked up my napkin off the floor.

"Hello, China," he said, putting the napkin back on my tray. "How long has it been? Twelve years? Fifteen?"

No. It hadn't been twelve years, or fifteen. More like twenty, that mad fling during the summer between our first and second year of law school. Chet Atwood and I were clerking in the Texas Attorney General's office in Austin that summer. We'd work late, sometimes till nine or ten o'clock, then go out with a couple of other law clerks. We liked the live piano music at Donn's Depot on West Fifth, in the old Clarksville neighborhood. The Depot had once been an early 1900s Missouri Pacific train depot. The entry area was a real railroad car and the ladies' restroom was a real caboose. Chet and I would have a couple of glasses of wine and dance, holding each other close on the crowded floor.

And then together, we would walk to his two-room student apartment over a garage just up the street, where we'd pour another glass of wine and lie on the bed and talk and finally, sweetly, make love. July and August was blazing hot that year, the nights were sultry, and the tiny apartment had no air conditioning. The window next to the narrow bed was open wide and Donn's piano, dreaming with the moonlight through the trees and over the rooftops, took us where we wanted to go. The night and the music were magic for two young kids on their way somewhere, not knowing where, just clinging to whatever temporary refuge they could find in each other, and then moving on.

But not together. I went back to class in the fall, and then on to a corporate career in criminal law. Chet—a laid-back guy with a large, soft heart—had already had enough of the constant push-push-push of law school. He wasn't ambitious and hard-charging. He preferred to let things happen rather than *make* them happen. The legal profession wasn't the right place for him, and our summer clerking job made that clear. He dropped out and disappeared.

76

Well, not quite. He sent me postcards from here and there, from Provence, from Spain, from the south of Italy—going with the flow, I assumed, moving wherever it took him. But he gave me no address where I could write to him, and anyway, I wouldn't have known what to write. I couldn't say "Come back to me" or "Where are you? I'll come to you." Other people had filled my life, and other dreams and ambitions, and whatever connection Chet and I might have had was broken.

And here he was.

"Oh my gosh, Chet," I babbled. "Chet Atwood. Is it really you? I mean . . . Well, golly. What a surprise! What are *you* doing here?"

He had put on some weight since I'd seen him last, but he still had that relaxed, Kevin-Costner, middle-America, good-guy look. He wore jeans and a short-sleeved blue polo shirt. His face was tanned and weather-beaten, the face of a man who refused to spend his days in an office, and the lines around his mouth were more pronounced. But his brown hair was still thick and dark and his right eyebrow still lifted in a crazy quirk, and he still had a problem with beard stubble. It grew darkly along his jaw and I knew without touching him that if he rubbed his face against mine, it would be rough and sandpapery. I flushed at the recollection, for with it came a flood of memories. Warm memories. Stirring.

Chet was watching me, his mouth crinkling into a familiar smile. I wondered if he could read my thoughts, and my flush deepened.

But all he said was, "I came over to restock Maddie's tasting room. I'm a part-owner of the vineyard on the other side of the river." He stepped around the end of the table and picked up a wine bottle. In the comically exaggerated tone of a French maître d', he said, "Madame will find that it's difficult to pair ze wine weez ze gazpacho, but I can recommend ze Sauvignon Blanc."

I laughed and he slipped back into his own voice. "And this—" He held the label so I could see the drawing of a vineyard with a Tuscan-style house in the distance. The label read *Last Chance Vineyard and Winery*. "This is it, China." His eyes met mine. "Our vineyard and winery. I hope you'll come over and visit us before you leave. I would love to show it to you."

Our vineyard . . . Visit us. He was married? I sneaked a glance—he wasn't wearing a ring. Some guys don't, of course, especially if they work outside. "Sure," I said. "I'd love to see it."

He pointed toward the table. "Find a seat and save the one beside it for me. I'll get some food and join you." He grinned. "I'll be the one with the bottle."

I had to grin, too. That was what he had always said, back in those half-forgotten days when we were students together. We would be planning to take a picnic to Zilker Park, or sail on Lake Travis with his longtime friends Jason and Andrea, or climb Mount Bonnell to watch the sunset. Chet would be the one with the bottle. And even then, he knew his wines. He made a game of it, knowing wine, but it had been a serious game. The wine would always be just right.

All that had been a very long time ago, and we were two very different people now. But when Chet sat down beside me, poured the wine, and we began to eat and talk, it was easy and relaxed and comfortable, and the years fell away like leaves from a tree.

We had plenty of catching up to do. He had spent a decade traveling. "Working and learning," he said, "mostly in southern Europe, in wine country. I wanted to learn as much as I could about the business, so I latched on to anybody who was willing to teach me."

He had been back in the Hill Country for only five or six years, partnered with Jason, who was now married to Andrea. Hence the *our* and the *we*. Andrea had grown up on a local ranch and knew the area. She had introduced them to Boyd Butler. They purchased a hundred acres from him, Chet said, and went into the grape business.

"Boyd Butler?" I asked. "So you bought a piece of the old Last Chance Ranch."

"Yep," Chet replied. "We call ourselves the Last Chance Vineyard and Winery. Jason is the business manager. I'm responsible for the vineyard and wine production. Andrea works with both of us. We're still a start-up and it'll be a few years before we have a decent harvest. We have vines in production, but they're still young. So mostly we buy grapes from local vineyards to make our wines—the one you're drinking, for instance."

"Nice," I said, tasting it again. "Very nice."

He nodded. "We're learning. Like the olive business, it takes a while. By the time we start harvesting our own grapes, we'll be expert vintners." He went on with his story, the personal side of it. He had been married briefly, then divorced, no children. "I was too footloose to manage a long-term relationship," he said ruefully. He quirked his eyebrow. "But you'd know about that, wouldn't you? I sort of ran out on you, if I remember right."

"I don't think either of us was ready for anything long-term back then," I said ruefully. "I had a lot of ambition and drive. You know. Things to do. Places to go."

"And I didn't have any." He laughed. "Ambition and drive, I mean. The way I remember it, I was one lazy sonovagun." He shook his head. "But not you. You used to scare the hell out of me, China, you were so motivated. You were *fierce*, you know? Ruthless."

"Yeah, that was me," I admitted. I was a little uncomfortable with *ruthless,* but *fierce* certainly fit.

"And then what?" He cocked his eyebrow at me. "You made the big time, you hung around for a while, and chucked it." When I looked surprised, he added, "Andrea kept tabs on you, from a distance. She wrote me that you'd left your legal career and moved to a small town and opened your own business." He twinkled. "I was married at the time, or I might have come looking for you. Might've tried picking up where we left off."

I wondered, fleetingly, what would have happened if he had. Probably nothing, I guessed. Chet and I were a summer thing. We'd been close for a while, but we always knew it was temporary. I said, "I got to the point where the career didn't mean anything to me. I was sick of living in the city. I needed to do something else with my life. Something I could care about."

"And now you've got an herb shop in Pecan Springs. And you're married." It wasn't a question. And he wasn't looking at me.

I nodded, busying myself with my soup. "I have my own shop, and I'm partnered with my friend Ruby in several sideline businesses. And yes, I'm married to an ex-cop, Mike McQuaid. Between us, we have two great kids: his son Brian, a freshman at UT, and Caitie, my niece, just thirteen." I laughed a little. "Kids, cat, dog, chickens, a big house and some acreage. Kind of a found family, you might say." At the thought of McQuaid, I felt a sudden cold in the pit of my stomach, and I shivered. I had successfully pushed the threat away for a little while, and I didn't want to think of what might be happening.

Chet frowned a little. "All going good back home, China?" He'd always had an almost uncanny way of reading me.

"Mostly," I said, trying for nonchalance. "You know how it is with real life. Ups and downs."

Still frowning, he touched my little finger with his little finger, a familiar, playful gesture. "Everything okay in the marriage?" he asked. Then, quickly, "Hey. If it's none of my business, just tell me to buzz off."

I met his eyes, feeling the need to be truthful. "Everything in the marriage is fine. It's just that my husband has this dicey ex-cop thing going on this weekend. It could be . . . well, dangerous. I guess I'm sort of nervous." With an uneasy laugh, I dug into my salad. "Not that I can *do* anything about it. I was already scheduled to come out here, and he didn't much like the idea of me hanging around, getting in the way."

Chet raised an eyebrow. "An ex-cop thing?"

"An escaped convict who's gunning for him." I held up my fork. "Look. Could we talk about something else? You mentioned Boyd Butler a moment ago. Ruby tells me that he's challenged Eliza Butler's will. He wants to take the ranch away from Maddie."

His mouth tightened. "So you know about that. Well, one way or another, it looks like he might get it." He looked at me, and the light seemed to dawn. "Hey, maybe you're here professionally. To help Maddie." He chuckled wryly. "Even if she asked me, I couldn't give her any help. If you'll recall, I left law school before I could take Curzon's accursed course on wills and estates." Even if she asked? I was wondering what that meant, but he was going on. "And Maddie's lawyer—Clarence—isn't much better equipped than I am. He's a local guy. Knows the players very well. Clueless about the playbook."

"No, I'm not here professionally," I said. "I took Curzon, but I'm no whiz on wills and estates. I'm interested, though. Maybe you can tell me. What's the deal?"

"Here's how I understand it," he said. "When Eliza's will was probated, Boyd was surprised—*incredulous* is probably a better word—when he found out that he wasn't in line to inherit the ranch. So he challenged the will. He charged that Eliza was mentally incompetent when she left her property— this ranch plus some oil leases out in Pecos County—to Maddie, who isn't a relative. He also charged undue influence on Maddie's part."

I emptied my salad bowl and pushed it away. "Alleging the usual nasty stuff?"

"Right." He pulled at his ear. "Of course, since then, he's changed his tune."

"Changed his tune? How?"

Chet gave me a look that I couldn't read. "Ask Maddie. If she wants you to know, she'll tell you. Anyway, her lawyer—good old Clarence—knew enough to ask for a jury trial. The probate jury found in her favor on both counts, and we all thought she was home free. But the judge—a friend of Boyd's named Tinker Tyson—reversed the jury's verdict. He found in favor of Boyd on both counts and awarded everything to his pal. The ranch, the West Texas property, everything."

"Reversed the jury?" I was surprised. But then, on second thought, not so much. I had read about similar happenings in Texas, where probate judges are elected in partisan elections, where their party affiliation is listed on the ballot. They frequently have no legal training. I picked up my sandwich. "His name really *is* Tinker Tyson?"

Chet nodded. "He's an old high school chum of Boyd's. Which explains a lot, of course."

I understood. "The reversal was appealed, I suppose," I said. Even good old Clarence ought to know enough to do that. "What happened to the appeal?"

"The appellate court found a handful of legal errors and sent the ruling back 'for judicial review.'"

I rolled my eyes. "Back to the judge who committed the errors in the first place. The plaintiff's buddy, Tinker Tyson." The name made me want to giggle. "Clarence didn't raise the issue of judicial misconduct?"

"He did. He filed a complaint with the Commission on Judicial Conduct, but you know how those things go. Exactly nowhere." He picked up his ham sandwich. "I did a little digging when this happened, China. You know, probate law is so complicated that lawyers need to take Curzon before they can even begin to read the fine print. But probate judges in Texas are political animals." He paused to chew a mouthful. "It turns out that only a couple of dozen in the state's two-hundred-and-fifty-some counties have any professional legal certification. The rest of them are farmers, car dealers, local politicians. They're even more clueless than I am when it comes to probate law."

That would make for some humongous problems, I thought. "So what happened when Tyson did his so-called 'review'?"

"Not much." Chet finished his sandwich. "He gave Maddie a survivor's tenancy in this house and in the West Texas property, and handed Eliza's half of the Last Chance and her share of the business to Boyd, as Eliza's nearest and dearest."

"Uh-oh," I said. The survivor's tenancy meant that Maddie could continue to live in the house as long as she wanted, which was something. But if Ruby was right and the oil reserves were depleted, the West Texas property was essentially worthless. The award was designed to prove to the appeals court that the probate judge had seriously reconsidered his original ruling, but it wouldn't help Maddie. And losing half of the business to Boyd would be crippling. I remembered her earlier comment about putting things on hold. She must have decided not to invest a lot of work in projects she would have to hand over to somebody else.

Chet nodded. "Uh-oh is right. Keep the house but lose the ranch and be forced to share the business. A compromise she can't accept. In his ruling, Tinker Tyson made a point of saying that if Maddie had been Eliza's daughter, the new will would have been honored and Boyd would have been out of luck. Blood is thicker than water."

I finished my sandwich. "Clarence is appealing again, of course."

"Yes, and he managed to get a stay until the appeal is heard—which could take months." Chet pursed his lips. "I don't have a lot of confidence in Clarence. He doesn't handle estate matters on a regular basis, and the appeals process is tricky."

"Doesn't sound like there's much anybody can do," I said. "At this stage of the game, anyway." I was wishing that Ruby had heard Chet's account, which made it clear that there was nothing *I* could do. Short of butting into Clarence's case, that is. Which I wasn't prepared to do, for a lot of good reasons.

"The whole damn thing has been one long, stinking headache for Maddie." Chet picked up his sandwich again. "Bad enough that she had to be the one managing Eliza's care for her last couple of years. Sofia helped, but Maddie did all the hard stuff. Then there were the accusations about the drowning." He glanced at me. "You heard about that?"

"Drowning, yes," I said. "Accusations, not really."

"Well, maybe *accusations* is too strong a word. It didn't come to that. But Boyd let it be known around the community that he thought Maddie had been careless." His mouth twisted. "That she'd left the door unlocked, which made it easy for Eliza to get out of the house that night and wander down to the river. That Eliza would have been safer in the nursing home where *he* would have put her, if only Maddie had agreed."

I cocked my head to one side. "Was there anything to it? To what Boyd was saying, I mean."

"Of course not. It's true that Boyd wanted to put Eliza in a nursing home, but if you ask me, it was only to restrict Maddie's access to her. The sheriff looked into the drowning, but didn't find any criminal negligence. And Maddie—well, for a while, she thought that Boyd himself might have had something to do with it. He came over to see Eliza earlier that evening." His voice held a bitter edge. "This whole thing has been damned hard on her, believe me. And it's all Boyd's doing, start to finish. That guy—he's a real piece of work, believe me, China. I wouldn't put *anything* past him."

I doubted that Chet was an impartial observer, but that was neither here nor there. "How's Maddie dealing with it?"

"The way she deals with everything. If it's getting to her, she doesn't show it. The good, the bad, the ugly—that woman keeps it all inside. You never know exactly what she's thinking. Or feeling."

If Chet could read me, I could read him. And the expression on his face—part frustration, part sympathy, part something else—told me that he and Maddie were more than just friends. Or that he *wished* they were more than just friends. Or something. Which probably accounted for his feelings about Boyd.

"Hey, China." Ruby put her hand on my shoulder, and I looked up. "If you're finished eating, Maddie wants to show you our cabin."

"Great," I replied. "I'm ready." To Chet, I said, "Are you going to be around this weekend?"

"You bet," he said firmly. "If you don't have plans for this evening, how about coming over to our place for supper? I'm sure Jason will be glad to see you again. And Andrea loves to cook for company."

"Sounds like fun," I said, thinking that it certainly beat sitting around, worrying about McQuaid. "How about if I bring Ruby?"

"Please do. Andrea will be twice as happy." He leaned over and kissed me on the cheek. "I'll drive over and pick you up around four thirty or five. We'll take a tour of the vineyards before supper."

"Looks like you and Chet are old buddies," Ruby remarked as we went outside. "Where do you know him from?"

"We interned together one summer." I shoved my hands in my pockets. "Actually, we had a thing going for a while, a couple of lifetimes ago."

"A thing, huh?" Ruby slanted me a look. "Well, for your information, he and Maddie have a thing going. Or maybe I should say 'had.'"

"Really? They're not seeing each other now?" That would be too bad. It sounded like Maddie could use a good guy to take her mind off the bad stuff in her life, and Chet was definitely a good guy. At least, he was when I knew him. A little footloose, but weren't we all, at that age? And now that he had the winery, he seemed to have settled down.

"Sofia told me that Maddie broke up with him when

Boyd—" Ruby stopped as Maddie came up to us, carrying a stack of folded sheets and towels.

"I'm heading for your cabin," Maddie said. "You guys can drive your van over there. Ruby, it's the one on the far end, where you usually stay."

"Yep," Ruby said happily. "Manzanilla. It's my favorite of all the cabins." She took my arm. "Come on, China. This is going to be *fun*."

Chapter Six

MCQUAID

Friday Mid-Morning

McQuaid got his third cup of coffee, took it back to his desk, sat down, and phoned Sheila. He needed to let her know there'd been another murder—*four, now there were four*—and ask her to call Royce and tell him she planned to station a team of armed cops in civilian clothes at the park where the Lions Club barbecue would be held on Saturday. Sheila was in a city council meeting, so he left the message with Connie Page, who promised to slap it into the chief's hand the minute she got back to the office.

"Top priority, Con," he added, although he didn't think he needed to tell her that. Connie had been his assistant during the five or six months he had occupied the police chief's chair, after Bubba Harris resigned and before the city council hired Sheila. She would understand from the tone of his voice that this was important.

"Got it, sir," Connie said. "Top priority."

"And another thing. Could you pull a Taser out of the equipment room for me?" He waited for her to ask why, or even say it was against departmental policy (he was sure it was). But she didn't.

"A Taser. Want a vest?"

That was Connie, always trying to be helpful. "I've got a vest," he said. "I'll stop in and pick up the Taser this afternoon, when I get back to Pecan Springs."

His next call was to Ian Abbott, the assistant Harris County DA, who had linked the dead body at the Ship Channel to Martha Kennedy, the key witness for the prosecution in the Mantel case. McQuaid introduced himself and gave Abbott the list of the detectives who had worked with him on the investigation. Bradley, Phillips, Lash, Songer, Dillard. It was a good bunch, the whole lot of them. But Carl had been the best. Best ever, now gone. McQuaid felt a sharp stab of regret and a sharper, hotter stab of guilt. If he had just pulled the damn trigger and given Mantel what he was asking for, Carl would be opening the fridge right now, pulling out a frosty Michelob, making himself a bologna sandwich.

"I'll see that we get a heads-up out to your guys," Abbott said. "I suppose you heard about Carl Zumwalt? Mrs. Zumwalt told us that Branson called to warn him."

"Yeah, I heard," McQuaid said flatly. "Be sure to let my guys know about Carl when your office talks to them. Maybe that'll give them a little more incentive to be alert. And let me know if you dig up anything on Mantel's whereabouts." He rattled off his cell number.

"I hope you're watching yourself," Abbott said, and McQuaid heard the tension in his voice, like a tight wire running through his words. "The last thing we want is for Mantel to score another hit. Especially under the circumstances."

"Damn straight," McQuaid said shortly.

He understood the "circumstances" Abbott was talking about, and that the man's concern was primarily political.

The DA's office would not want the story of the Watkins' murders linked to Max Mantel's escape until *after* Mantel was safely under lock and key. They especially wouldn't want any attention from newspapers or television. Which was exactly why McQuaid wasn't going to tell Abbott about his plan to use the media to lure Mantel to Pecan Springs. If it turned out well, Abbott would hear about it. If it turned out in some ugly, unpredictable way—well, he'd hear about that, too.

The next call went to the *Enterprise*. McQuaid tapped his fingers impatiently as he waited for the receptionist to go in search of Harkness Hibler, the editor, who—it turned out—was keeping score for the senior men's horseshoe tournament in the yard behind the building.

"Sorry, McQuaid." Hark's chair squeaked as he sat down in it. "The horseshoe tournament is hot news in the weekend sports section, and I needed to get the flavor before I write the story."

"Who's winning?" The horseshoe tournaments and domino playoffs were a relic of times past in Pecan Springs, but lots of folks liked to know that they were still going on. It made them think the town was still the way they imagined it had been, back in the day. Which of course it never was, except in their imaginations.

Hark chuckled. "Herb Mayo, that old reprobate. He's good as long as he stays off the sauce. Let him get a couple of beers under his belt and his game goes to hell." Another chuckle. "How's things with you, buddy? The PI business keeping you occupied?"

"You know how it goes," McQuaid said casually. "Some days are more occupied than others."

"Same here," Hark said. He was an easygoing guy with

a shambling gait and a baggy-pants slouch that always reminded McQuaid of Garrison Keillor. But when it came to the *Enterprise,* Hark was all business. Several years before, he had bought the faltering Pecan Springs weekly from the Seidensticker family and immediately began bringing it back to life as an honest-to-God newspaper that lived in the real world. While small-town newspapers were going under by the dozens, Hark had made the *Enterprise* locally relevant and (more important) a must-read for every citizen. He had also shocked the town by instituting an editorial policy designed to put news—real honest-to-God *news*—back on the front page.

In the days when the Seidenstickers were managing the paper, it was partnered with the local chamber of commerce. Every story was scrubbed, sanitized, and pasteurized before it was offered for public consumption, with the aim of making Pecan Springs look like the coziest, cleanest, most idyllic place in Texas. As far as the *Enterprise* was concerned, this was a town where every law was obeyed to the letter, where seldom was heard a discouraging word, and the skies were not cloudy all day.

But Hark was a serious journalist who insisted on covering all the news, good, bad, ugly, and downright indecent. On his front pages, you could read about the meth lab the sheriff's drug squad closed down just outside of town, the bribery case that involved three members of the town council, and the arrest of a prominent businessman on child porn charges—stories that the previous editor would have reduced to single bland paragraphs hidden below the fold on the back page, along with the livestock auction notices. Hark's editorial policy put him seriously crosswise with the C of C folks who preferred to portray Pecan Springs as a town so clean it squeaked. But he was as stubborn as a Texas mule, journalistically speaking, and stubbornly committed to telling the plain, unvarnished truth, however politically incorrect it might be.

"It is what it is," he liked to say. "That's the way I'm going to print it. You don't like it, damn it, don't read it. Simple as that."

McQuaid went straight to the point. "Got an idea I want to float past you, Hark. I just got off the phone with the guy who's in charge of the Texas Rangers' Special Response Teams. Could be a story about to break—a big one."

"Rangers?" Hark's chair squeaked again, and McQuaid knew he was sitting bolt upright. "Somebody's getting traded? There's an injury? They didn't threaten to fire Banister again, did they?" Hark was a Rangers fan. He didn't miss a game, even when the season was as disappointing as this one.

"Not baseball," McQuaid said. "Texas Rangers, as in law-and-order." He paused. "There's been a murder. Four of them, in fact." *Four murders that he could have prevented with one single bullet. One.*

"Four murders? Rangers? Jeez. When? Where? Here?" Hark's computer keyboard began clicking rapidly. He was taking notes.

"Not Rangers," McQuaid said. "And not here. Not now. Not yet." He paused. "But maybe we can put an *end* to it here—with a little help from you and your friends in the media. If this works, you'll get an exclusive."

"Ah," Hark said happily. "An exclusive. I am all ears, my friend. Shoot."

McQuaid told Hark what he knew and followed that up with what he planned—tentatively, that is. He still had to firm up the details with Sheila and talk to Reilly, president of the local Lions, who needed to know what was in the works. It was dicey to run a sting in a crowd situation.

But the important thing, the immediate thing, was to get as much of the story on the wire as quickly as possible. It was still possible to make the noon news on the TV affiliates—NBC, CBS, ABC, FOX—in Houston, Austin, and San Antonio. McQuaid knew that Bad Max had an insatiable ego. He loved publicity, loved seeing his name in print, his face on television. He'd be watching and listening to find out how his escape was being covered in the newspapers and on TV and radio.

And the media would jump on this story, for damn sure. It had all the right ingredients, the gory, grisly stuff that fed the appetites of readers and listeners. Husband and wife murdered in swank Houston neighborhood, retired cop gunned down in his front yard, witness killed and dumped beside the Ship Channel. They'd jump on *his* name, too, as the lead police officer on the investigative team that had built the case that sent Mantel to Huntsville. They would feature his insistence that he wasn't letting an escaped convict scare him out of his home or keep him from doing his job at the Lions Club barbecue. Then all he had to do was wait for Mantel to pick up the bait.

Hark took a couple of quotes from him to incorporate into the story, and then the computer keyboard stopped clicking. "This thing is a little on the dangerous side, wouldn't you say?" he asked. "Not to mention monumentally stupid. Advertising where you'll be. Putting yourself out there front and center, when this badass character is gunning for you. You'll be live bait. A sitting duck."

"Nah," McQuaid said, leaning back in his chair, acting the part of somebody who knew what he was doing. "The chief will have plenty of guys on hand. The Rangers will be here, too." He neglected to say that Royce wasn't sure whether he could send anybody. "They'll spot Mantel. They'll have him cuffed before he has a chance to make a move." And if they didn't, he'd wait until Mantel made a move and he would make *his*. He would have his weapon. *The same gun he should've used when he'd had the chance. One bullet would have saved four lives.*

"All the same," Hark said. "You know what those Lions Club barbecues are like. There you are behind the serving table, a spoon in your hand and a mob scene all around. Somebody could walk up to you, stick a knife in your ribs, disappear into the crowd. Or hop up on the back side of the stage and sight down on you. *Bam.* Nobody will even know you've been shot until you pitch facedown in the fajitas." There was a frown in his voice. "China know about this little stunt? She's okay with it?"

"China's out of town," McQuaid said.

"Damn good thing for you," Hark said drily. "If she were here, she'd be on your case about it."

McQuaid looked at the clock. Nearly eleven. He put some urgency into his voice. "Listen, Hark, if this plan is going to work, we need to get the story out there. You going to stop talking and make it happen? We don't have time to be fooling around."

Reminded of his journalistic duty, Hark grunted. "I'll do it," he said. "But China better not blame me if you wind up dead." Another few clicks. "Okay if I use that photo I took the day you gave that talk at the high school?"

"Photo?" McQuaid asked, startled. "Of *me*?"

"Hell, yes. One of you and one of Mantel, which I can get from the guys at Huntsville. You want this story on TV, some producer will want a photo. May want an interview, too. Okay?"

"I guess," McQuaid said slowly. He hadn't thought that far ahead. "If it's necessary."

"Don't turn your cell off," Hark advised. "I've put your number in as contact. You'll get a call if somebody decides they need an interview. And don't forget our deal. You get Mantel, it's my story. Mantel gets you, that's my story, too." He chuckled grimly. "Either way, I get the exclusive."

"You get the exclusive," McQuaid said. He clicked off the call, scratched his nose, and thought about what Hark had said about the photo and the interview, neither of which he liked but was prepared to go along with, just to get the job done. The other thing bothered him, though. *Monumentally stupid*? He believed that was probably an exaggeration, but he didn't like the idea of getting shot. It might be a good idea to have another backup on hand.

He picked up his phone again. He and Blackie had an appointment with a new client in Austin—a lawyer with a couple of promising jobs—at two o'clock. They were planning to drive separately and meet there. But he needed to talk to Blackie. Now.

After three rings, Blackie picked up. "Yo, McQuaid. What's up?"

"Hey, partner," McQuaid said. "Got something I need to talk over with you. How about if I stake you to chicken-fried at Beans'—say, noon?" Bob Godwin, the proprietor of Beans' Bar and Grill, served the incontestably best chicken-fried steak anywhere in the Hill Country.

"Offer I can't refuse," Blackie replied. "Hey, what's this I hear about some escaped con killing people all over the place—and looking for you, especially?"

McQuaid narrowed his eyes. Some days it was good to have a partner who was married to the chief of police. Some days it wasn't.

"I'll tell you over chicken-fried steak and a beer," he said, and clicked off.

Lunch arrangements settled, McQuaid made one more call—to China's cell phone. She'd said she probably wouldn't be within range of a cell tower, and she was right. He got her voice mail, said a quick hello, then got to work on something he'd been supposed to do a couple of days before: fill out an invoice for the job he'd completed the previous week. A San Antonio corporation had called him in when the company's outside auditor detected a hefty outflow of funds from the corporate bank account into several employees' private pockets. After the arrests, McQuaid had conducted a full financial check on the errant employees to determine where the money had gone and whether it was recoverable.

It wasn't his favorite kind of work—he preferred a job that had more action. But it paid the bills.

BY the time McQuaid walked into Beans' Bar and Grill, the place was already crowded with Friday lunch-hour regulars. The usual pool game was going on in the back, and the steady buzz of voices was occasionally punctuated by the sharp *crack!* of a cue ball. The Missouri Pacific tracks were on the other side of the parking lot, not fifty yards away, and every now and then, the sound of the TV high on the wall was drowned out by the rumble of a passing freight train, which shook the windows and rattled the glassware behind the bar. There was nothing trendy or upscale about Beans'. It was just a down-home Texas place that served good food and drink and lots of it. Nobody expected anything else.

Blackie Blackwell had already claimed their usual table by the window. Thick-shouldered and stocky, with sandy hair and a square jaw, Blackie had the look of a guy who could be counted on to do his part in any situation, no matter how difficult or dangerous. There was a sturdy, solid, rock-like dependability about him, McQuaid had always thought. He always felt better when they were on a case together—especially when it was really dicey, like the recent oil-field thefts that had taken them into cartel territory across the border. He knew he could rely on Blackie.

As McQuaid pulled up a chair and sat down, Bob Godwin sauntered up with a basket of warm tortilla chips, a crockery cup of fiery salsa, and two frosty Lone Star longnecks. An ardent Second Amendment champion, Bob wore a red T-shirt emblazoned with a picture of a pistol and the words *Keep Calm and Carry On*. His golden retriever, wearing his usual red bandana and leather saddlebags, followed him to the table to say a friendly hello. McQuaid gave his ears a good rub. Budweiser, Bud for short, was a long-time Beans' favorite. The dog toted beer bottles and wrapped snacks from the bar to the tables, and money and credit card chits from the tables to the cash register. People liked to tip him with stuff from their plates, so Bob had lately taken to hanging a hand-lettered sign around his neck: *Do not feed me. Bob will bite you!*

"Hey, guys, how ya doin'?" Bob took his order pad out of the canvas apron he wore around his waist. "Got cabrito fajitas on the menu today." He gestured toward the chalkboard behind the bar, under a fly-spotted sign that said *7-Course Texas Dinner: A 6-Pack & a Possum*. "Or there's meatloaf, ribs, chicken-fried, and catfish. Chili, too. What's your pleasure?"

"Chicken-fried," McQuaid said, and Blackie nodded.

"Same here." Bob's signature chicken-fried steak—a sizeable chunk of round steak pounded thin, breaded in Bob's secret blend of herbs and spices, and deep-fried—came smothered in cream gravy, with mashed potatoes, a vegetable, and a coleslaw side. It was too much for lunch, but McQuaid reminded himself that since China was out of town, he wouldn't be having a regular dinner. This would be his main meal for the day.

"Two chicken-frieds, comin' up," Bob said. He pocketed his order form and left, Bud at his heels.

Blackie picked up his longneck and took a slug. "Sheila tells me you're cooking up a little sting at the barbecue tomorrow night." His tone was neutral. If he didn't like the idea, McQuaid knew, he wouldn't show it—until he heard all the details. Then he'd tell you what he thought.

"That's what I wanted to talk to you about." McQuaid dipped a tortilla chip in salsa and popped it into his mouth. He and Blackie had teamed up as private investigators after Blackie left his position as the sheriff of Adams County, a much-loved third-generation job that his father and grandfather had held before him. Blackie liked to joke that his son—the baby Sheila was carrying—was going to grow up and become the Adams County sheriff, just to bring the job back into the family. Meanwhile, he and McQuaid were doing the investigative work they both liked to do. They were good together.

To bring down the salsa's temperature, McQuaid swigged a slug of beer. "I got a phone call from Houston Homicide early this morning," he said.

"I know," Blackie said. "Sheila told me. But maybe you'd better fill me in. She was in a hurry. She might have left a detail or two out."

McQuaid told Blackie the story. But not from the beginning, not from the arrest and his consequential choice not to shoot. *The choice against which he had to measure four deaths. Four.* He left that out and started the story with Mantel's escape from Huntsville, then went on to the morning's telephone conversations with Sheila, Royce, Abbott, and Hark. Blackie listened with his eyes half closed, without questions or comment, but McQuaid knew he was processing the whole thing.

"Hark says he'll do his best to get the story out there," McQuaid said. "And if I know Mantel, he'll be watching the media, hoping to get a look at his own ugly mug. Now all we have to do is wait and see if he shows up at the park tomorrow."

Blackie was thoughtful, very quiet, absently turning the beer bottle in his fingers. "Could work," he said after a moment. "Only thing is the crowd—unpredictable. Still, Sheila was saying she can put a dozen people there. Royce told her he could send one or two, as well." His voice became ironic. "You know Royce. He'd like to be in on the takedown. The Rangers always get their guy."

McQuaid chuckled. There might be competition on this one. Sheila would like to get credit for the arrest. "You'll be there?" He thought he knew the answer, but he needed to be sure.

"You bet," Blackie said without hesitation. "Right beside you." He tipped his bottle up and drank, then put it down again and glanced at McQuaid, calculating. "Sheila told me you hustled China and Caitie out of town. You thinking Mantel might show up at your house tonight, ahead of the thing tomorrow?"

"It's possible," McQuaid said slowly. That scenario had occurred to him but he'd been so focused on getting all the pieces in place for the barbecue plan that he hadn't given it much thought. "You got something in mind?"

"Not exactly," Blackie replied. "Wondering, though, whether Mantel has any relatives or friends in the area. Would you happen to know?"

"No," McQuaid replied slowly. "But Harry Royce might. I'll give him a call. It could be worth checking them out. If Mantel heads over this way, he'll be looking for someplace to hang out."

Blackie nodded. "Do that. And as I say, I don't like crowd scenes. Too unpredictable—dangerous, too, especially with this new open carry situation. People who carry guns don't always know how to use them." He picked up a tortilla chip. "If we could think of a way to lure this guy into coming after you at your place, it might be better to—"

He was about to say more, but Bob came up to the table at that moment, carrying their food. "Hey, McQuaid," he said, with a nod over his shoulder. "Ain't that you, up there on the TV?"

Startled, McQuaid looked up. The television set was tuned to the noon news on KXAN, channel 36, the Austin NBC affiliate. And that was his photo, all right, the one Hark had shot when he was talking to the Pecan Springs senior class about careers in law enforcement, back when he'd been acting chief of police. Next to his photo on the screen was Mantel's mug shot. Both of them were big as life and clearly recognizable. He couldn't quite hear the audio, but he supposed that NBC had picked up Hark's story, including the information about the barbecue tomorrow.

It was good, no, better than good. Hark had done what McQuaid asked, faster than he had any right to expect. He could only hope that Mantel couldn't resist taking this exactly as it was meant: a personal, hand-engraved invitation to Pecan Springs, issued by the cop who had refused to shoot him when he asked for it. Who had instead handed him a death sentence that he had to wait for, in prison. It was a come-and-get-me double dare. A taunt. A thumb of the nose.

Bob put their plates on the table. "That's one mean-looking SOB," he said, shaking his head. "Escaped out of Huntsville, is what they're saying. Killed the DA over in Harris County. Killed an ex-cop, too, buddy of yours." He eyed McQuaid. "That true?"

"All true," McQuaid said, and wondered what Abbott would say when he saw it—*if* the Houston TV channels were carrying it. It was exactly what the DA's office didn't want. He was picking up his fork when his phone vibrated in his pocket. He pulled it out and checked it, then pushed back his chair. "Excuse me," he said. "It's my son." He left the table and went outside, where he could hear better.

"Dad?" Brian asked excitedly. "Dad, is that really *you* I'm looking at on the TV? It looks like you and they say it's you, but—"

McQuaid interrupted: "What channel are you watching, son?"

"Channel 24. KVUE. They're saying that some really bad guy escaped from Death Row, and that you're out to get even with him for shooting one of your cop friends. Is that *right*?"

"More or less." *Get even?* That must be the story Hark had peddled to the wire service—not quite what McQuaid had had in mind, but whatever worked. KVUE was ABC. "Are you where you can switch over to KEYE or FOX? See if they're carrying the same story?"

"Hang on." Brian was off the line for a moment or two, then back. "They are, both of them. They've got your photo, and they're saying the same thing, that you're looking for this guy because he killed your friend. They make it sound like you're a lone wolf. On your own, I mean. A rogue ex-cop." He sounded anxious. "What's happening? What's going on, Dad?"

"Nothing for you to worry about," McQuaid said. "And I'm not on my own. The Rangers are in on this, and so is the PSPD. We're all working together to get this guy." KEYE was CBS. All four affiliates had the story now, which raised the chances that it had already been picked up in Houston and maybe on cable, too. "Was that why you called?"

There was a moment's silence. "Actually, no," Brian said, and cleared his throat. "I got a call from Sally a little bit ago, just before I saw you on TV." Several years ago, Brian had decided to call China *Mom*. At the same time, he began calling his mother by her given name. Sally had objected, but when she spoke to McQuaid about it, he'd told her to take it up with Brian. She had, but obviously without success.

"I see," McQuaid said, remembering his ex-wife's call on the answering machine. *I'm in trouble, and I've exhausted every other option. You're my last chance, Mike. My absolutely, positively* last *chance.* He'd returned the call to her voice mail and hadn't heard back from her yet.

"What did she want?" he asked, swallowing down the irritation. This was so like Sally, imposing herself on her son when she hadn't done anything to help the boy. She hadn't picked up her share of his school expenses, the way she'd promised. She hadn't even bothered to send a card on his birthday. Brian had his own life, his friends, school, even a job. It wasn't fair for her to call him up and unload her problems on him.

"She was . . . well, she was pretty incoherent," Brian said. "She kept saying something about a 'last chance.' After I got her calmed down, I figured out that she was looking for a place to hide out. She's afraid of something—she won't say what. She wants to come up to Austin for a few days." There was a quaver in his voice, and he paused to get it under control. "Come here, I mean. My place."

Brian had lived at one of the off-campus co-op houses during his first year at UT. But when the spring term ended and he got a part-time job at The Natural Gardener, he had found a small house to share in South Austin. Brian had emailed his parents a photo—a cute little yellow bungalow with green shutters and a large live oak in the front yard.

Now, listening to Brian, McQuaid felt the anger tighten his belly. "Damn it," he muttered. "That woman needs to grow up." Immediately sorry, he bit off the words. He'd always been careful to keep his feelings about Sally out of his conversations with their son. But he couldn't help wondering which woman had called Brian with this "last chance" plea, the same one she'd used on him. Had it been Sally? Or Juanita? Or some third personality who hadn't yet made a name for herself?

Brian cleared his throat. "The thing is that . . . well, it doesn't work for Sally to come here right now." He sounded uneasy, uncomfortable, not like himself. "I told her that this place is pretty small and there's not a lot of room. Just two bedrooms, I mean. I kind of thought maybe she could . . . well, stay with you and China. She could have my room while she's there. She said it was just for a few days. She wouldn't be any bother."

Where had he heard that before? McQuaid thought. Anyway, it was out of the question. "She'll have to find someplace else," he said. "China's out of town." He hesitated. "And there's a thing."

"Huh," Brian said. "A thing. Like with this guy on TV? The guy who shot your buddy?"

"Yeah. That thing." He'd gotten Caitie and China safely out of the way. It would make him crazy if Sally started hanging around Pecan Springs when he was trying to deal with the Mantel business. "Is your mother calling you back?"

"I don't think so. I pretty much told her she couldn't come here, so I guess she'll try calling you." He took a breath. "Listen, Dad, I'm sorry if I put my foot in it. I didn't know China was away. I told her she could probably—"

"Don't worry about it, son. We'll work it out." McQuaid thought fast. Maybe Ruby would give Sally a place to stay for a while, until her current storm blew over. Ruby knew her and seemed to be able to connect with her, maybe because they were both pretty flakey. But then he remembered that Ruby was with China, so that was out. Maybe Amy, Ruby's wild child?

"Any idea what her problem is?" he asked.

"I got the impression that she was afraid of somebody. Really afraid, I mean. Like maybe some guy was after her and she needed to stay out of sight for a while." Brian sighed heavily. "But you know Sally. It's hard to tell what's real and what's . . . well, made up. She can be pretty dramatic."

She sure could. "Well, if she phones you again," McQuaid said, "tell her to stay where she is—wherever the hell *that* is—until she talks to me."

"Thanks," Brian said. "But about this thing. I mean, I hope you're not . . . you know, putting yourself in any danger." His voice thinned, and he sounded like a very young boy, half-scared, half-excited. "You're *not*, are you, Dad?"

"Nah," McQuaid said dismissively. "Sometimes stuff just . . . you know, happens." He put a smile in his voice. "You going anywhere this weekend?"

"Nope. I'm off today, but I'm working tomorrow and

Sunday. Tell China I like the job, and the hours are working out."

"She'll be glad to hear that." John Dromgoole, the owner of The Natural Gardener, was a friend of China's. "Have a good weekend, you hear? And don't worry about your mother."

"I'll try," Brian said. "I'll try not to worry about *both* of you." He paused to let the subtle snarkiness sink in. "You'll take good care of yourself, won't you, Dad?"

McQuaid said he would and clicked off. He stood for a moment, looking at his phone and wishing that he could talk things over with his wife, could tell China about Carl, and what he and Hark had cooked up, and the plan for tomorrow. And about Sally. Yes, Sally, definitely. He considered calling the ranch landline number that China had given him and decided against it. Maybe she hadn't arrived yet. Or if she'd arrived, she was with a gang having lunch or out somewhere. And anyway, it wasn't a good idea to talk to her. She'd be upset about Carl, and he couldn't tell her about tomorrow. If he did, she'd turn around and come straight back home.

But he wanted to hear her voice. So, even though he knew he wouldn't get through, he called her cell again and got her voice mail prompt. Listening, he closed his eyes, thinking how weird it was that a few recorded words could make him want her so damn much.

Thanks for calling, whoever you are. Sorry I missed you, but I'll return your call as soon as I can. Leave a message— and have a wonderful day.

He was tempted to redial, just to listen to it again, but the beep came and he said, "Hey, babe, just thinking of you. Hope you and Ruby are having a great time—and staying out of trouble. Nothing doing here that's very important. Talk to you later. Love you." He took a breath and added, "*Really* love you."

When he got back to the table, his chicken-fried steak was cold. He ate it anyway.

Chapter Seven

Every time we go to the grocery store to buy olive oil, we come face-to-face with a conundrum. The oil on the shelves—the oil we would like to purchase for its health benefits and its Mediterranean appeal—may not be what we think it is. That is, while the label may say that the bottle contains "pure olive oil," it may also contain less expensive oils, such as canola and sunflower-seed oil, and colorants. It may also have been treated with heat or chemicals to alter the taste or preserve the oil.

And even though you may think you're buying *Italian olive oil*, chances are good that the oil in the bottle comes from Spain, Tunisia, or somewhere else, shipped to Italy and rebottled there. What's more, it may not be the kind of oil promised on the label. A recent California study found that 69 percent of the imported "extra virgin" olive oil sold in supermarkets was not actually extra virgin.

In other words, you're not getting what you think you're paying for. You're being scammed.

China Bayles
"Virgin Territory"
Pecan Springs Enterprise

Our cabin was located about a half mile from the ranch house, at the end of a narrow, wooded lane, past three other cabins, each about fifty yards apart. As we drove along, I noticed to my surprise that they all looked like *real* log cabins.

And they were. They had been moved, Ruby told me, from the nearby village of Sisterdale, which had been settled as a German Utopian community in the 1840s. "They were being torn down," she said. "Eliza thought they should be preserved, so she bought all four and had them taken apart and rebuilt here. She restored the exteriors and renovated the interiors of three of them for guests. Sofia lives in the other one." She smiled slightly. "It was another of Eliza's big projects. That woman never said no to an idea, no matter how ambitious."

"Is Maddie renting them to guests?" I asked. "Like a B&B, I mean?"

I was thinking of what Chet had told me about the probate judge's award to Boyd of half of the business—Eliza's half, I assumed. It was a Solomon-like ruling that recognized Maddie's legal claim to *her* half. But while the award might be reasonable in principle, it made absolutely no practical sense. How could Maddie be expected to work with a man who was determined to snatch her inheritance?

"Maddie rented them for a while," Ruby said, "but she stopped when things got so uncertain. I don't think she wants to build the business just to hand it over to Boyd. Anyway, we're the only guests this weekend. Sofia lives in that one. Picual." She gestured toward the third cabin, the one we were passing. "Eliza named the cabins after olive trees—*Spanish* olives. Ours is Manzanilla." She jerked a thumb over her shoulder at the two cabins we had passed. "Those back there are Arbequina and Arbosana."

108

"Interesting names," I remarked. "And the cabins are very attractive." They were built of weathered gray logs, with limestone fireplace chimneys, porches across the front, and corrugated metal roofs. They were landscaped with native shrubs—salvia, Mexican oregano, esperanza, and hummingbird bush—and built on land that sloped down to the Guadalupe River, a hundred yards away. To the north, behind them, the hill rose up sharply, covered in impenetrable thickets of cedar, yaupon holly, and elbow bush.

"Just wait until you see the inside of ours," Ruby said as we pulled up in front of the last cabin and parked beside a small desert willow tree, covered with frilly pink and lavender orchidlike blossoms. "You'll love it."

I did. It was compact and attractive, with a living-dining area; a corner kitchenette with a refrigerator, a stovetop, and a microwave; a pleasant, airy bedroom with two quilt-covered beds; and a bathroom—obviously added to the original cabin—with a whirlpool tub. The floors were polished planks, the pine ceilings were beamed with massive cypress logs, the furniture was simple and rustic, and an open stair led up to an airy sleeping loft under the low roof. The fireplace, which had a gas log, was faced with limestone all the way to the ceiling. Framed drawings and photographs of olive trees hung on the walls. It was a wonderful weekend retreat.

"Perfect," I said, dropping my duffel bag on the floor. "And so quiet." I cocked my head. "Listen. Not a whisper of traffic. Isn't it glorious?"

We stood listening—and heard absolutely nothing except for a few birds in the nearby trees. Then a vehicle pulled up outside and a door slammed. A moment later, we heard footsteps on the porch, and Maddie was opening the door. "Hi," she said. "I've brought you some extra linens. Let me put them away, and we'll take our tour of the ranch."

Ruby stretched lazily. "Changed my mind," she said. "That bed looks so inviting, Maddie. I think I'll skip the grand tour and curl up for a nap."

"You're sure?" Maddie asked. "I've put Bronco in the back, so there's room for all three of us up front."

"I'm sure," Ruby said. "You and China go and have fun." She gave me a significant look. "I'm sure you won't run out of things to talk about."

A half hour later, Maddie and I were bouncing along a rutted ranch road near the river, with the pickup windows open to the breeze and Bronco in the back of her beat-up green Dodge. We had made nearly a full circle of the ranch, looking at the small groves of olive trees that Eliza had planted in different locations.

"Eliza loved to experiment with her plantings," Maddie said, stopping the truck to show me a small grove of a couple hundred trees at the foot of a long, south-facing slope. "Those are Chemlali. It's a Tunisian olive that begins to bear early, after just a couple of years. The fruit is small but really delicious, and the oil is mild and fruity. Eliza liked the trees because they do well in a dry spell. And they're cold hardy." She waved toward the slope. "She planted them at the bottom of the hill because in the winter, the cooler air settles here. She thought the Chemlalis would do better in this spot than, say, the Manzanillas. She put them higher up on the slope, where it's a few degrees warmer in winter." She turned and gestured toward several other rows of trees, with longer, sweeping branches. "And those are Pendolino. They're pollinators for the Manzanilla—universal pollinators, actually. The Chemlalis are self-fertile."

"And I thought an olive was just an olive," I said, shaking

110

my head. "There's so much to learn." I heard a sharp *yip* as Bronco scrambled out of the truck in hot pursuit of a jackrabbit. "Will he catch it?" I asked, as he and the rabbit disappeared into the neatly planted orchard.

Maddie laughed. "In his dreams. Our local jackrabbits are speedsters. But Bronco has high hopes. He always gives it his best, so we need to wait for him." She switched off the ignition and leaned back in the corner of the seat, facing me. "Do you know Chet from somewhere? I saw you two talking together at lunch. You seemed like friends."

Her tone was carefully casual, but I remembered the look on Chet's face when he talked about her. I remembered, too, what Ruby had said: that Maddie and Chet had had a thing going. Past tense. Was that true? If so, what had pulled them apart?

Matching her tone, I said, "We did a summer internship together a couple of lifetimes ago. It was good to see him and catch up on what he's doing." I chased a fly out through the open window. "Nice that he's into wines again. That was always one of his passions."

She regarded me curiously, as if she was thinking of asking whether I had once been one of Chet's passions. But she only said, "He gets discouraged about the vineyard sometimes. There's a lot of work, and the weather and irrigation are always big uncertainties. It'll be easier once the vines are established. But a vineyard is like an olive orchard. There's never any end to the work—and to the worry." She paused and added tentatively, "Did he mention that he and his friends Jason and Andrea bought the land from Boyd? And that Boyd is—was—Eliza's nephew?"

"Yes." I paused, then added, "He told me about the probate problem, too."

Maddie turned to look out the window, so I couldn't read

her expression. But I could hear the worry in her voice. "Oh, dear God. The probate problem." She sighed.

"Sounds like a raw deal," I said sympathetically. "I hope the appeal is successful."

She turned to face me. "It feels like I've been in limbo for such a long time. I don't know if Ruby told you, but in Eliza's last days, her care was pretty demanding and I had to let everything but the orchards slide. After she died, I dug in and started building up the other parts of the business—the nursery, the guest cottages, the ranch tours. I was going to work on the café next, but . . ." Another sigh. "When Boyd contested the will, I didn't have the heart to continue building. I kept thinking that if the appeal was denied or the ruling went against me, all the land and half of the business would go to Boyd." She looked out the window again. "Unless we could . . . maybe, work out our differences."

Work out their differences? They were considering a settlement? I wanted to know more about that. But first I wanted to hear her take on Boyd. "Chet told me a little," I prompted tentatively, watching her face.

"Oh, Chet." Maddie pulled down her mouth. "Don't believe what he says, China. I'm afraid he's hardly neutral on the topic. It's because of . . . well, what happened between us."

"I got that feeling," I said. I had guessed right. There had been something going on between Maddie and Chet. "But still . . . I understand that Boyd suggested there'd been negligence in Eliza's death. Something about leaving a door unlocked?"

She nodded ruefully. "That was it. Eliza had been suffering from dementia for some time, but we were managing. Sofia spent as much time as she could with her during the day and evenings, and I slept in the room next to hers at night. Both Sophia and I hated the thought of putting her in a nursing home. We loved her very much." Her voice was trembling. "We wanted to keep her with us as long as we could."

"I expect she felt more comfortable here at the ranch," I said. "Surrounded by everything she loved."

"That's what I thought, too." She cleared her throat. "But Boyd . . . well, he saw it differently, which I can sort of understand, I guess. He was worried about her safety. He thought she'd be better off where there were more people—nurses and so on—to monitor her." She dropped her glance. "Anyway, he kept bringing doctors to see her. They would examine her and write these terribly gloomy reports, saying that she ought to be institutionalized."

"That kind of pressure must have been hard to cope with," I said. "And then she . . . drowned?"

Maddie shook her head sadly. "I've never understood how that happened, you know. Sofia and I—we were so careful about keeping the doors locked. And toward the end, Eliza was afraid of going outside after dark. I didn't think she would ever go out, unless somebody actually led her. I even thought—" She tapped her fingers on the steering wheel. "I feel terrible about that now, China. Really terrible."

"You even thought what?" I prompted.

"Well . . ." She drew out the word. "The evening Eliza died, Boyd came to the house to have supper with us. At the time, I wondered whether he might have unlocked the side door before he left, so he could come in later that night and . . ." She pressed her lips together.

I finished her unspoken thought. "And take her to the river?"

She nodded reluctantly. "I know I shouldn't have been

113

imagining something like that when I didn't have a shred of evidence. Anyway, I couldn't think why he might want to do it. And now . . ." Her voice trailed off and she looked away.

She couldn't think *why* he might want to do it? It seemed to me that Boyd had a pretty powerful motive for wanting his aunt out of the way. I thought about that for a moment, remembering what Ruby had said about Maddie's being inexperienced when it came to men, maybe even naïve. Was she seeing things clearly? Had she been charmed by Boyd?

"Ruby tells me that there's some sort of issue with Boyd's olive oil," I said, feeling my way into that part of the story. "Something about fraud?"

"Well, that's what people have said." She shifted uncomfortably. "There's no law against marketing a blend," she added a little defensively. "Of course, if it's a blend, you're supposed to label it. Which Boyd intended to do, except . . ." She took a breath. "Well, he explained the whole thing to me. It was Mateo's fault, really. Mateo—he works for Boyd—mixed up the labels when the oil was bottled. Boyd didn't discover it until after it happened the second time. It was an honest mistake."

An honest mistake? Apparently Eliza hadn't thought so. "Ruby says that Eliza knew about the blend and threatened to do something about it."

"Yes. She heard about it from Sofia's niece Sarita, who also works for Boyd. Eliza planned to have the oil tested, but. . . . Well, that was about the time she began to go seriously downhill. It didn't seem important then. Like a lot of other things, the idea got dropped."

"But Boyd knew that Eliza was aware of what he was doing—the adulterated olive oil, I mean."

"Yes, of course. She told him straight out that she intended to get the oil tested."

I gave her a direct look. "You said you couldn't think of a reason why Boyd might want his aunt dead. Wouldn't that be a reason?"

She frowned. "Oh, gosh, I don't think so, China. Not over . . . not over something like that. Especially when it was just a mistake. The mislabeling, I mean. And that was Mateo's fault, not Boyd's."

If it was just a mistake. Maybe it wasn't, and Eliza knew it. I had known killers who pulled the trigger with less provocation.

But I had something else in mind. I said, "Well, maybe not. Maybe you're right, Maddie. But Ruby told me that Boyd was expecting to inherit his aunt's ranch. And with good reason. He had a copy of an earlier will in which Eliza left everything to him."

"That's true," she said slowly. "He was shocked when he found out that she had rewritten her will and left everything to me." She made a face. "*Shocked* isn't the right word. I was there when he got the news. He was stunned. He looked like somebody had punched him in the gut. The next day, his lawyer challenged the will."

"And you don't think the expectation of an inheritance might have given him a reason to do away with his aunt?" I raised my hand against her quick protest. "You don't have to answer that. I'm not making any accusations. I'm just pointing out that Boyd had more than one reason to be relieved and even thankful when his aunt died."

Not that there was anything that could be done about it, of course. Eliza had been dead for almost two years. And Chet had said that the local sheriff had looked into the drowning and didn't find anything suspicious. If there had been any evidence of anyone's complicity in her death, it was long since gone.

"I hear what you're saying, China." Maddie sighed. "Chet says I'm way too easy on Boyd, after all the grief he's caused me." She ran her finger along the scar that crossed her cheek, her voice softening. "But I'm beginning to think there might be light at the end of the tunnel."

"Ah," I said, remembering her remark about working things out. "Your lawyer thinks there might be a settlement?" If there's room for real compromise, a settlement can be the quickest and best way to end a long and expensive stalemate.

Half smiling, Maddie ducked her head. "Yes, I guess you might call it a settlement. But not in the way you're thinking. It's Boyd and me. The two of us, not the lawyers." She didn't look up. "Boyd says we ought to get married, and I'm considering it. That would fix everything."

I stared at her. You know that old saying about being knocked over with a feather? Well, that's just how I felt. "Boyd says you ought to *get married*?" I repeated, blinking stupidly. I wasn't sure I'd heard her right.

She nodded. "Don't you think it makes sense? The Last Chance Ranch was divided into two separate pieces a long time ago, when Eliza's father died. Half of it went to Eliza, and half to Boyd's father. Getting married would bring the two halves back together again. The business would be under one management—ours." She paused, and her voice became harder, more fierce. "And I wouldn't have to give up Eliza's olive groves. They would be protected, forever. Boyd has promised me that."

"Well, yes," I said slowly. "When you put it that way, I suppose it might make a certain kind of sense. But . . ."

But it didn't make sense to me—at least, not the kind of sense a marriage proposal *should* make. She had left out the answer to a very important question.

"Do you love him, Maddie?" I asked. "I mean, Boyd has been giving you a lot of grief over the past couple of years and—"

"Oh, but that wasn't *Boyd*," Maddie put in quickly, in an I-can-explain-everything tone. "He had nothing to do with it, really. Challenging the will was his lawyer's idea. Boyd didn't even know about it, to start with. And then he . . . well, he just sort of went along with what his lawyer told him to do."

"Wait a minute." I frowned. "It was his *lawyer's* idea?" An attorney isn't supposed to initiate a legal proceeding without a client's knowledge and approval. I mean *never*. An attorney who does something like that ought to be fired. On the spot. If he hasn't been fired, he has a fool for a client. Or . . . or somebody's not telling the truth.

"Right. Boyd explained the whole thing to me," Maddie said earnestly. "To understand it, you probably have to know something about the family history. You see, Jimmy Bob Elliott—that's Boyd's lawyer—is an old friend of the Butler family. Mr. Elliott knew Boyd's grandfather and Boyd's father, and he helped Eliza draw up her original will—the one that left all the land and everything to Boyd. Mr. Elliott was so upset when the new will was probated and he saw that Eliza had named me as her beneficiary that he went straight to the judge and filed a challenge. Boyd didn't even know what was happening until it was too late."

"But it *wasn't* too late," I said. "All he had to do was withdraw the challenge and let the probate proceed."

"I suppose that's true." She spread out her hands, still not looking at me. "But Mr. Elliott can be pretty persuasive.

Boyd let himself get talked into going along with it, just to see what would happen. He realizes now that he made a big mistake. He should have told Mr. Elliott to drop it. He's really sorry about the whole thing. He wants to make it up to me. He wants us to get married. Right away, before this legal thing is settled."

Oh, come on, now, I thought. *Give me a break*. This suit has dragged on through a court hearing, a jury verdict, a reversal, an appeal, a ruling, a second ruling, a stay, and a second appeal—and Boyd is just now "realizing" that this entire affair was his lawyer's fault? To make amends, he is offering to marry the woman who (he claimed) took advantage of his mentally incompetent aunt, maybe even contributed to her death? And he wants this to happen right away?

Excuse me, but I wasn't believing this. It sounded to me like the man had decided to find another way to get his hands on Maddie's half of the long-divided Last Chance Ranch. He would marry her. It also sounded like Maddie—who would do anything to hold on to her trees—had decided to believe that Boyd was truthful. And trustworthy. But who could blame her? She was probably sick to death of fighting and wanted to get the whole thing over with. Marriage seemed like a way out. Under those circumstances, she might not be ready to listen to arguments from opposing counsel.

But I had to try. "When did you start talking about getting married? Was this sudden, or had it been going on for a while?"

She shifted in the seat. "Well, I've always kind of had a soft spot in my heart for Boyd, ever since I was a little girl. But he's so good-looking that I never thought . . ." Unconsciously, her hand went back to her scar. "I had no idea he liked me, really. He never showed it. Anyway, a couple of weeks ago, he came over to apologize for what his lawyer had done and tell me how sorry he was about everything. We started talking and . . . well, it just seemed like all of a sudden, both of us realized how much we have in common. When it comes to the land, I mean. We both love the olive trees. And we both think that Eliza would be very happy if the two pieces of the Last Chance could be reunited."

"But *marriage*?" I asked. "That's a pretty serious step, isn't it?" She hadn't answered the question I'd asked a moment before, and I asked it again. "Do you love him, Maddie?" I wanted to ask how she felt about Chet, too, but this wasn't the time.

Her fingers went back to her scar. "He says he loves me. He says he's loved me for a long time and he just didn't know it." She turned to me, almost defiantly. "That happens, you know. You can love somebody without knowing it." Her cheeks had reddened. "I'm . . . I'm still thinking about it," she said, looking away. "This is all pretty new."

Thinking about whether you love him? I opened my mouth to reply but there was a clatter in the back of the truck and a loud *woof*, and we both turned around to see Bronco, his pink tongue hanging out, grinning at us through the back window of the truck.

I turned to look at Maddie. She wouldn't meet my eyes. She wasn't going to answer my question, either. Or maybe she was using her silence to tell me that it was none of my damned business, which I could certainly understand. Love is a very personal, very private matter. It isn't something you discuss with a perfect stranger. I was meddling in her life, and if she didn't want to answer my question, well, that was her business.

I glanced back at the dog. "Looks like Bronco didn't get that rabbit he wanted."

Woof, Bronco said again, apologetically. It was as if he were saying *I tried my best, but that blasted rabbit outran me. Outsmarted me, too.*

Maddie turned the key in the ignition and put the truck in gear. "We can't always get what we want," she said quietly. "No matter how much we want it. Sometimes we have to compromise."

I didn't think she was talking about Bronco and his rabbit.

Chapter Eight

MCQUAID

Friday Afternoon

Some months before, McQuaid had installed a hands-free cell phone device in his truck. The system turned the long, empty hours he spent on the road or doing surveillance into productive work time. With the addition of a clever folding keyboard, he was fully equipped. Almost anything he could do in his office, he could do in his truck. He wasn't sure he liked it.

The thing was that road time had always been thinking time for McQuaid. There was something about climbing into the truck and getting out on the road. He could turn up the volume on the radio and fill the cab with his favorite country-western music. Or he could turn it off and fill his head with his thoughts. Or he could do both. Listening to music didn't keep you from thinking. But when you got down to it, time on the road—or time parked along some dark curb, keeping an eye on a house—was time *alone*, with no intrusions or interruptions from the outside. Hands-free or handheld, the smartphone let the world into his vehicle when he would rather be alone.

But right now, he was glad to have it. He needed to check with Sheila on the situation in Houston and find out from Harry Royce whether Mantel had any relatives in the area. He had an appointment with that Austin attorney in forty minutes, so there wasn't time to sit in the parking lot and talk on the phone. He swung out onto Nueces, took LBJ Drive to I-35, made a left onto the onramp, slid into the fast-moving northbound traffic, and called Sheila for an update. He got Connie.

"I've checked out a Taser for you, sir," Connie said. "It's here at my desk when you need it."

"Thanks," he said, grateful that Connie seemed to consider him an adjunct PSPD officer. "I'm on my way to Austin. How late will you be in the office?"

"Way past when I should be at home." Connie sighed. "I'm working on the budget. It has to go to the council on Monday, and I still don't have enough in there for the body cams we need. And that's assuming we get the federal grant, which I haven't written yet."

"About as much fun as wrestling grizzlies," McQuaid said with genuine sympathy. He had enjoyed his stint as acting chief, except for that budget crap. The council wanted the police department to fight crime but they hated like hell to pay for it. McQuaid had felt that they took a special delight in seeing him grovel for every nickel. The price of body cams had come down, but they were still selling for seven or eight hundred dollars. Getting the money to buy them for all the patrol officers wouldn't be easy. And then there were the policy issues to decide. Did the officers initiate the recording, or should the cams run continuously? Who in the department would be authorized to view the footage, tag it, and archive it? How would open records requests be met? People thought it was a simple matter—just pin a camera on every cop and turn it on. But there were lots of issues to deal with, big issues that took serious thought.

"Looks like the boss is still on the other line," Connie said. "Do you want to hold?"

"Yeah." McQuaid glanced out the truck window. He was just crossing the Blanco River, between San Marcos and Kyle. You couldn't see the damage from the highway bridge, but the Blanco—long known to meteorologists as "Flash Flood Alley"—had been the site of a devastating Memorial Day flood. A six-inch rainstorm twenty miles upstream of Wimberley had produced a killer flood that swept down the river, taking a dozen lives, destroying more than a thousand homes, and knocking out roads and bridges, some of which hadn't yet been rebuilt. The day after the disaster, McQuaid was supposed to attend a meeting in Austin. But water was still flowing over this very bridge and he had to use a round-about detour. The flood was a reminder, if anybody needed one, of the impact of extreme weather. It had forced FEMA to redraw its outdated floodplain maps.

Sheila came on the line, her voice flat, matter-of-fact. "I was just talking with Ian Abbott. The DA's office got a tip that there was a body in one of the gravel dumps at the Turkey Bend Wharf, on Buffalo Bayou. You know the place?"

"I do," McQuaid said. It wouldn't be the first time that area had been used to dispose of a body. "Another one of the witnesses in the Mantel case?"

"Yes. They've ID'd her as . . ." Sheila rustled a paper. "Karen Kingsley."

Kingsley. McQuaid felt his gut tighten. The girl had been fifteen at the time of the trial, but she'd had the look of a lost child barely out of elementary school. She'd be—what? Mid-twenties, now? But now she wasn't. Now she was dead.

He felt the weight on his shoulders again. This made five. *Five people who would still be alive if he had pulled the trigger.* "Time of death?"

"It's still a rough guess. Abbott says they're putting it at about the same time as Kennedy's. Sunday, maybe Monday. Multiple gunshots. They'll know more after both autopsies, but there's apparently some evidence that the two women were killed together, or at least around the same time. Abbott didn't go into specifics."

"Sunday, Monday. *Before* Mantel escaped," McQuaid muttered. But then, they already knew that he had to be working with somebody, or several somebodies. It didn't change anything. Just reminded him that they needed to watch for at least two people at the park tomorrow. And that they had a photo only of Mantel. They had no idea what the other man looked like. Or men. Or men and women.

"*Before* Mantel escaped," Sheila repeated, with emphasis. She added, "By the way, Abbott is royally pissed at you. He saw your photo with Mantel's on the noon television news over there in Houston. The DA's office was trying to keep a lid on this thing. They didn't want the media to make a connection between Mantel's escape and the shooting of the DA and his wife—at least, not right away. Your neat little media trick blew that effort, and now the reporters are banging on their doors. Abbott wants to know what the hell is going on with you and Mantel."

"I'll bet he does." McQuaid checked the mirror, then pulled to the left to pass a slow-moving Postal Service eighteen-wheeler with *We Deliver For You* painted on the side. "What did you tell him?"

"Nothing. That information has to come from the Rangers. If Royce thinks the DA's office needs to be cued in to what we're working on over here, he'll tell Abbott. If he doesn't, he won't." She paused, and when she spoke again, her voice was less tense. "What have you heard from China? I imagine she's having a quieter day than you are. Maybe she's even having fun."

"Haven't heard, but yes, I'm sure she is. Fun, that is. What kind of trouble could she and Ruby get into out there at that olive ranch?"

Sheila chuckled. "Better not ask." There was a silence. "Connie says you're picking up a Taser."

"Right. I'm on my way to Austin now. I'll stop for the Taser when I get back to Pecan Springs. Connie promised to keep a light on for me if I'm late."

"We'll both be here," Sheila said. "I'm working on that damn budget, too."

The traffic was picking up now, but all three northbound lanes were moving well. He had just passed Kyle, twenty-two miles south of Austin. The village had begun as a railroad depot on the International and Great Northern Railroad's route from Austin to San Antonio and was until recently a sleepy little town. At the turn of the millennium, it had boasted some fifty-three hundred citizens. The latest headcount put it at over twenty-eight thousand, one of the fastest-growing cities in Texas. Kyle straddled the freeway, its growing subdivisions pushing east across the rich blackland prairie and west into the Hill Country.

McQuaid had one more call to make. Harry Royce opened the conversation with "Ian Abbott is out to get you, man. He's mad enough to spit nails."

"He is?" McQuaid played dumb. "What about?"

"He saw you on the noon news. What's more, he specifically recalls telling you that the DA's office didn't want the media to connect any dots until after his office could tell the public that Mantel was back under lock and key. He thinks you set him up."

"I set *him* up?" McQuaid grunted. "If it's all the same to you, Harry, I'll let the apology wait until after you've made the arrest."

A flashy red Porsche 911 with the top down was coming up behind him fast, and he moved back into the right lane to let the car shoot past him. The blonde driving the Porsche, her hair flying, must have been doing upwards of ninety, and McQuaid saw, with a flare of irritation, that she was holding a cell phone to her ear. As he watched, she dodged into the far left lane, cutting in front of a pickup pulling a travel trailer.

"Damn," he muttered, as she whipped back out of the left lane and into the middle lane, just ahead of a motorcycle.

"Sorry," Royce said. "Didn't quite get that."

McQuaid raised his voice. "I don't suppose you happened to tell Abbott that *you* knew about that little media play before the networks picked it up."

"You suppose right," Royce replied. "Abbott's not in my line of command. If he's pissed, it's no skin off my nose. Yours, either. You're an independent." He paused. "If you want to know the truth, McQuaid, I didn't think you'd pull it off. That you'd get the media to put that story where Mantel could see it, I mean."

"So now you know the story's out there, are you going to put a couple more guys in Pecan Springs tomorrow?"

Royce was cautious. "I'd like to have some evidence that Mantel is headed in your direction—something more than that voice mail message he left on your phone. Anyway, your local constabulary seems to be on the job. Dawson said she's calling in some off-duty guys to keep an eye on things."

McQuaid glanced into the mirror. A black-and-white was looming behind him, light bar flashing, siren sounding. He looked down at his speedometer. Sixty-five. The trooper wasn't after him. "Did Abbott tell you about finding another body?"

"Yes. Number five. Makes it pretty clear that Mantel is working with somebody." Harry paused. "That siren I'm hearing. He isn't pulling you over, is he?"

"Nah," McQuaid said as the black-and-white sped past. "He's probably after the blonde in the Porsche who's doing ninety while she's holding her cell phone to her ear." He thought of Blackie's suggestion for getting a line on Mantel's local connections. "Listen, Harry, if somebody hasn't done this already, how about getting Huntsville to pull the names and addresses of the people who visited Mantel in the past five or six months?" He hesitated. This was an unofficial request, and Royce would probably tell him to forget it. On the other hand, he might just be so short of field personnel that he'd agree. "Also, maybe dig into his file and see whether he has any family or friends over this way. San Marcos, Kyle, New Braunfels, San Antonio. Ex-wives, women friends, buddies. If there are any locals, I could do some checking for you. Ask around, see whether anybody's heard from him."

"Well," Royce said slowly. He paused, then: "Seeing that it's you asking, and that you led the original arrest team, I guess I can do that. If we find anything that looks useful, how do you want it? How fast?"

"You can email it to my phone," McQuaid said, and gave him the address. "Quick as you can find it would be nice."

"If we can dig it up, you'll have it by quitting time," Royce said.

"Quitting time." McQuaid grunted. "That's for you guys

drawing a state paycheck. Us indies, we don't know what quitting time is."

"Maybe so," Royce said. "But I'm stuck here in this office. I don't even have a window. You guys out there on the road are the ones having fun."

McQuaid looked ahead, down the highway. He was gratified to see that the trooper had caught up with the blonde in the Porsche and pulled her over.

"You got it, man." He grinned as he moved into the center lane to pass the trooper and the woman who was about to get a ticket. On this stretch, if she was clocked at ninety, she'd be paying five hundred plus another hundred in court costs. He gave the trooper a wave. "Some of us, anyway."

Royce barked a sarcastic laugh. "Say, do you ever wish you'd just blown Mantel's head off when you had the chance? When you were making the arrest, I mean. Would have saved the state a bundle of money and a lot of grief." He paused. "And five lives."

Five lives. Five. McQuaid took a breath. *He had to face the truth. The painful truth.* "Yeah," he said softly. "Yeah, Harry. I sometimes wish that."

THE large legal firm that was interested in hiring McQuaid, Blackwell, and Associates had an office near the state capitol. McQuaid ran into the usual traffic tie-up on East Twelfth, and by the time he finally located a parking space and made his way to the seventh floor of the building, he was late. Blackie was already there, thumbing through a magazine, one blue-jeaned leg crossed over the other, his black Stetson—a Blackwell trademark—perched on the chair beside him.

"Thought maybe I was going to have to do this alone," he said, when McQuaid came into the reception room.

"Traffic," McQuaid replied. "Should have given myself more time." He sat down, glancing at the thick pale gray carpet, the tastefully upholstered furniture, the glossy blond receptionist at a desk near a window that framed the capitol building. "Impressive. Why don't we find ourselves something plush like this up here in Austin, instead of hanging out in that fleabag down in Pecan Springs?" Their little strip-center place of business was a standing joke between them, although both of them rather enjoyed its noir-ish ambiance.

Blackie dropped his magazine—*Texas Fish & Game*—on the table. "Because we're country boys, that's why. We wouldn't know how to behave in a place with a view of the capitol. It'd feel like Big Brother was looking over our shoulders." He paused. "Did you check with your Ranger pal on Mantel's local contacts?"

"I did. Royce says he'll try to pull that information, plus the names of people who visited Mantel in prison. If he's got anything, I should have it this afternoon." He leaned closer to Blackie and lowered his voice. "They found another body. One of the witnesses, a young woman. The DA's office was tipped to look in a gravel dump at a wharf on Buffalo Bayou."

"Another body." Blackie's mouth tightened. "Five?"

"Five and counting," McQuaid replied tersely. *Five. And one bullet—one bullet from* his *gun would have kept them all alive.*

A phone buzzed on the receptionist's desk. She picked up, then glanced in their direction with a frosty smile that just missed being condescending. "They're ready for you now, gentlemen. Down the hall, to your left."

"Thank you, ma'am. I reckon we can find it without a

map." Blackie clapped his hat on his head, hooked his thumbs in his belt, and gave the young woman a broad Paul Newman wink that she pretended to ignore.

McQuaid grinned. Blackie was a quiet guy, but every now and then, when he was pushed a little, he liked to put on his western act. "Don't mind my friend," he said, sotto voce to the receptionist. "They don't let him off the ranch very often these days."

The two young lawyers—McQuaid thought they looked like they were just out of law school—were seated at a polished conference table that could have accommodated sixteen. They were looking for experienced investigators who could do pre-deposition background checks and interviews on two dozen witnesses in a criminal fraud case the firm was preparing for trial. The lawyers would supply the questions, but the interviewers would have to know the case well enough to anticipate a range of answers, decide whether the person being questioned was telling the truth, and know just how to worm the truth out of them, within legal limits. It was the kind of job McQuaid enjoyed, for it gave him the opportunity to do what he did best: ask the right questions and analyze the answers, verbal and nonverbal.

The meeting lasted a half hour and concluded with a round of cordial handshakes. "We'll get back to you next week," one of the lawyers said. "The partners have to approve our recommendation."

"But don't take on any other major work in the meantime," the other lawyer said.

"THAT seemed to go well enough," Blackie said, when they were out on the street again. "Good to have another paying job next month, too."

After a cool morning, the sun had come out briefly, sending the temperature into the upper eighties. The sky was darkening to the southeast, though, which might mean rain. A pair of young girls in brief denim shorts and tank tops sauntered past on the sidewalk. Eyeing them, the driver of a Dirtnail Pedicab—masked and caped as Batman—gave them an appreciative whistle they pretended to ignore. A ponytailed kid wearing a tie-dyed *Keep Austin Weird* T-shirt and carrying a guitar case painted with rainbows crossed the street in the middle of the block, and a mounted patrol cop on a horse stopped him for a lecture.

The afternoon was warm enough to make McQuaid want to take his jacket off, but he was mindful of the Glock in his shoulder holster. Instead, he loosened his tie. "If we get the job, it'll keep us busy for a while." He said *if*, but he agreed with Blackie. The meeting had gone well, and he was feeling confident. "Depending on the trial date, we might need to rearrange the calendar." He glanced at his watch. It was later than he expected—nearly four. "You headed back to Pecan Springs?"

"Yep. You?"

"While I'm up this way, I think I'll get off the freeway at Oltorf and swing over to South Congress. Brian's renting a little house over there and he's been after me to drop in and see it. I won't stay long. Probably be a half hour behind you."

"South Austin, huh? Nice place to live." Blackie tipped his Stetson to the back of his head. "Doesn't seem possible your boy could be in college already. I keep thinking of him as a little kid, same way I think of mine." In addition to the baby he and Sheila were having, Blackie had a couple of grown sons by an early marriage.

McQuaid nodded ruefully. "When Brian was little, I kept

thinking how great it would be when he grew up and we could do more guy things together—hunting, fishing, climbing. Now, he's busy with school and we don't seem to get together very often." Which didn't mean they weren't good buddies. In fact, he cherished his relationship with his son, whom he had raised after Sally left. He didn't like to brag, but there probably wasn't a closer father-son duo in the whole state of Texas. There wasn't anything they couldn't talk over together.

He pulled out his phone and checked his email. "Nothing from Royce yet. If he comes up with an address, I'd like to check it out this evening. You available?"

"Sure," Blackie said. "Sheila's working on her budget, so I'm on my own this evening. Thought I'd pick up some takeout when I get back to Pecan Springs and drop it by the office for her. Give me a call when you know what you want to do. I can go with you or meet you where you're going, whatever works best." He gave McQuaid a stern look. "Don't even think of going by yourself, you hear? You *call*."

"You got it. Thanks, partner," McQuaid said. "Catch you later."

Back in the truck, he took off his tie, folded it into his pocket, and unbuttoned the top button of his blue shirt. A moment later, he was heading north on San Jacinto to East Fifteenth, hooking a right and then another right at the front-age road, and merging left into the stream of cars heading up the I-35 onramp. The southbound afternoon traffic was packed tight and frustratingly slow-and-go across the river and down to Oltorf. McQuaid was tempted to give it up and stay on I-35. Royce might be calling him any minute with a list of names.

But his conscience bothered him. It was too bad that Sally had unloaded on Brian—well, not unloaded, maybe, at least, it hadn't sounded quite that way. But she had let the boy know that she was in trouble and that she needed his help. That was Sally, never around to let her son know that she loved him, but always the first one to ask for money or a place to stay or a shoulder to cry on when she was faced with a problem—and there was *always* a problem. And Brian was a thoughtful kid, a great kid, sensitive to his mother's needs. He was probably feeling terribly guilty, maybe even depressed, because he couldn't give her a place to stay. The least McQuaid could do was drop in and let the boy know that his dad was here to give him a hug. He thought of calling, letting Brian know that he'd be dropping in. But he was only a few minutes away. He'd let it be a surprise.

He swung off at the Oltorf exit, heading west past Travis High School and the Blunn Creek Nature Preserve, a pretty green oasis for the students at nearby St. Edward's University. Wilson Street was a few blocks on the other side of South Congress. It was pleasant, McQuaid saw, a typical South Austin tree-lined street of small, one-story 1950s bungalows with inviting front porches, vegetable gardens in the front yards, and sidewalks, real sidewalks. There were young moms pushing strollers and kids riding bicycles and jumping rope. The neighborhood had a homey, family feel.

It was a change for Brian, and a good one, McQuaid thought approvingly, away from the West Campus frat environment where there'd been too much drinking and drugging—not that Brian did that kind of thing. He had always been a good student who cared about keeping his grades up. He'd done well in his first year at UT, pulling As and Bs and proving that he could handle the challenging course work in his environmental science major. Now that he had a part-time job, it made sense for him to get away from the campus. Kids had to strike out on their own sooner or later, anyway.

McQuaid drove slowly down the street, looking for the number. He couldn't recall whether Brian was sharing the house with one or two other boys—he should have paid more attention to what China had told him. But from the size of the houses, he thought there probably wasn't room for three, so it was probably just Brian and somebody else. A couple of blocks off Oltorf, he spotted it, a small yellow house with green shutters, white trim, and a large live oak in the front yard. And there was Brian's car in the driveway.

Good, McQuaid thought. The boy was at home. He found the nearest empty spot along the curb on the other side of the street, two or three houses down, parked his truck, and took the key out of the ignition. But as he was getting out, he saw the front door of Brian's house open. His son— shirtless, barefoot, wearing olive-green cargo shorts—came out onto the porch and walked toward the car that was parked out in front. With him was a very pretty black girl in white terry shorts, a pink tank top, and pink sneakers. She had a bag over her shoulder and a tennis racquet in one hand. Brian was holding the other.

McQuaid quickly got back into his truck, hoping he wouldn't be seen. But he didn't need to worry, for Brian had eyes only for the girl. As he watched, the two of them walked around the car. Brian opened the driver's door and the girl tossed her bag and the racquet into the back and started to get in. But the boy caught her shoulders, pulled her to him as if she were the last real thing left on the earth, and bent his head to hers for a long, deep kiss.

McQuaid found himself holding his breath, not sure he should be watching. No, he was sure he should *not* be watching. This was his son's private life, and the boy was over eighteen. No. Brian wasn't a boy now. He was a man, and he was clearly involved—in love? in lust?—with this young woman. This young black woman.

The kiss ended. Brian touched the girl's face tenderly and they bent forward, foreheads together, for a moment. Then she got in the car. Brian stepped back and stood in the street, watching until she turned the corner, out of sight. Then, his hands in his pockets, he went jauntily up the walk to the house, skipping—actually skipping—a couple of steps.

McQuaid sat back in his seat, feeling a little like Spencer Tracy in *Guess Who's Coming to Dinner.* But wait—he wasn't prejudiced, was he? Or *was* he? If he wasn't, why was he sitting here wondering how he was supposed to react? He thought back quickly over the talks he and Brian had had about sex, conversations about safe sex and unsafe sex and pregnancy and commitment. Conversations he thought he had handled pretty well at the time, helped along by his comfortable relationship with his son, with whom he could talk about anything, everything.

But he had never thought to bring up the issue of . . . well, interracial love. Interracial . . . sex. It just hadn't crossed his mind. Not until now. Not until he had seen his son pull that girl to him and kiss her, kiss her intimately. Kiss her as if they had just—

McQuaid shook himself. Whatever the two of them had been up to before they came out of that house, it was their business, not his. So what if Brian was involved with her, even in love with her? Interracial relationships were a lot more common these days than they were when he was growing up, even here in Texas. Yes, it might be a rocky road. It might end unhappily, even painfully, and he certainly didn't want to see his son get hurt.

But wasn't getting hurt part of growing up, becoming an adult? And didn't you learn by taking chances, challenging accepted ideas, testing yourself? Brian was young, yes, but he had a good head on his shoulders. McQuaid had always trusted him to make wise choices—and learn from his mistakes. He had no reason to start distrusting his son's common sense now, just because he'd seen him kissing his girl.

Still trying to figure out what to do, he put the key in the ignition and drove around a couple of blocks. Making up his mind, he circled back to Wilson and pulled into the empty space where the girl had parked. It was hot, and he wanted to take off his khaki jacket. But he was still wearing the damn Glock, and he didn't want to take it off and leave it in the truck, even locked. He got out, walked up the steps to the door, and knocked briskly. When Brian came to the door, clearly surprised to see him, he said, with an assumed casualness, "Hey, guy. I was on my way back to Pecan Springs after a meeting downtown and I thought I'd take a chance and see if you were at home. Okay if I come in?"

"Oh, sure, Dad," Brian said, opening the door. He pushed his fingers through his tousled dark hair, smoothing it. He had pulled on a black T-shirt and was wearing a pair of flip-flops. "Gosh, this is . . . this is a surprise. I wasn't expecting you."

Obviously, McQuaid thought, stepping inside. The living room was small but neat, dominated by a large-screen TV in the corner. He looked around. "Nice place you've got here, son. A lot nicer than the co-op." He hesitated. "Am I going to get to meet your roommates?"

"Roommate, singular." Brian ducked his head. "Sorry. Casey just left."

Casey, McQuaid thought. So his roommate's name was Casey. But Casey could be a guy—or Casey could be the girl he had seen Brian kissing. He'd known a woman named Casey once. Damned good patrol officer, as a matter of fact. He'd seen her take down a guy twice her size.

"Too bad," McQuaid said. "Well, another time."

He stopped, waiting for Brian to tell him about the girl. After all, he and his son had always been close. There had never been anything they couldn't talk about together. Surely he would tell his dad about this girl he was seeing—or living with.

But Brian only stuck his hands in his pockets. After an uncomfortable pause, he said, "Want to stay for supper? I could open a can of baked beans. There's some hamburgers in the freezer. And cheese. And beer." He brightened. "Want a beer?"

McQuaid hesitated. It looked like the boy wasn't going to say anything about the girl. Should he tell Brian that he had seen her? He hesitated, then sidestepped the issue. "Will Casey be back in time to join us?"

Brian shifted from one foot to the other. "I don't . . . I don't think so. Tennis practice."

Tennis. He didn't have to wait for Brian to tell him who Casey was. He nodded and glanced at his watch. It was nearly five, quitting time, and there was still no word from Harry Royce. But there might be.

"I'd like to stay for supper," he said truthfully, "but I need to hang loose. I'm supposed to get a call about somebody I want to see tonight."

Brian frowned. "Does this have anything to do with you being on TV at noon?" His blue eyes were serious, worried. "Have they caught him yet? The guy who killed that DA over there in Houston, I mean. And the cop you used to work with." He bit his lip. "I remember Carl Zumwalt, Dad. He gave me a toy badge once. I wore it all the time, even on my pajamas. He was a really nice guy. I'm sorry . . . I'm sorry he's dead."

Dead. McQuaid hadn't thought about the murders since he had pulled off the freeway, and the reminder was like a splash of cold water. He took a breath. "Haven't had an update on the situation for a couple of hours," he said soberly. "So far as I know, Mantel is still on the loose." Another breath, and he tried for a grin. "Hey. Before I go, maybe you can give me the grand tour."

But Brian was still frowning. "I don't like the idea that you're kind of daring that killer to come and get you, Dad. I wish you wouldn't do stuff like that." His voice was thin. "I'm not telling you how to do your business. I'm just telling you how I feel. I mean, I trust that you wouldn't do something . . . well, stupid. Or anything that was *really* dangerous. Something that might get you killed." He stopped uncertainly. "Would you?"

McQuaid gave him a straight look. They were both dealing with issues of trust here, weren't they? "I guess a man does what a man has to do, Brian. I've always tried to stay out of trouble, best I can. I wish you wouldn't worry."

Brian nodded slowly. "Yeah, I get it, Dad. The thing is that I feel the same way about you as I do about Sally—all that stuff she gave me about needing a place to stay, about it being her last chance. And she sounded *afraid*." The look on his face and the tone of his voice reminded McQuaid that Brian was still his parents' child. "I don't want either of you to get hurt."

McQuaid put his hand on Brian's shoulder. "That's how families are, son. I hate seeing you taking chances, too." He held Brian's eyes for a moment, remembering that kiss, wishing he could say something to Brian that would let him know that he knew about Casey. That he had seen them together, there by the car. He took a deep breath, searching for the right words. But he couldn't find them—and when you got right down to it, the secret was Brian's to keep, not his to give away.

So he said, "Look, Brian. I know there are some risks you feel *you* have to take. If things don't turn out the way you hope, you're going to get hurt. That's the way life is. We just have to trust each other, do what we think is right, and hope for the best. And if it doesn't work out, we learn whatever we can from the experience. And we go on from there."

McQuaid flinched. True enough. But he was talking all around the real subject, which was his son's relationship with a black girl. And what he'd said sounded like a shallow, simplistic philosophy without much depth to it.

But Brian squared his shoulders and nodded. "You're right, Dad. We learn what we can and go on. Well, let me show you around." He waved around the room. "It's not a palace, but it's comfortable. I like it here. A lot fewer distractions than at the co-op. I don't go out much. Casey's in pre-med, which is tough. When summer school classes start up next week, we'll both be hitting the books."

The house was sparsely but nicely furnished and surprisingly tidy. Brian's bedroom contained his usual scramble of books, science equipment, rocks, animal bones and skulls, and his computer and printer. McQuaid noticed that the bed was neatly made up with the quilt China had given him when he went off to college. The door to the other bedroom— Casey's—was shut, and there was nothing in the house that gave any hint that Casey was the girl McQuaid had seen. Nothing, that is, until they stepped out onto the back porch and McQuaid spotted a pink sweatshirt draped across the railing and a pink headband on the floor. Brian noticed it, too, and his neck reddened. McQuaid waited, thinking Brian might say something. But he didn't, and neither did McQuaid.

Before they said good-bye, McQuaid went back to the subject of Sally. "I hope your mom didn't lay too much of a guilt trip on you," he said.

"Well, she did, sort of." Brian looked away. "I felt bad that I couldn't . . . you know, ask her to stay here, especially because she sounded so scared." With a lopsided grin, he added, "But you can see that there's not a lot of extra room. It would be pretty hard for Casey and me to study—with my mother hanging out here, I mean."

"True," McQuaid agreed. But he thought he understood. Brian believed that his mother—who wasn't the most liberal person in the world—wouldn't be able to deal with Casey, which was undoubtedly right. Hell, he thought *he* was pretty liberal and he wasn't exactly having an easy time dealing with it.

Brian ducked his head. "I love Sally, but to tell the truth, Dad, the Juanita thing scares me. I used to sort of like it when Juanita showed up, you know? She was funny. Funny ha-ha, I mean, always clowning around, good for a lot of laughs. Now I know there's nothing funny about it."

Then, watching his son, McQuaid understood something else. Brian was worried that Casey, or maybe he and Casey together, wouldn't be able to deal with his skitzy mother, whose behavior was totally unpredictable.

"I'm sorry, son," McQuaid said, with genuine sympathy. "It's a tough situation."

"Tougher for Sally than for us," Brian said. "I wish there was something I could do for her. But as long as Juanita's around, she's going to go on jumping into the deep end and yelling for somebody to throw her a life preserver." He sighed. "So there's no point in feeling guilty about it, I guess."

Reassured by what seemed to him to be an entirely adult assessment of the situation, McQuaid put his arm around his son's shoulders, gave him a warm hug, and said good-bye.

But as he got in his truck and drove away, he felt a deep regret, wishing he had been able to tell Brian that he had seen him with the girl, wishing that they could have talked about it—what it might mean, where it might go, where it might end.

All he could think about was the two young people, Brian and Casey, holding each other against the world in a long, deep kiss.

Chapter Nine

The Manzanilla is a highly productive olive that originated in Spain many centuries ago and is widely grown in the Middle East and the United States. The trees are moderately resistant to cold weather and begin bearing when they are about five years old. The medium-size olives are primarily used for the table. The stuffed green olives and black olives you buy in the supermarket are most likely Manzanilla. The fragrant oil has a slightly peppery bite.

The Picual is an early-ripening, cold-tolerant olive cultivar from Spain. Picual olives, which are primarily grown for their oil, account for a quarter of the world's olive oil production. The oil is known for its floral aroma (you may detect a tomato-leaf note), its complex flavor, and its stability, which gives it a longer shelf life. Extra-virgin oil from Picual olives has a high level of polyphenols, an organic compound which is known to have antioxidant effects. Diets that contain antioxidant-rich fruits and vegetables are linked to lower risks for diseases like cancer, heart disease, stroke, cataracts, Parkinson's, Alzheimer's, and arthritis.

China Bayles
"Virgin Territory"
Pecan Springs Enterprise

It was just after three when Maddie dropped me off at Manzanilla, circled around, and drove back down the lane toward the ranch house. I watched her go, thinking about my question: *Do you love Boyd enough to marry him?* Yes, I'd been meddling, and she had every right to keep her own counsel.

But all the same, I thought, she had given me an answer. She might be flattered by his unexpected attention and hopeful that marriage might keep her from losing her trees, but she didn't love him. Which didn't mean that she would tell him no. In fact, I had the feeling that she might be all too ready to say yes.

So now I really wanted to meet the man who had asked her and form my own opinion about him. I also wanted to know what Ruby knew about this potential marriage. Was *this* why she had brought me out here? To find a way to keep Maddie from marrying this guy?

At the cabin, I went into the bedroom to wake Ruby from her nap. But her bed was neatly made and empty, and there was a note on the dining table. *Pete came by and we're going for a walk along the river,* she wrote. *Sofia asked me to remind you to drop in and see her at her cabin this afternoon. She has something she wants to talk to you about— seems pretty urgent.*

Pete? Oh, yes. Pete Lawrence, the guy I had talked to in the lunch line. Tall and lean, broad shoulders, gingery hair, wide smile, very blue eyes in a pleasant, sun-browned face. A nice guy who managed the ranch's olive groves. And looked like a cowboy.

I rolled my eyes. Ruby has a tendency to go off the rails about cowboys, like the bull rider she'd fallen in love with

143

at the rodeo. But the bull rider was *last* summer, almost a full year ago, and he'd followed the rodeo out of town. She and Hark Hibler, the editor of the *Pecan Springs Enterprise,* had seemed pretty serious for a while—at least Hark had. The same flame hadn't seemed to light Ruby's fire, though. While she and Hark still went out together, they were mostly just friends. And as far as I knew, she hadn't lost her heart to a cowboy yet this year. She was due, and Pete—who had seemed pretty nice—might just be the one.

Well, since Ruby was out for the afternoon, I might as well go next door and see what Sofia wanted to talk to me about. Maybe I could get her to tell me something about Boyd. I picked up a pencil and added my own note to Ruby's.

Heading next door to see Sofia.

To the southeast, over the trees, a bank of dark clouds was rising, and the afternoon sunshine was come-and-go, scattering cloud shadows along the lane. I remembered that the previous night's weather forecast had said something about a storm moving up from the warm waters of the Gulf of Mexico, but I'd been busy and hadn't paid much attention. It was almost oppressively warm, and the still air was heavy with the fragrance of the honeysuckle that clambered up the lattice at one end of Sofia's porch. The outside of the cabin—Picual, it was called, in honor of another of Eliza's Spanish olive trees—looked very much like ours: hand-hewn gray logs, metal roof, wide front porch with a time-worn floor. A path lined with large round river rocks led from the lane up to the porch steps. Beside the steps: two large clay pots of bright red geraniums and a shallower pot containing a big mother aloe vera plant and several baby plants—pups, they're called. The collection looked very pretty.

But while the interior of our cabin had been remodeled and completely modernized, Picual looked very much as it must have looked when it was first built. I assumed that this was the way Sofia preferred to live: in a single room, about twenty by twenty, with a door in the front and in back, a small cooking and eating area tucked into a corner, a narrow bed pushed against a wall, and a tiny lean-to bathroom built against the back of the cabin. For some, the living space might have been a tight fit. But the bed was covered with a bright woven blanket and heaped with pillows, there were several colorful rugs on the floor, and the space was cozy with painted furniture, a pair of low bookcases, and interesting Mexican and macramé hangings on the walls. There was a cast-iron pot of simmering *frijoles* on the stove, its rich fragrance wafting through the air. The fireplace, like the one in our cabin, was built of stone, but there was no gas log and what was left of a recent fire was still visible on the hearth.

The cabin's small windows didn't let in much light, and it took a moment or two for my eyes to adjust to the dimness. Sofia was sitting in a chair beside the fireplace, her feet resting on an upholstered ottoman, a brightly striped serape spread over her lap.

"You'll forgive me for not getting up," she said. "It's been a long day already."

It was quite warm in the room but the old woman wore a rust-colored knit shawl over her shoulders. The silvery crown of her coiled hair shone in the dim light. When she put out her thin, wrinkled hand to me, her fingers felt like brittle twigs. But her dark eyes were alert and searching, filled with questions. I felt again as I had earlier, that she was looking inside me for something—what, I wasn't sure, and I felt vaguely uncomfortable.

"Our tea is waiting for us on the table." She spoke slowly, not stiffly but with an endearing formality, as though she considered each word, each phrase important enough to choose and arrange it carefully. She gestured toward the square table in the kitchen corner. Covered with a red-checked gingham cloth, it held a bright blue teapot, two green and orange mugs, and a yellow honeypot. "Bring me a mug, please, with honey, and one for yourself. Then come and sit beside me."

In a moment I was seated on a low stool, near enough to touch her. The tea was a cheerful mint with a spritely lemon tang—lemongrass, I guessed. We sipped in appreciative silence for a few moments. Then I asked, "You wanted to see me?"

Sofia's voice was soft and I found myself leaning forward to catch her words. "Ruby tells me that you understand about Maddie's inheritance."

I spoke carefully. "I understand that Eliza left the ranch to Maddie and that Boyd—or rather, Boyd's lawyer—has challenged the will in court. There was a ruling, then an appeal, and another ruling."

She put her mug down on the small round table beside her, next to an intricately carved wooden box about the size of a hardcover book. She pulled her dark brows together, watching me, and again I saw the canny intelligence in her eyes.

"Jimmy Bob Elliott is a silly old fool," she said sharply. "But he's not enough of a fool to act on his own account, especially where Boyd Butler is involved. It was *Boyd* who challenged Eliza's will."

"Speaking on behalf of lawyers, I'm glad to hear that."

146

I smiled. "It's a very bad idea for an attorney to go around filing suits that his client hasn't explicitly approved."

"Yes." Sofia pursed her lips. "The legal actions were all Boyd's, despite his lies to Maddie." She slid a glance at me. "Sarita has told me that Boyd and Jimmy Bob Elliott have had many long conversations about how to get Eliza's will set aside so that Boyd can inherit."

I raised my eyebrows. The words *his lies* had been spoken with severe contempt, and she had checked with a glance to be sure I understood her point. But I wanted to know more about her informant, whom both Ruby and Maddie had mentioned.

"Sarita—she's your niece, isn't she?"

"Yes. She is the daughter of my sister. Sarita knows very well what goes on in Boyd's house, and she tells me." Sofia smiled, obviously pleased with Sarita's private communications. "She has worked there for many years, as his cook and housekeeper. Her husband, Manuel, oversaw his father's olive groves. Now it is her son Mateo who manages the trees and produces the oil. Sarita knows what Boyd is up to."

Sarita was also the person who, according to Maddie, had told Eliza about the adulterated olive oil. Boyd seemed to have blamed Mateo for the so-called mix-up in the labels, which would have been a natural and very sufficient reason for Sarita to come to her aunt, protesting the innocence of her son. This back-channel communications between the households wasn't at all surprising. Skilled employment in outlying ranches is often a family affair, and the families of neighboring ranches tend to intermarry. And of course there is always a lot of gossip and tittle-tattle back and forth, just as there is in every extended family.

But there might be something else going on here, something more purposeful and well, underhanded. Or if not underhanded, at least, not quite aboveboard. Sofia might look like somebody's sweet little grandmother, but she struck me as a shrewd old lady who knew exactly what she was doing—and what everybody else was doing, too. I wouldn't put it past her to use her niece as a spy, and perhaps to spin her report just a little.

Or a lot. Was Boyd the villain that he was being painted? Chet certainly had a reason to bad-mouth him. And what about Sarita? Had *she* been honest? Had *she* told the truth? Or had she come to Sofia with an invented story she thought her aunt might be glad to hear? When it came to tale-telling, the truth is often the first victim.

"And you've told all this to Maddie?" I asked. "What Sarita told you, I mean."

"Oh, yes. Yes, of course." She pursed her lips disapprovingly. "I love Maddie like a daughter, but I am sorry to say that the girl is not listening to me, or to her head. She stupidly chooses to believe Boyd's explanations—not just about Jimmy Bob Elliott challenging the will but about the labels on the olive oil." She gave two sharp clucks of disapproval. "The *bad* olive oil. You know about that?"

I nodded.

She was silent for a moment, staring down at her hands. When she lifted her head to speak, her expression was profoundly dark. "And about Eliza? You heard how she died?"

"I know that Eliza drowned." I gave her a probing look. "Is there something else to know?"

She returned my look, straight and direct. "Not to *know*, if you are talking about proof. But I am very sure in my heart"—she pressed both hands together over her chest—"that it was Boyd's doing. In her last days, Eliza was terrified of the dark. She insisted that the curtains be drawn against the night, and she slept with the light on beside her bed and in

148

her bathroom. She would never have gone out into the dark by herself. *Never.* But she would have gone with her nephew, especially if he gave her some sort of convincing explanation." Her voice quavered, intense. "And he was here that night, you know. He could have unlocked the side door before he left and come back later. Sarita has said that he did not return home until very late that night, which seems suspicious to me." She sighed. "But the authorities could find no proof."

Exactly. No proof. Nothing but inference, hints, insinuation. There wasn't even enough here to construct a circumstantial case.

"So you and Sarita have talked about this," I said. "Who else have you discussed it with?"

"Only Maddie." A pause. "And you."

I heard the emphasis on the last two words. "And why me?"

But she only shook her head. I gave her a moment to answer the question and then I said, "Maddie tells me that she and Boyd are discussing marriage. She seems to be considering it seriously. Do you think she really wants to marry him?"

"No!" Sofia spit out the word. "I do *not* believe she wants to marry him, no! But she is afraid of losing the trees. Maddie is like Eliza in that way, you see. The trees, the trees, always the trees—you would think they are the only things in this world that matter." She raised her hands and let them fall back into her lap. "The trees are what she worries about. She thinks marriage might be the easiest way to solve her problem. To keep the trees."

I chuckled wryly. "If that's her whole reason, she's likely to be disappointed. Marriage—especially under these circumstances—can create a great many problems, rather than resolve them."

"And there's something else." Sofia put her hand on my arm and leaned toward me. Her voice was urgent. It held a quaver that seemed almost exaggerated. "Maddie is in danger, you see. I believe Boyd killed his aunt because he expected to inherit her half of the Last Chance Ranch, and more. Now, he wishes to marry Maddie and then he will—"

"Hold on." I pulled my arm away from her. "Inherit . . . more? What *more* do you mean?"

"It's not the ranch. Why should Boyd want more land when he can't manage what he has? And he isn't interested in the trees, either." She gave me a knowing glance. "It's the Butler oil land in West Texas. In Pecos County. When the probate judge—Tinker Tyson—gave his second ruling, he said that Maddie can keep that property, and the income from it, as long as she lives. That's when Boyd decided he must marry Maddie. He wants—he *needs*—that money."

I frowned. This wasn't making a lot of sense. "But Boyd must know there's no income from that land. Ruby says that the oil has been depleted." In fact, when Chet told me that the probate judge gave that land to Maddie, I had assumed that it was the kind of award that might look good on paper but was in reality a meaningless consolation prize.

"It is true that the land has produced no income in over two decades," Sofia said. "But the drillers have found a new way to get oil out of the ground. The Butler leases are due to expire before the end of the year, all of them. There will be a great deal of money to be made when they are renewed or sold." She gave a wry chuckle. "Boyd understands that Tinker Tyson made a mistake. He should never have given that land to Maddie. But now it is done and Tinker says he cannot undo it."

"Ah," I said slowly. "I see." I had read recently about the West Texas oil boom—quick profits, high returns—created by the new hydraulic fracking technologies. The boom would last only as long as the drillers were able to get oil out of the ground, and then it would be over and the land would be fit only for grazing again. Or, because fracking is an even greater polluter than drilling, the soil and ground-water could be so contaminated that cattle couldn't graze on it. But Sofia was right. Until the oil ran out or prices took a tumble, whoever owned that property stood to make a substantial amount of money. The leases in Maddie's pocket were a compelling dowry.

"Yes, exactly," Sophia said, as if she had followed my thought. "And Boyd, I am sorry to say, needs money. His father lost most of his share of the Butler oil land through drink and bad management. Boyd has gambled away what was left of it." She added reproachfully, "He has even mort-gaged his half of the Last Chance."

I wondered whether the information about the gambling was more of Sarita's back-channel communications to her aunt, or whether it was locally common knowledge. But if it was true, Boyd wasn't exactly a safe marriage bet.

"Does Maddie know about the gambling? And the mort-gage?" Surely that would give her second thoughts.

"She has heard of both from her lawyer, Clarence Coo-per. Boyd has told her that the mortgage has been paid."

Ah. Chalk up one in good old Clarence's column. Well, the existence of a mortgage, if there was one, would be a simple matter to confirm. All it took was a trip to the county clerk's office and a look at the property records.

But that wasn't the point, was it? The point was that, on all counts, and whatever the truth of these accusations against Boyd, Maddie seemed to prefer to believe him.

"She must want to keep those trees very badly," I mur-mured, half to myself.

"Yes, she does." Sofia's glance was a sharp-pointed dart. "But marriage between these two is impossible. That is what I have told Boyd. It is what I am telling you."

"Well, I certainly agree that it's a terrible idea to marry someone just to save a few olive trees," I said firmly. "I suggest that she ask her lawyer to draw up a very careful prenuptial agreement, spelling out exactly what belongs to both her and Boyd *before* the marriage."

Texas is a community property state. In the absence of a firm agreement, Maddie would have trouble protecting whatever income her separate property brought her after the marriage—and if it was true that Boyd was a gambler, she was likely to need protection. I thought of my friend Justine Wyzinski, the Whiz, who practices family law in San Antonio.

"If Clarence doesn't have experience in this area of the law," I added, "I can put Maddie in touch with a very good lawyer who—"

"You don't understand, my dear." Sofia lifted her chin, speaking with an almost ringing authority. "It must not be done. It is *impossible*."

I frowned at her. "Impossible? I don't quite understand. They're both of legal age, aren't they? If she wants to marry him and he wants to marry her—"

Sofia interrupted me. "This is why I asked to speak with you this afternoon: to learn whether you are the person I want to advise me on this matter." She smiled slightly. "I believe that you are, and I will show you the papers that prove that what I say is true. You will tell me what you think about these papers—whether they are sufficient—and what you think I should do."

"You're asking me for a legal opinion?" I asked, frowning. "But I'm not—"

I was about to say that I wasn't a practicing attorney, but she broke in again. "Yes, a legal opinion. Yes, exactly. I have money. I will be glad to pay whatever is reasonable." She picked up the carved wooden box on the table beside her and put it on her lap. "I trust you will understand that what we are about to speak of is a very difficult, delicate family matter, to be discussed only between the two of us and no one else." She paused, running her fingers over the polished surface of the box. "Eliza brought this box with her from Spain," she added reminiscently. "It is very old, made of olive wood from the Spanish orchards. She kept her most precious papers in it."

So there it was. Sofia wanted to engage me to give her a legal opinion about the papers in the heirloom box she held on her lap. Eliza's important documents. Maybe they had to do with the trees, or with the production of olive oil—some sort of secret recipe or formula, or instructions for managing the orchards. Maybe she wanted my opinion on their potential value, in case they might be of use to Maddie. Or maybe she wanted to keep the documents—whatever they were— from Boyd, and hoped I could tell her how to do that.

But I had just met this woman. For all I knew, she was a little wacky, even a whole lot wacky. This whole thing might be a figment of Sofia's imagination, or something else: a way to make herself seem important, a way to get attention from an outsider. At the same time, though, I was intrigued. There was no shortage of lawyers hanging around the fringes of this affair. I could understand that Sofia might not trust Jimmy Bob What's-his-name, Boyd's attorney, to keep his mouth shut about anything important. But she could certainly ask good old Clarence for an opinion. She didn't need to bring in a complete stranger. Unless, of course, there was some sort of very special reason she didn't want a local lawyer dipping into Eliza's secret recipe for olive oil—or whatever was in that box.

I was about to open my mouth and ask that question, point blank, when there was a knock at the door. Sofia frowned and raised her voice. "Yes, who is it?"

"It's me," Chet said loudly. "May I come in, Sofia? I've brought you a present. And I'm looking for China."

Sofia closed the carved box and put it back on the table beside her. She smiled at me. "It is our friend, yours and mine. Go and open the door. There will be time to talk about this matter later. But please remember that it must be kept between us."

I opened the door to see Chet, standing on the front porch with a bottle in his hand. "Hey," he said. "Ruby told me you were here. It's threatening to storm, so I thought we might get an early start on our tour. I'd like to show you around the vineyards before it starts to rain."

I glanced over his shoulder. The clouds that had been building to the southeast now covered almost half the sky. The sun had disappeared and a fitful wind stirred the leaves of the live oak tree in front of the cabin.

Before I could say anything, Sofia called out, "Come in, please, Chet. Especially if you have brought me some wine."

I stepped back and held the door open. "I have," Chet said with a laugh, coming into the room. He raised a bottle. "I've brought you a red from our Dolcetto and Sangiovese vines. Would you like a small glass now? And Jason and Andrea have asked me to invite you to supper. China is coming—right, China?"

"Right," I said. "I'm also looking forward to seeing your vineyard. Unless we have to postpone because of rain."

"Not a chance," Chet said confidently. He grinned at Sofia. "When I left Jason's place, Andrea was baking your favorite lemon olive oil cake. If you come, the occasion will be even more grand."

"I would love a small glass of your wine." Sofia gestured toward a cupboard. "But I won't go to supper with you and your friends. I am very tired." She smiled primly. "And I'm an old, old lady. You young people can do very well without me."

"That's not true," Chet protested. "We love your stories about the old Last Chance."

She shook her head and we had to accept her refusal. Later, when I thought about her words, I would deeply regret that Chet and I didn't keep on insisting. If we had taken Sofia with us, things might have turned out very differently, and a great deal of loss and pain might have been spared.

But we didn't. Chet handed us each a glass of wine and—quite earnestly—said some of the things that used to make me smile, back in the days when we sampled wines together.

"Can you taste the blueberry tones, and perhaps a bit of tart cherry?" he asked hopefully. "Maybe a hint of coffee? It's a nice, complex red, don't you think?"

I smiled. I do enjoy drinking wine, but the language used by connoisseurs has always seemed a little . . . well, unclear. Lawyers prefer definitions that they can nail down, and that everyone can agree to.

Sofia sniffed. "I don't know about coffee and cherry, but your wine is very good, Chet." She smiled at him and I got the idea that he was a favorite of hers. Perhaps she thought he was a better marriage bet for Maddie than Boyd. "The next time you come," she added, "please bring another bottle. I'll drink it down to the bottom and tell you if I can find any blueberries in it."

Chet and I laughed at that and finished our wine. I bent

over her chair and whispered my promise to come back in the morning and look over her papers. "And I'll bring you a piece of Andrea's olive oil cake," I said.

She patted my hand and said, with a smile, "Thank you, China Bayles. I'll be waiting."

We said our good-byes and left. Outside, on our way to the dusty yellow Jeep parked out in front, Chet looped his arm in mine. "A sweet old lady, isn't she?"

"A very shrewd old lady," I said. "Quite canny." I thought about her questions of me, her penetrating glance, her thin hands on the box of documents, which might or might not contain something valuable. "She plays her cards close to the vest."

"Cards?" Chet cocked an eyebrow. "That little old lady is holding cards? I didn't have her figured for a player."

I realized that I shouldn't have spoken. "Oh, you know me, Chet," I said lightly. "I'm the one who sees a plot under every rock." The rumble of thunder helped me change the subject. "Hey. If we're going to beat that rain, we need to pick up Ruby and be on our way."

"Ruby said to tell you that she's not coming with us," Chet replied. He stopped beside the Jeep. "How about giving me a hand with the soft top? We'd better put it up now. It's no fun to try to get it in place when the wind is blowing and we're getting wet."

I went around to the other side of the Jeep. "Ruby's not coming with us? That's too bad. What's she doing?" Together, we raised the top and began to fasten it to the front windshield.

"She and Pete are going for a ride," Chet said. "Then dinner and country dancing." Chet checked the fastenings to make sure they were secure. "I saw them just now, getting into Pete's pickup. They seemed quite simpatico." He stepped to the back. "We need to zip in the back window. You start over there on that side."

I followed directions. "Simpatico?"

Chet grinned. "Yeah. They were holding hands. I was glad to see it. Nice for Pete to have a little fun for a change. Lately, he's had more trouble than he needs."

"Well, Pete's a cowboy," I said flippantly. "So I guess I'm not surprised." When I saw the puzzled expression on Chet's face, I thought I'd better explain. "Ruby falls in love with a cowboy every so often. She's about due."

Chet's glance was serious. "I hope it's not a game with her, China. Pete's just beginning to get himself together after a bad situation. He was engaged to a girl in San Antonio, but she threw him over for somebody else. He's a super-nice guy. I'd hate for him to get hurt again."

I sobered guiltily. "I didn't mean to make Ruby sound like a heartbreaker." We finished zipping. "She never intends to hurt anybody." I paused, thinking that it wasn't always Ruby who called it quits. Sometimes it was the cowboy who ended it—like Shane, riding away with never a backward glance. Maybe Pete was what Ruby needed. Maybe he was a different kind of cowboy.

Chet was frowning. "With Pete, I'm not sure it can ever be easy come, easy go. He's not that kind of guy." He went to the driver's-side door and got in, and I followed suit— after I moved a length of rope, a pair of work gloves, a wire cutter, and a box of ammunition into the backseat, where it joined several bottles of olive oil, the labels crossed out with a dark marker.

"Rancid," Chet replied when I asked him. "I got them from Boyd, who had some bottles go bad. Andrea intends to use it in her next batch of soap."

"Smart," I said. "That's a good use for bad oil."

"Bad oil works pretty well as a rust preventative on outdoor equipment and tools, too. And I used it to polish up a couple of my wood carvings." He went back to the previous subject. "Say, could you maybe . . . like, talk to Ruby, make sure she understands Pete's situation? He might be looking for something, well, something sort of permanent."

"I suppose I could," I said reluctantly. I love Ruby like a sister, but I don't like to get involved in her romances. Colin Fowler, the love of her life, was killed three years ago, and while I keep telling her it's time she got over it, she still hasn't recovered from the tragedy. She was madly in love with him, and when Ruby is truly in love, she flings herself into it with all her heart and absolutely no common sense, like a woman jumping out of a plane at ten thousand feet without a parachute, in complete ecstatic free fall. Since Colin's death—his murder, to be accurate—she's been involved with several guys for a month or two at a time, but the flames never quite took hold. Still, considering what Chet had said, I thought it would be a good idea to have a little talk with her. I liked Pete. If he was in a vulnerable place, still getting over being jilted, Ruby might not be good for him.

Love is a tricky, tricky thing, you know? It can be right for us, it can be wrong. What's right at one time in our lives—witness my relationship with Chet that summer when we were clerking together—can be wrong at another. And even when it's right, it can go badly.

When it's wrong, it can be a nightmare.

Chapter Ten

MCQUAID

Late Friday Afternoon

Still thinking about his son and the girl with the tennis racquet, McQuaid took East Oltorf under the freeway to the Sonic Drive-In and ordered a burger, fries, and a chocolate milkshake. While he ate, he reminded himself that one kiss does not a long love affair make, and that they were only sharing a house. They weren't married. And there was no point in dwelling on the situation. Brian would tell him what was going on when the boy was good and ready. Anyway, he had to think about tonight—assuming Royce came through with the contact information—and about his plan for luring Mantel out into the open where he could be captured. He clenched his jaw. Or shot. *Five dead.* This time, if the man stood in front of him, asking for it, he was likely to get it. Right between the eyes.

Finished eating, he doubled back under the freeway, made a left on the access road, and took the on-ramp, heading south on I-35. The gray clouds were grimly ominous, the wind was picking up, and an occasional brief shower splattered the windshield. He turned on the wipers, but they left muddy arcs across the glass. As he flicked the windshield washer on, he remembered that the Lions barbecue had been rained out the year before, and they'd had to reschedule. His Plan A would be scuttled if they were rained out again, and he had no Plan B. Irritated, he wished he'd paid more attention to the weather forecast.

He was still thinking of this when Harry Royce called.

"I dug out Mantel's local connections. Two addresses in New Braunfels and San Antonio. If you still want them, I'll email them." Royce's voice darkened. "Nobody says you have to do this, McQuaid. It's your own private undertaking."

"Understood," McQuaid replied. Royce was right. Tracking down Max Mantel, putting him back where he belonged or—

Or whatever. It was his own private crusade. He checked his mirror, then swung out to pass a big yellow school bus that was trucking along at the speed limit, nearly seventy. It was empty, but it was still moving fast for a school bus. "Who are they? The local connections, I mean."

"One of them is Mantel's stepbrother," Royce said. "A guy named Lester McGown, age thirty-seven, three priors. Two misdemeanor possession, one felony armed robbery. Lives on Chisholm Road, outside New Braunfels. I pulled the Huntsville prison visitation records. McGown is on the list. He saw Mantel about two weeks ago, and a couple of weeks before that."

The inside of the windshield was fogging and McQuaid turned on the defroster. "So McGown might have been in on the escape," he said. "And the shootings."

"Maybe, maybe not." Royce was matter-of-fact. "I had a trooper do a drive-by on the Chisholm Road address. It's a single-wide, looked to be occupied but nobody was home. If I had the manpower, I'd put somebody on the place."

"I'll get on it this evening," McQuaid said. "Maybe I'll have better luck." The defroster wasn't clearing the windshield fast enough, and he swiped at the glass with a paper napkin, leaving a streak of mustard. "The San Antonio address—what's the connection?"

"Turns out to be a wrecking yard owned by a cousin," Royce said. "Joe Romeo. No priors, no record of prison visits. Probably not worth checking out." McQuaid heard papers rustling. "I've got the full list of friends and associates, but everybody else is in the Houston area. The two I gave you are the only ones in your neck of the woods. Long shots both of them, if you ask me."

McQuaid grunted. "In this business, everything is a long shot." Including tomorrow's barbecue setup. Yeah, Hark's story on the wire had helped him put the bait out there. But the odds of Mantel's snatching it up couldn't be better than sixty-forty. Forty the man would show, sixty he wouldn't. Hell, they might even be worse than that. Seventy-thirty, eighty-twenty. There was no way to tell. And now, rain—which was coming down so hard at the moment that the glowing taillights of the car thirty yards ahead were a foggy blur.

"Any news from Houston?" he asked. "No more homicides, I hope."

"If there are, nobody's bothered to tell me."

"Wouldn't they? Aren't you in charge?"

"Am I?" Royce's chuckle was ironic. "Abbott sure as hell thinks *he's* in charge. He's still hot as a two-dollar pistol over your TV sucker play this afternoon. He's phoned over here twice, pumping me for the details. I was glad to be able to plead ignorance. Told him I had no damn idea what kind of dirty tricks you might have up your sleeve." His voice grew clipped, stern. "Don't you contradict me on that, my friend. I do not want to see your name connected with this office in any public way, shape, or form. Whatever you do tonight, tomorrow, next week, you are out there on that skinny limb all by your lonesome." He paused for emphasis. "You got that, McQuaid?"

"Got it." McQuaid wasn't perturbed. Royce had to protect himself. He couldn't admit to letting a civilian trespass on cop turf, even if the guy was an ex-cop and a licensed PI who was doing something useful. "You know, Harry," he added, "I feel for Abbott, I really do. Today must've been a helluva day in the DA's office—losing the boss the way they did. But if Abbott thought he could keep a tight lid on the political pot for more than an hour or two, he's dumber than a box of rocks."

"I'm with you on that, fella." Royce must have looked at the clock, because his voice had become suddenly cheerful. "Hey, looka that. It's an hour past quitting time. I'm outta here, quick as I send you this email."

"Put your cell number in that email." McQuaid slipped into his mock gangster growl. "Us indies, man, we don't got no quittin' time. But hey, old buddy. If Blackwell and me find us some fun tonight, we'll be glad to let you know, so you can come and give us a hand."

Royce gave a sharp laugh. "You can forget that, 'old buddy.'" McQuaid heard the clicking of a keyboard. "Glad to hear Blackie's going with you," Royce added. "He's a good man. I'll put my cell number in, but if you've got to call me, it'd better be good. My kid's pitching tonight. Western Hills Little League. If we don't get rained out, I aim to be in the front row of the bleachers." He paused. "Haven't you got a boy in Little League? Seems to me I remember something about that."

McQuaid thought of Brian and the girl. "Hell, Harry, that

162

was seven, eight years ago. Brian's in college now. He's got a place of his own, off Oltorf in South Austin. With a roommate."

"No shit," Royce said. "My, how time flies."

"It does that," McQuaid said softly. A place of his own, with a roommate. A girl roommate. A lover. It was enough to make a man feel old. "Time sure as hell does fly."

LIGHTNING was flickering but the rain was still stop-and-go a half hour later, when McQuaid slowed for a left turn off Limekiln Road west of Pecan Springs. He drove down the narrow gravel lane that led to the large Victorian house where he and China lived with their adopted daughter, Caitlin. He had already arranged to pick up Blackie at the Pecan Springs cop shop, where his partner was enjoying take-out Tex-Mex with the chief of police. Then they would drive down to New Braunfels to see what they could learn, if anything, at the Chisholm Road address Royce had emailed him. No point in going all the way down to San Antonio. Likely wouldn't be anybody at the wrecking yard on a rainy Friday night.

But Blackie—with whom McQuaid had talked by phone several moments before—was occupied, and the chores came first. McQuaid would feed Winchester and the cat, look in on Caitie's flock of pet chickens, and pick up his bulletproof vest and a few other items. He ran mentally through his checklist for nighttime action: Glock and ammo, pepper spray, vest, LED Maglite, raingear, spotlight. He was trying to remember where he'd put that spotlight when he made the last turn and saw the beat-up red Ford Fiesta parked in his drive.

His jaw dropped open then snapped shut. He narrowed his eyes. Hell and damnation. That was Sally's car, the one she'd been driving since she totaled her Subaru last winter. What the devil was *she* doing *here*?

And then he remembered Brian saying that he'd told his mother to check with his dad and China about staying with them. Taking her cue from the boy, Sally had apparently figured that the McQuaid house in Pecan Springs was a pretty good place to hide out from whatever she was afraid of. But instead of checking, she had pulled one of her usual dumbass tricks. Sally—or maybe Juanita was running things this week—had just shown up, here at the house, with the idea of doing whatever she damn well pleased first and asking permission later. That was the way she'd always operated. She was never going to change.

He pulled up next to Sally's car and turned off the ignition. The kitchen light was on, and there was a light in the dining room, too. She had obviously managed to let herself in, which wouldn't have been hard, if she had remembered from the last time she'd stayed here that they kept the back door key under the third flowerpot to the right of the steps. He scowled, noticing that the back screen door was hanging open. She had probably let Winchester out, and there was no telling where the hell he'd wandered off to. The little guy was still new to the place. He couldn't be relied on to stay in the yard—or find his way back home once he'd left it.

McQuaid could feel the anger rising inside his chest like the world's worst case of heartburn. Before he could do what he'd been planning to do tonight, he would have to hunt for the dog, as well as deal with his out-of-control ex-wife and her psycho sidekick. He narrowed his eyes. Well, he wasn't going to let Sally get by with this kind of ill-mannered, immature behavior. Not this time, and not ever again. He was drawing the line. She wasn't staying in his house and that was all there was to it. Period. Paragraph. The end.

He yanked his phone out of the device holder and speed-dialed his mother in Seguin. After a brief chat with Caitie—who was a) worried about her chickens and b) excited about going fishing that afternoon with her Pawpaw and catching two *big* striped bass, bigger than the biggest striped bass Pawpaw himself had ever caught in the San Marcos River—he got his mother on the phone. She knew Sally pretty well, given that her son had been married to the woman for over five years, and she'd had enough acquaintance with Juanita, she often said, to last her for three or four lifetimes.

"What is she hiding from *this* time?" she asked tartly. "Somebody she owes money to, I reckon."

Which brought McQuaid up short. Was it a good idea to put her up at his parents, where his daughter was also staying? What if Sally's pursuer, whoever the hell he was, managed to track her to Seguin and cause trouble for Mom and Dad and Caitie? He considered that possibility for a moment, but it was so remote a chance that he discarded it.

"I think she just needs a place to stay for a couple of days, Mom," he said in a placating voice. "Everybody can use a break now and then, you know."

There was a silence. "Well, I suppose," his mother said at last. "But she can't come tonight. We're going to have Caitie's fried fish for supper and then she and I are going to the nursing home for my regular Friday night Bingo. Mr. Rizzo from down the block and Mr. Reilly Junior and Senior from the hardware store are coming to play poker with your father. If Sally can't find anyplace else to stay, I suppose she can come tomorrow." Her voice grew steely. "But you tell her she can't come at all if she's going to bring that friend of hers. That Juanita person." McQuaid flinched, recognizing that I-am-laying-the-law-down tone from his high school years, when he and his friends had not always trod the

straight and narrow. "You tell her if she's thinking of bringing Juanita, they can both stay at the Motel 6 out on the
highway. Your father and I are not having that one in this
house ever again. You tell her now, you hear, Michael?"

McQuaid sighed and said that he understood her reser-
vations and he would certainly share them with Sally. He
pocketed his cell phone and got out of the car, muttering
curses. His ex-wife had to pick tonight, of all nights, to
impose herself. Well, he supposed there wasn't any harm in
letting her stay, since it would be just one night. He wouldn't
be back from checking out McGown's address until pretty
late, and China surely wouldn't mind if Sally slept in Brian's
room. He wasn't entirely sure about that, but he figured he
could explain the situation in a way that would help his wife
understand why he had invited his *ex-wife* for a sleepover.
First thing tomorrow, he would make sure Sally got down
to Seguin, where his mother would make her behave—or
pack her off to the Motel 6. Either way, she would be out of
his hair.

It wasn't just the door to the screened-in back porch that
was open, McQuaid saw as he went up the steps. The kitchen
door was wide open, too, and when he went inside, he saw
to his horror that Sally or Juanita or both must have had a
meltdown. The kitchen—neat and tidy when McQuaid left
that morning—was a huge *mess*.

A blue nylon duffel bag was lying on the floor, a woman's
purse, open, next to it. Chairs lay on their sides. The door to
the pantry was open, and cans and boxes were scattered
across the pantry floor. Mr. P, Caitie's orange tabby cat, hissed
at him from the top of the refrigerator. In the corner, Winchester's basket and water bowl were both upside down, and
there were kibbles spilled across the floor. The knife rack on
the counter beside the sink had been knocked over and the

knives scattered. A saucer was broken in the sink. The flour canister that usually sat beside it had tipped onto the floor and the lid had come off. The flour was strewn in a powdery white arc, with footprints tracking through it and around the table and out the hallway door.

"Sally?" McQuaid shouted furiously. "Sally, where the hell are you? What in the devil do you think you're doing? What—"

He heard a plaintive whimper, and Winchester pushed one of the lower cupboard doors open and crept out, trembling all over. His large brown eyes were filled with apprehension, his lifelong expectation of calamity and catastrophe fully realized. He threw back his head, closed his eyes, and gave one long, doleful, desolate howl.

"Winnie, poor boy," McQuaid crooned, and gathered him up in his arms. "What has she done to you?" He checked to be sure the dog was all in one piece, then righted the basket and deposited Winchester in it, giving his head a reassuring pat. "You'll be fine, guy. Just hang in there while I get to the bottom of this." The dog gave him an accusing look, turned around in his bed, and tucked himself into a ball, his long ears draped over his eyes.

McQuaid straightened up and raised his voice again. "Sally! Sally, damn it, what the *hell* is going on here?"

No answer. He strode out into the hallway, following the floury footprints into the dining room, where a couple of chairs were upset and a potted fern on a stand in the corner had been knocked onto the floor, spilling damp dirt and a handful of decorative rocks across the carpet.

And then on the opposite wall of the room, just above the wainscoting, he saw something that made his heart stop. It was a bloody handprint, the fingers widely splayed out, smearing a bloody trail several inches down the wall. And on the floor a few paces away lay a knife—a butcher knife from the rack in the kitchen—on a crisscrossing welter of white flour footprints. A pair of footprints left the welter and tracked the length of the room to the French doors, near which lay a woman's white tennis sneaker, the laces still tied. The doors stood wide open. The tracks led out onto the brick patio, in the direction of the driveway. It was raining again, and the air in the room was damp and chilly.

For a moment, McQuaid stood very still, staring at the bloody handprint on the wall, the knife, the open French doors, the sneaker, trying to put it all together. But then the irritation surfaced, on top of the confusion of other emotions. He knew Sally all too well, unfortunately. He thought it was entirely likely that she (or she and Juanita) had staged this melodramatic little charade to make it look like the guy she was running from—the guy she was afraid of—had followed her here and made off with her.

And there was plenty of reason for him to think this. Sally had pulled a similar stunt once, when Brian was a baby. Clothes strewn across the floor, dishes broken, books pulled out of a bookcase, both baby and mom gone. Mc-Quaid was a cop and cops always worried about the safety of their families. He had swallowed her cute little trick, hook, line, and sinker. He had felt pretty damned stupid—and mad as hell—when she showed up with the baby while the guys from the local station house were still investigating their "abduction."

But that was then and this was now, and when he knelt down to look carefully at the footprints, he saw that one set was small, a woman's tennis sneaker, most likely a match to the sneaker beside the door. The other set—the pair leading to the French doors—had been made by heavy work boots. Large boots, size twelve easily, and the indentation in the plush carpet suggested that the wearer was pretty hefty, perhaps even carrying Sally, slung over his shoulder. What happened here looked like it had involved two people, one of them the man she was afraid of. Who was he? An angry lover? Somebody she owed money to? A business partner she (or Juanita) had double-crossed?

But there was no point in standing around speculating. He had to get moving. He closed the doors and quickly searched the house: the downstairs room he used as an office, the laundry and utility rooms, the living room, the upstairs bedrooms, the bathrooms. He called Sally's name, stopping frequently to listen for any sound. But there was no sound and no sign of her—no floury footprints on the stairs or in the other rooms, either.

Back in the kitchen, McQuaid stood indecisively for a moment. He wished he could walk out, get in his truck, and forget about Sally until tomorrow or the next day—*after* Mantel was back in custody again. But he couldn't. There was a lot of cop left in him, and he knew the drill.

He pulled out his cell phone. The house was in Adams County, so he'd have to call the sheriff's office and report this as an apparent abduction. The sheriff—Curt Chambers, another of his and Blackie's fishing buddies—would dispatch a deputy or two, probably even come himself. The investigation would go on for a couple of hours at least, and like it or not, take priority over everything else. He would have to phone Blackie to let him know that their plan to check out McGown's address in New Braunfels was on hold while he dealt with whatever had happened to Sally. He should probably also phone Royce and update him on the situation.

But first, the sheriff.

He was poised to punch in 911 when his phone buzzed

in his hand. He felt a cold chill in his belly as he recognized the number.

"Sally," he said urgently. "Sally, where the hell *are* you? What happened? What's going on?"

There was a silence, then a grating, gravelly voice. An unmistakable voice. "You missin' somebody, McQuaid? You lookin' for your wife? Well, you can stop lookin', right now. I told you I'd come for you, and I have, by damn. Lucky me— I've got your nearest and dearest. Pretty little thing, too."

McQuaid's blood turned to ice. But when he replied, he managed an even, conversational tone, even a chuckle. "My wife? No, I'm not looking for my wife, Mantel. She's out of town, where you can't lay hands on her. That's my *ex*-wife you've got." Another chuckle, rueful now. He added, "You want her, Max, you can sure as hell keep her. But I'm telling you, man, you'll be sorry. She may look cute and cuddly, but take it from me, that woman is the worst kind of trouble. You know what's good for you, you'll drop her off at the nearest shopping mall and forget you've ever seen her."

"Don't give me that horseshit, funny man," Mantel growled. "What would your *ex*-wife be doing in your kitchen, feedin' your damn dog? Nope, I got me the right one. Snatched her right outta your house." His voice took on an edge. "Dunno about cute and cuddly, though. She's a reg'lar wildcat. We had us a tussle over one of them big kitchen knives before I knocked her silly and hauled her outta there." He snorted. "You don't believe me, McQuaid? Just you listen to this."

There was a scuffle and a muted scream, and then Sally's voice, low and frantic, terrified. "Mike! Mike, they're going to kill me! Come and get me, Mike. Please!" She was sobbing hysterically now.

They're going to kill me. So Mantel wasn't alone. "Where

are you?" McQuaid asked roughly. She probably didn't know, but it was worth a shot.

"In a single-wide, out in the country somewhere, no idea where. Please, Mike," she wailed. "Help me. Oh, help—" But her plea was cut off, as if somebody had clapped a hand over her mouth.

"Believe me now, funny man?" Mantel laughed, that crazy, unmistakable laugh.

"You've made a stupid mistake, Max," McQuaid growled. "She's not my wife. But I don't suppose that makes a helluva lot of difference to you. Where are you? What do you want from me?"

"What do I want?" Another laugh, broken off sharply. "Well, hell, you're such a smart fella, McQuaid, college grad, hot-shot cop. You oughta be able to figure it out. *You're* the one who sent me to Huntsville. You could've ended it, quick and easy, the night you pointed your gun at me. That would've been the polite thing to do. Instead " He made an ugly noise. "Instead, I've been buried in that damn prison, waiting for my execution. But that don't matter none now. I got the prosecutor and your old partner and a couple of witnesses, and you're next on my list. I'll be more'n happy to trade your pretty little wife for *you*." His voice roughened. "But you'll have to come and get her. I ain't runnin' no delivery service."

And then McQuaid understood.

Instead of walking into the silly little trap he had set— the Lions Club barbecue, which had been a stupid idea from the get-go—Mantel had just set a trap for him, with Sally as the bait. And he was being pulled into it. He had no choice.

There was a despairing wail in the background. "Mike,

please! Don't argue with him. He's a brute. Just come and get me!"

He forced himself to be cool. "Okay, Mantel. So give me an address. Where am I supposed to pick up this ex-wife of mine?"

Mantel snickered. "You keep calling her that, man, she's gonna be really pissed at you. She's hot enough now—I'd hate to see her when she's *really* mad."

"Tell me where I can find you," McQuaid said tersely. He was thinking of the two dead girls in Houston, the witnesses at Mantel's trial. Of the DA and his wife. Of Carl. Of Sally and what they might do to her. And then he thought: *But it's not Sally that Mantel wants. She's just a means to an end. I'm the one he's after.* "Come on, give me an *address*, Mantel."

"Not so fast." Mantel's voice hardened. "I ain't ready to hand this chick over just yet. You stay with your phone and hang tight, McQuaid. I'll get back to you with instructions." The call went dead.

McQuaid thrust his phone in his pocket and strode toward the gun safe in his office.

No need to call the sheriff now.

Time to get his gear, pick up Blackie, and hit the road.

Time to *move*.

Chapter Eleven

Texas is the site of the first vineyard in North America. Established around 1659, a century earlier than plantings in Virginia or California, it was the work of Franciscan priests—and the start of something big.

The fifth-largest wine-producing state in the nation, Texas now has almost 4,500 acres of vineyards under cultivation. Some 350 commercial wineries that currently produce over 1.5 million gallons of wine a year, from some two dozen different grape varieties. The flourishing wine industry contributes more than $1.88 billion annually to the Texas economy. Recently, *Wine Enthusiast* magazine rated the scenic Texas Hill Country region outside of Austin among its ten top wine-travel destinations worldwide, saying that wine lovers can enjoy "the romance of the Old West" as they navigate "a sea of cowboy hats and pickup trucks."

Texas Department of Agriculture

The skies were gray and lightning flickered around the rim of the low, dark clouds. But the rain held off long enough for Chet to take me on a walk through his Last Chance Vineyard, some thirty acres planted with several different kinds of grapes—Merlot, Cabernet Sauvignon, Dolcetto, and Sangiovese. As far as I could see, the vineyard was a lovely, lively patchwork of shimmering greens, moving with the wind: Kelly green, emerald green, mint green, pine and pistachio and shamrock green. All green, every green, many greens, everywhere I looked. The amazing variety of shades of green made up a little, or so it seemed to me, for the regularity of the rows.

Chet parked his Jeep beside the field, and we got out and walked between the trellised vines. The rows were oriented north to south, Chet told me, for the best solar exposure. The vines were only four years old and just beginning to bear, the small green berries half-hidden by the canopy of leaves. Harvest, Chet said, was some seven or eight weeks away, depending on the weather.

"We're irrigating, of course." He pointed to the plastic drip-irrigation tubes that ran along the rows. "Grapes are drought-tolerant, but it's too risky to depend on rainfall. Anyway, we would never get enough rain in the summer, when the grapes are really heat-stressed. And the soil here isn't right for dryland grape growing. We've put in our own wells—three of them."

"Your wells are on the Edwards Aquifer?" I asked. The Edwards is the aquifer that supplies our water back home in Pecan Springs. With that came the thought of McQuaid, and I glanced at my watch. It was nearly six. I knew he'd had an afternoon appointment with a law firm in Austin, but he should be home by now, feeding Winchester and Mr. P and checking on Caitie's chickens. Or maybe he would stop at Beans' for supper and a quick game of pool with the guys. I thought of his scheme to bait Mantel, and then just as quickly made myself stop thinking about it. That was tomorrow. Whatever he was doing tonight, he was safe.

"Not the Edwards," Chet was saying. "We're on the Trinity here. Unfortunately, the water level in the aquifer is dropping because of the drought, and it's likely to get worse because of climate change. I saw a computer model the other day that said that at the current rate of use, the water level in parts of the aquifer will drop by as much as a hundred feet in the next couple of years. If that happens, we'll have to put in deeper wells. In fact, they're saying the aquifer could be entirely depleted in another fifteen or twenty years." He reached out to touch a green leaf. "It sounds pessimistic, but it turns out that the Last Chance Vineyard may be just that. The last chance to build a producing vineyard in this county."

"Depleted?" I whistled softly. "Gosh, Chet. If that happens, what will you do?" I glanced across the river, in the direction of the olive groves. "What will Maddie do?" Assuming that the trees still belonged to Maddie, of course. "And all the other farmers and ranchers?"

Another shake of his head, very serious. "I don't know, China. Everybody is worried—worried enough to get serious about conservation, which is a good thing, of course. Maddie's olives will likely be okay, since they're fairly well established, and since quite a few of Eliza's plantings are dryland olives. They're sustainable. But for Jason and me, the other vineyard owners, and the market farmers, it's a big question mark. What we need are three or four back-to-back really wet El Niño years to replenish the aquifer—and give the grapes enough time to get established. But I'm afraid that's only part of the picture. There are other problems."

I fingered the velvety leaves of a nearby vine, thinking how glad I was to be growing herbs. They're a lot more cooperative—and tolerant. "Other problems? Like what?"

"Like late frosts, for example. April a year ago was one of the coldest on record in the Hill Country, and the vines were hit by the worst late spring freeze in a century. Bud break typically occurs here in the last week of March or the first couple of weeks of April, and a late spring freeze can stunt the new growth. In some cases, it can kill the entire vine."

"Bud break?"

He grinned crookedly. "You'll be sorry you asked."

"Maybe so." I returned his grin. "But I'm a gardener, remember? And I'm curious."

He reached for one of the vines and pulled back the leaves. "The grape starts its annual growth cycle in the spring with bud break. The buds appear between the vine and the leaf stalk. Right here." He pointed. "Every bud is already pre-packed with everything it needs to produce grapes: the shoots, leaves, tendrils, even the berries. By mid-April, the buds are pushing out shoots at the rate of an inch a day. Then the leaves start unfolding."

"And then the temperature drops below freezing," I said, remembering my own garden disasters and misadventures. "Always at the worst time."

"Exactly. It's harder on some varieties than others. The Chardonnay, for example, likes to bud early. So if we get a few warm days in February, the Chardonnay gets the urge to surge and the buds start coming out. Which means that by late March or early April—when other varieties are just beginning to think about budding—the Chardonnay has already put out lots of green shoots and leaves, maybe even a few flowers." He gestured at the vines around us. "But almost all grapes are susceptible. If there's a freeze warning in early spring, you'll see us rushing out to the vineyard to set up heaters or fires or even fans, anything to keep the cold air from settling on the vines."

I frowned. "You know, I don't remember ever seeing a grape flower. What do they look like?"

"They're tiny," he said. "And wind-pollinated. Each flower has both male and female parts." He cocked a suggestive eyebrow at me, and I laughed.

"Yes. Very convenient," I said. "Saves dating, making arrangements with the local bees, that sort of thing."

He nodded. "Once they're fertilized, they get down to business and start setting fruit. Voila! Grapes. Unless, of course, there's a bad set, which can happen if the weather is rainy or you get a hailstorm or powdery mildew. And then there are the bird problems—" He lifted and lowered his shoulders in a shrug. "It's always something."

"Birds?"

"You bet. Here, mockingbirds and grackles are the worst, especially around harvest time. Some growers put up balloons with colored eyes, hoping the birds will think they're predators. Or they run an audio system that broadcasts bird distress calls."

We had turned around now and were headed back to the Jeep. "Sounds terribly dicey, Chet." I gave him a sympathetic look. "Are you having second thoughts? Do you ever wish you'd stayed in law school? Become a lawyer, found a cushy job in a nice quiet law firm in Houston or Dallas?"

"Law school?" He laughed. "Oh, hell, no. Leaving when I did was right for me. And getting hooked up with Jason and this place—that was right, too. But sometimes things sort of seem to gang up on you." He hunched his shoulders. "Between the extended drought and the late freeze, some of the local growers took a really bad hit last year, and a couple of them gave up. Small growers are always operating on the margin, financially. A tough year can break us."

"That's true for most small businesses," I reminded him, although I had to admit that growers and farmers are in an even more precarious place than the rest of us. We rely on the local economy for our livelihoods. They have to rely on the weather, as well.

"I guess you're right." He turned to look out over the sea of green vines. "Life is a learning curve, you know. And the way things happen, well, it's always pretty random. Take this vineyard, for instance. Boyd needed money and had to sell off some of his ranch property. Jason and Andrea— they've both always wanted to work on the land—found out about it and told me. I was looking for a place to grow grapes, and put down my own roots at the same time. And I gotta say that life here has been good for me, especially after Maddie and I—"

He stopped and gave me a long look. "You know about us?"

"Ruby told me that you've been seeing each other." Thunder rumbled not far away. "Between your grapes and her olives, you obviously share some common interests."

He nodded. "She came back here to the ranch after she finished college. That was when Jason and Andrea and I had just bought the land, and we were trying to figure out how to make the vineyard happen. I knew plenty about making wine, and a lot about growing grapes, but next to nothing about growing grapes here in the Hill Country, which is a whole other thing. Maddie understood about that, and she was willing to share her experience. So she began helping us out, and I gave her a hand with the trees, whenever I could. It was a good arrangement, practically speaking. And before long . . ." His voice trailed off.

I made an encouraging noise. But I could sense that Chet didn't need any encouragement. He wanted to talk, and I was an old friend, convenient and safe. He remembered our good times together. He knew he could trust me.

He took a breath. "And before long, things between us were pretty comfortable. We were spending days together at work, on our side of the river or on hers. And in the evening, she'd come over here or I'd go over there and we'd read or watch TV or play Scrabble. You know, fun stuff."

I slid him a questioning look. "Just Scrabble and TV? No huggy face kissy poo?"

He ducked his head. "Well, some of that, I guess. We're both over twenty-one, aren't we?"

"I was remembering the summer we worked in the AG's office together," I said with a teasing laugh. "If you'll recall, we didn't play a lot of Scrabble or watch TV after work. We danced at the Depot. We drank wine. We did . . . other things."

"Right." He gave me a boyish grin. "Yeah, well, Maddie and I did a few other things, too. More than a few, I guess. We're good together, that way—or at least, I thought we were. And we began to talk about getting married, in general terms, sort of. I was pretty happy with the status quo, though, and I thought she was, too. And to tell the truth, I was . . . well, I was kinda scared that if I asked her and she said no, it would mean the end of what we had, which was pretty comfortable."

I can read between the lines. What he meant was that he'd been afraid that if she said no, there wouldn't be any more huggy face kissy poo. I frowned. "So you didn't actually ask her?"

"Not in so many words, no." His look was puzzled, maybe a little hurt. "What are you getting at, China?"

I lifted my shoulders, let them fall. "Just trying to see where things are." Actually, I was thinking that his relationship with Maddie was so much like the Chet I had known in the old days. A sweet and laid-back Chet who sort of drifted along with life as it happened, partly because he was more or less content with the status quo but also because he was uncertain and . . . well, not the kind of guy who seized life by the throat, shook it a couple of times, and *made* it do what he wanted.

"Uh-huh." He sighed. "But you're right. I thought it was sort of understood that we'd be getting married, but I didn't come right out and ask her. Then Eliza died and Maddie's legal troubles began, and I thought maybe I ought to wait until she had a better idea of how . . . well, how it was all going to end up." He pulled his brows together. "Which made it pretty uncomfortable for me, either way it went."

"Uncomfortable? I don't think I understand."

And then I did. He meant that if Maddie ended up with the ranch, it might look to her like he was marrying her for her land, for financial reasons. And if she didn't—

He gave me a straight look. "I don't really have a lot to offer Maddie. I mean, I've gotta be honest about this, China. I'm no big, wonderful bargain. I've been married before and it didn't work out—mostly my fault. I don't know how to do much else in this world except make wine. I'm part owner of a vineyard that may or may not survive—and if it doesn't, Jason and Andrea and I are going to owe the bank a big bundle of money, without any easy way to pay it off. I don't even have a place to live—a real house, I mean. I'm bunking in a little room at the back of the barn where we make our wine." He scratched his ear. "I love Maddie—I love her a lot, actually—but my prospects aren't very damn good. If the winery fails and she loses her olives, we'd be stranded. We wouldn't have much of anything to live on."

"I see," I said, but actually I didn't. If the two of them really loved each other, they'd be willing to take a risk, wouldn't they? Lovers took risks all the time.

"In the end, though," he added, "I have to admit that I waited too long. I should have spoken up before—" He stopped.

I prompted, "Before Boyd beat you to it?"

"Right. Before Boyd jumped in and screwed everything all to hell." He sounded disgusted with himself. "That guy is a damn snake. But to be honest, this situation is my fault, too. I shouldn't have been so slow on the trigger."

I certainly agreed with that, but I wasn't going to tell him so. "I don't want to mess with your love life," I said. "But do you think that's what Maddie wants? To marry Boyd?"

He gave a helpless shrug. "I really don't know, China. Like everything else, it's complicated. She told me that when she was a kid, she had a major crush on him, but he acted like she didn't exist. Jason has known Boyd since high school and he says the guy has a record of hanging out with cheerleaders. You know, popular girls, bimbo blondes, with—" He made a curving shape with his hands. "Maddie is smart as a whip. Competent in everything she does, loves her trees, knows how to manage her business. But she's not a bimbo blonde and she's not—" Another curvy gesture. "She's always been terribly self-conscious about that scar, too. She thinks people are peering at it, wondering what happened to her. They aren't, but she doesn't know that." He threw up his hands, let them drop. "And now Boyd gives her this big song and dance about loving her all along. And she thinks marrying him might solve her problems with the land." He gave me a lost-kid look. "He's holding all the cards. There's no way I can compete with the guy."

I was insistent. "But does she *want* to marry him?"

He bent over and pulled a weed, then straightened up again, giving the question some serious thought. "You know, I don't think she does. But there's a lot on the line, so she figures she has to take his offer seriously—like it's a kind of business decision, which I guess maybe it is. And while she's thinking about it, she says she doesn't want to see me." He twirled the weed in his fingers. "She says it's too confusing."

I chuckled wryly. "Well, if I were you, I'd take that as a promising sign."

"Promising?" He was puzzled. "What are you talking about?"

Really. Guys can be so dense. "If Maddie *wanted* to marry Boyd," I said patiently, "she would tell him yes. If she's confused, maybe it's because her head is telling her that marriage might make a certain business sense, but her heart is telling her something else. Have you stopped to think that she might love *you*? That she might prefer to marry you—if you'd ask her?"

He gave me a look that was part hopeful, part already defeated. After he thought about it for a moment, though, defeat won. "Maybe. But what am I supposed to do, China? Jump up and down and yell? Bang some sense into her? Beat up on Boyd? If that's what it takes, forget it." His shoulders slumped. "You know I've never been any good at confrontation. That was one of the reasons I didn't do so well at law school. I don't like to push people, one way or another."

That was certainly true. I had never seen Chet go mano a mano with anybody. But if he was going to get somewhere with Maddie, he needed to take a different approach. "I don't think it's a matter of confrontation, Chet. If I were Maddie, I'd simply want to understand all the options open to me. I wouldn't want to guess."

He frowned. "So what are you saying?"

"I'm saying don't push her. Just tell her how you feel. Let her know you love her, you're standing behind her all the way, you want to marry her, if she decides that's what she wants to do. Be clear, be straight. She may be confused about a lot of things, but don't let her be confused about *that*."

As if to endorse my recommendation, a bolt of lightning launched from one cloud to another, almost overhead. There was a sharp clap of thunder and a sudden shower of chilly rain came pelting down. We yelped and dashed for the Jeep.

In the car, Chet turned to me. "One of the things I admired about you in law school, China, was your ability to get down to the nuts and bolts of an argument. You did it back then and you're still doing it. Thanks, Counselor."

"Don't bother to thank me," I said firmly. "Just do what the hell I say."

"Yeah, maybe." He gave a discouraged sigh and turned the key in the ignition. "I'll give it some thought."

I rolled my eyes.

JASON and Andrea lived in a nearly new three-bedroom double-wide about fifty yards from the very large barn where the wine was made. Andrea was expecting us for dinner, Chet said, so he suggested that we postpone our tour of the winery until after we ate. We pulled up behind a big red Dodge RAM truck parked in front of the house. Like most ranch trucks, this one was a working vehicle, a heavy pickup with dual wheels in the rear. The truck bed was filled with fencing tools, a thick roll of barbed wire and some rusty metal fence poles, and a crate holding five or six large bottles with olive oil labels. The labels had been X'd out with a heavy black marker.

"Lucky you." Chet made a face. "That's Boyd's truck. Now you'll get to meet the devil himself."

"Great," I said, with unfeigned enthusiasm. "I'm curious about this guy."

I was, too. Opinions differed on the man and I wanted to see what the fuss was all about. According to Ruby, Boyd Butler was extremely good-looking, charming, and accustomed to having his way, especially with women. He had apparently persuaded Maddie that the problems with the olive oil labels were somebody else's fault and that *he* was not the one who was responsible for the legal battle over her inheritance. Maddie thought marriage to him might be a good plan, but Sofia thought it was a terrible idea—to use her word, *impossible*. Chet thought he was a snake, but that view might be based on the fact that Boyd had adroitly managed to insinuate himself between Chet and his heart's desire. I was eager to form my own judgment.

But if I'd hoped to learn anything concrete about Boyd Butler during this close encounter, I was immediately disappointed. He came out the front door as we stepped up onto the porch, slamming the door behind him. He was in his mid-thirties, something over six feet and muscular, with a sun-darkened face. He was dressed in worn jeans, cowboy boots, and a gray Western shirt. He had blue eyes, chiseled features, dark blond hair, and a thick blond mustache. He was indeed good-looking.

And edgy. He wasn't smiling, and he didn't pause for introductions. He scowled at Chet, nodded curtly and without curiosity at me, clapped his black Stetson on his head, and strode to his truck, arcing a cigarette butt off to one side. He climbed in, slammed the door, and drove off with an irritated spray of gravel.

"Aww," I said, and wrinkled my nose. "And I wanted to ask him for a date."

Chet was chuckling at that when Jason opened the door to us.

"Hey, guys," he said, stepping back. "Come in and make yourselves at home."

"What was that all about?" Chet said as we followed Jason into the living room.

Jason made a face. "More trouble. Boyd's east well has stopped producing and he wants to irrigate the olive orchard on his side of our fence. Our well is deeper. He wants to tie into it."

"I hope you told him no," Chet said seriously. "There's not enough pressure in that well as it is."

"That's what I told him, all right," Jason said. "But you know Boyd. He hates to take no for an answer." With a wide grin, he turned to me and stuck out his hand. "And here's China Bayles, for heaven's sake. Chet's heartthrob from his law school days. China, so glad to see you! How many years has it been?"

"Way more than any of us want to count," I said, and felt my hand clasped hard in his. Jason was just as I remembered him—short and round and full of fun, and by now almost bald. But he had always had a very strong sense of who he was and what he wanted, and I wasn't surprised by the sudden thought that his was probably the creative energy behind the Last Chance Vineyard and Winery.

Jason looked from one of us to the other. "Hey, I thought you were bringing Ruby."

"She had a better offer." Chet grinned. "Pete's taking her country dancin'."

185

"Glad to hear that," Jason said. "Ruby is just the woman to take Pete's mind off his troubles."

For a moment, I was a little taken aback by his comment. Jason knew Ruby? But then I remembered that she had been coming out to the Last Chance for years. Of course Jason knew her. She and Pete had probably known each other for a while, too.

Andrea—auburn-haired, slender, and cute in jeans and green sleeveless top—came into the living room just then. She had a quick, friendly smile and an engaging manner, and since we hadn't seen each other in years, we had a lot of catching up to do. Like Chet and Jason, she seemed dedicated to the idea of the vineyard and winery.

"It's not an easy business," she said to me in the kitchen a little later. "There's so much to do—and to worry about. The grape harvest and the weather and the aquifer, just everything." She went to the oven to pull out a baking pan filled with four beautifully browned Cornish hens and began clipping the strings that held the legs together. "And of course Boyd loves to throw monkey wrenches into the works."

"Like the well he wants to tap into?" I sniffed. "Gosh, that smells gorgeous, Andrea. What's in that stuffing?"

"Wild rice and mushrooms—and rosemary," she said. "And yes, like the well." She plated the game hens on individual plates and put them on the table. "And the fence—his cows keep getting into the vineyard. And the road he's supposed to maintain and doesn't. And the situation with Maddie's inheritance." She gave me a questioning look. "That's the worst, of course. You know about that?"

"Ruby told me." I nodded. "Do you think it was really his lawyer's idea? Challenging Eliza's will, I mean."

"Not a chance," she said firmly. She picked up a pan filled with hot mashed potatoes and began spooning them into a glass bowl. "Jimmy Bob Elliott wouldn't pick up a six-pack at the 7-Eleven without getting Boyd's written instructions. If Maddie would just *think* for a minute or two, she would realize that." She nodded at a large bowl of salad greens on the counter. "Would you mind grating some Parmesan into those greens?" She reached into a drawer and pulled out a vegetable peeler. "I like to use the peeler for that—grated Parmesan gets all clumpy."

"Exactly the way I do it," I said, and got to work slivering curly Parmesan peels into the fresh green romaine and arugula. Over my shoulder, I asked Andrea the same question I'd asked Sofia and Chet. "Do you think Maddie really wants to marry Boyd? I mean, if she loves him—"

"She doesn't," Andrea said firmly. "In fact, if Chet would just open his eyes and look, he'd see that she's in love with *him*."

I stopped peeling. "Oh, really? I guessed that might be true, but I don't know Maddie well enough to be sure."

"Yes, *really*. Until the last few weeks, he and Maddie were over here for supper regularly, and the four of us used to go fishing and swimming together. But that legal business has boxed her into a serious corner, and Boyd seems to be holding a door open." She pulled down her mouth. "Not to be snarky, China, but Chet is such a dunce. I wish he'd be more assertive. He let Boyd elbow him out of the picture."

"Assertive isn't Chet's nature." I picked up the salad tongs and began to mix the Parmesan into the salad greens. Quickly, I added, "I'm not being critical, either. Just stating a fact."

"And you're exactly right," Andrea said. "By nature, he's low-key and easy-going. You can't ruffle him, which I like. And which in an odd sort of way makes him just right for Maddie."

I put the tongs into the salad bowl. "I talked to Sofia this afternoon," I said. "She told me that it would be wrong for Maddie to marry Boyd." I paused. "Actually, she said it would be impossible."

Andrea cocked her head. "Sofia is a smart old gal. And she's right. Marrying Boyd would be a disaster for Maddie. I don't believe the guy loves her—he just wants to get his hands on her property. All of it. Not just the land here, but the West Texas land as well."

I frowned. "I don't think Sofia meant that it would be a mistake, or even a disaster," I said. "She used the word *impossible*, as if she knows of an actual bar to the marriage. Any idea what she means? I'm curious."

"I gave up trying to figure Sofia out a long time ago." Andrea was half frowning. "That woman is sometimes simply inscrutable. But she was born on this ranch, you know. She and Eliza were sisters, and now that Eliza's gone, Sofia is sort of the resident spirit of the place. If you find out what she's talking about, please tell me. I'm curious, too." She slid me a glance. "I heard Chet say that Ruby has gone out with Pete this evening. That's why she's not here."

"Uh-huh." Something Andrea had said puzzled me—I thought I had misheard, actually. But I was distracted from that by her mention of Pete. "Chet told me that Pete's had girl trouble lately," I said.

Andrea nodded. "Ruby is a sweet, thoughtful person and I'm sure she wouldn't intentionally hurt him. But . . ." She poured the gravy into a bowl and added a spoon. "Pete's had a rough time. If you think it's appropriate, you might let her know that his heart's still a little bruised."

"I will," I said. "But I don't know the full story. Okay if I ask her to talk to you, if she feels she needs some background?"

"Of course." She glanced at the salad bowl. "Looks like you're finished there. Let's get the food on the table and call the guys. I'm sure they're hungry."

The dinner was excellent. We had salad, the Cornish hens with wild-rice-and-mushroom stuffing, garlicky mashed potatoes, carrots with a zingy ginger sauce, and, of course, Chet's wine. After dinner, Jason pushed back his chair and announced that he and Chet were in charge of kitchen cleanup.

"Nobody's going to argue with that," Andrea said. The rain had let up, so she and I walked out to the barn and she gave me a tour of the winery, an impressive production facility that had obviously required quite a financial investment. I thought of Chet's remark about owing a bundle to the bank and hoped that the Last Chance Vineyards would turn out to be profitable—at least, profitable enough to pay the bills and give the three of them something to live on.

I also thought of what Andrea had said earlier—the thing that had puzzled me—and brought it up again. "Before supper, I thought I heard you say that Sofia and Eliza were sisters. I meant to ask you about it, but the conversation took a different turn. I'm curious. Did I mishear?"

"Nope." Andrea gave me a sideways look. "You heard it right. They were sisters."

I frowned. "But Ruby told me that Sofia's father was the ranch foreman. And that her mother was the cook-housekeeper." No, that wasn't quite right, now that I thought about it. She had simply said that Sofia's mother was married to Emilio Gonzales, the ranch foreman—not that he was Sofia's father. I was the one who had put the two together—and jumped to the wrong conclusion.

We were standing beside a shoulder-high stack of shelves filled with wine bottles, all of them bearing the Last Chance label and the name of the wine. Andrea picked one up and looked at it. "Ruby's mother was a good friend of Eliza's—I'm sure she knows the truth." Her smile was faintly ironic. "Rena Gonzales was Sofia's mother, yes. But her father was old Mr. Butler. Roy Butler, Eliza's father." She put the bottle back. "They're half sisters."

"I see," I said slowly, as pieces of the story fell into place. An old story. It wouldn't be the first time the lord of the manor had exercised *le droit du seigneur*. "I assume that Sofia knows this," I said. "And that Eliza knew it, too."

Andrea nodded. "I don't think there was ever any effort to keep it a secret, especially after Emilio Gonzales died. *I* knew it, when I was growing up. I don't even remember who told me. My mother, probably." She walked along the shelf, looking at the bottles. "Anyway, the girls grew up knowing they were sisters, and they were close when they were children. But Eliza went away to college and to New York and Paris to work, and then followed her lover to Spain." She picked up another bottle. "Sofia stayed here. After her mother died, she took on the task of caring for old Mr. Butler—her father." She handed the bottle to me. "Here. Give this to Sofia when you go back to your cabin. It's a Dolcetto and Sangiovese red. It's her favorite."

"Didn't Sofia think maybe life was a little unfair?" I asked, taking the bottle. "She did all the work, while her sister got all the advantages?"

"Oh, no," Andrea said hurriedly. "I'm sure it wasn't like that at all, China. Sofia *wanted* to be here. She thought it was her responsibility to take care of her father—who loved her, in his way. In fact, I think he was closer to Sofia than he was to his legitimate daughter. Eliza was rebellious. Growing up, she was always in his face, you know? Typical teenager, maybe. But Eliza pushed it a little far. She was defiant. When she left for New York, he made it clear that he didn't care if she never came back. She was gone for over a decade, you know."

"While Sofia stayed," I said, reflecting. Two very different daughters with seemingly different loyalties.

"Yes. Sofia loved the ranch, you see. She didn't want to leave. And then, of course, when Eliza came back to stay, she was overjoyed. And the old man, too—old Mr. Butler. All was forgiven, I guess. He and Eliza buried the hatchet, and the three of them were together for a time—half a year, maybe." Andrea bent over and took another bottle off the bottom shelf. "Then, after he died, Sofia had her sister with her. That was really all she ever wanted, I think." She looked at the label, then held it out to me. "Here. This is for you and Ruby. It's a very nice white."

"Thank you," I said. "We'll enjoy it." I thought back to my conversation with Sofia, who hadn't struck me as quite so compliant as Andrea pictured her. And there was something else—money.

"Ruby told me that Mr. Butler divided his fortune between Eliza and her brother," I said. "He didn't leave Sofia a dime. You don't think she might have resented being left out of the inheritance, after she had given him her undivided time and attention for . . . what? Ten years? Fifteen?"

"If she resented it," Andrea said, "she never gave any sign. She knew she was born on the wrong side of the blanket. She didn't expect an inheritance. Her father loved her. That's all she wanted."

Well, maybe, I thought. But was it really that simple?

"And she knew her sister would always take care of her," Andrea went on. "She had no worries on that score."

Maybe again. But then, families live by their own familial logic, impossible for outsiders to understand. "And after Eliza died and left everything to Maddie?"

"She knew Maddie would take care of her." Andrea sounded confident. "Maddie has been like a daughter to both of them. And of course Maddie knows—that Sofia and Eliza were sisters, I mean. She's committed to making a home for Sofia."

I was beginning to see the larger picture. But there was something Andrea was leaving out. On purpose? And did it have anything to do with what Sofia had said to me about the impossibility of Maddie marrying Boyd?

"Maddie may *not* be able to take care of her," I said quietly. "If she loses the ranch to Boyd—" I stopped, musing. "I suppose Boyd knows. That Sofia is his aunt, I mean."

Andrea pursed her lips. "Yes, but there's something of a mystery about that. I don't know whether it was a moral judgment or race prejudice or something else. But Howard—Boyd's father—was never happy with the fact that he had a Hispanic half sister. Boyd ignores Sofia. He simply pretends she doesn't exist."

"Families," I said, shaking my head. "There's always a backstory, isn't there?"

"Oh, you bet," Andrea said with a laugh. "Don't get me started on *my* family." She flicked off the light. "The guys have been at it long enough. Let's go see if they've finished their cleanup."

Back at the house, Jason and Chet came out of the kitchen and served us slices of Andrea's lemon olive oil cake, which had a nicely rustic look and was a light, lemony finish to our dinner. Jason played his guitar, we sang and chatted and enjoyed a last glass of wine. Then, as dark fell, it began to rain lightly again, and I thought it was time I went back to the cabin.

"Tomorrow's a busy day," I said. "Looks like we'll have quite a few people at the workshop."

"Maddie told me she's really pleased at the turnout," Andrea said. "She asked me to come over and give her a hand, so I'll see you. Will you need any help with the setup?"

"That's what I've got Ruby for," I replied with a laugh.

"Well, let me know if I can help," Andrea said. "Hang on while I cut a piece of that cake for Sofia. She likes it."

In a moment she was back with a slice of cake in a small plastic container and a bag for the two bottles of wine. With hugs all around, Chet and I said our good nights and went out to the Jeep.

"What a lovely evening," I said, as we got into the vehicle. "That's quite an impressive wine-making operation you have there. And Jason and Andrea are wonderful people."

"Yes, they are," Chet replied emphatically. "They're the best friends I have in the world." He paused. "Except for Maddie, of course."

"I hope you're thinking seriously about what I told you."

He turned toward me and I could see his crooked grin in the light of the dash. "You got it, Counselor," he said, and turned the key in the ignition.

We could have returned to the ranch the way we came, across the bridge on the county road. But since we weren't going back to the vineyard, Chet elected to take us on a shorter ranch road that forded the Guadalupe at a low-water crossing, a place where the shallow water ran clear and just hubcap-deep over a firm, thick bed of flat limestone rocks. The washboard road was a rocky, rutted lane connecting the two halves of the old Last Chance, navigable by truck and unused except for ranch vehicles. The Jeep bounced from one rut to another and I bounced with it.

After the rain, the night was warm as bathwater and black as pitch—not a sign of the moon or stars. Once we had left the winery yard and Jason and Andrea's house behind us, there were no visible lights, only a distant glow in the south-eastern sky over San Antonio and another, closer and to the southwest, over the smaller town of Boerne. Once I saw a small pair of yellow-green eyes glowing in the tall brush beside the road. A raccoon, Chet said, and then changed his mind as the unmistakable tang of skunk drifted into the Jeep, mixing with the fragrance of sage, cedar, and damp earth. At another point, a stunning whitetail doe and twin spotted fawns bounded effortlessly across the road in front of us. That was the only traffic—until we forded the river and climbed the rise on the other side and headlights rounded a bend and came toward us, eighty yards or so in the distance. Truck headlights, with three lights unevenly spaced beneath them.

"Boyd's truck," Chet remarked. "I recognize his bumper light bar. Should be four lights on that bar but there's only three. One of the bulbs is burned out, and he hasn't gotten around to replacing it." He shook his head. "The guy is like that, you know? He's got good ideas, but he's kind of careless with—"

At that moment, the truck lights disappeared. "What's going on?" I asked, puzzled. "Did he turn his lights out?"

"Switched them off or pulled off the road," Chet said. "Or both. That is *weird*. Wonder what he's doing—and where he's been."

"To see Maddie, maybe," I suggested, and then bit my tongue. I didn't need to remind Chet that Boyd and Maddie were a thing.

"Probably—although this road is a little out of his way." Chet's mouth tightened. "And I don't understand why he'd cut his lights. No reason for him to do that—unless he's trying to keep us from seeing him. In which case, he's probably pulled off. There's a cottonwood grove up there on our right."

"You're sure it's him?"

"Without a doubt. That burned-out light is like a missing tooth. At night, you can spot it a couple of hundred yards away." Chet sighed. "You're probably right—he's been with Maddie. They've been spending a lot of evenings together, that's for sure." His voice took on an ironic edge. "I guess she's trying to figure out if she wants to spend the rest of her life with the jerk."

There was nothing much I could say to that, and Chet seemed to have lapsed into despondency. As we drove past the clump of cottonwoods where he thought Boyd had pulled off, we peered into the darkness, searching. But we couldn't see a thing. We made the rest of the drive in silence.

The lights were on in our cabin and Pete's truck was not parked in front beside Big Red Mama, so I figured Ruby was already home from her date and it was safe to go in. I wouldn't be interrupting anything . . . well, intensely personal.

I picked up the bag Andrea had given me and glanced toward Sofia's cabin, wondering if it was too late to deliver the cake and wine. But the lights were out. Sofia must have gone to bed. Her goodies would have to wait until tomorrow. I turned to Chet with a smile.

"Thanks for the evening. It was fun." I reached for the door handle. "Will you be around tomorrow after the workshop? Maybe we—"

"Wait, China. There's something I need to say." Chet put

his arm across the back of my seat and leaned toward me. The Jeep was still running and the dash lights cast a shadow on his face. "I know I haven't been very upbeat about the situation with Maddie and Boyd. But that thing you said, about being straight with Maddie and letting her know how I feel—I needed to hear that. You're right. Maddie needs to know that Boyd isn't her only option. I may not be much of a choice, but I'm here. And I really do care for her."

"I *know* I'm right," I said firmly. "What's more, you should talk to Andrea about this. She has the idea that Maddie is in love with you."

"Huh?" Chet pulled back sharply, eyes wide. "How does she—I mean, what makes her think—" He stopped, staring at me. "Are you *foolin'* me, China? Andrea really said that?"

"She really said that. Talk to her. Ask her for her opinion. Then go talk to Maddie." I touched his arm. "But don't put it off, Chet. In fact, it'd be good if you did it this weekend. There's no point in leaving Maddie in the dark."

He stared at me for a moment longer. "Okay," he said slowly, "I'll talk to Andrea. Tonight, if she and Jason haven't gone to bed already." He leaned forward and kissed me on the cheek. "If I'd known you were so damn smart, China Bayles, I might not have left you back in Austin all those years ago."

"Huh," I said. "You left me back in Austin all those years ago *because* I was so damn smart. Remember?"

Which made us both laugh. I put my arms around him and hugged him, thinking how interesting—and nice—it was to reconnect with someone I had loved briefly, in another lifetime, and discover that he was pretty much the same person now as he had been then. In an odd way, it was comforting.

We said good night. Carrying my bag, I got out of the

Jeep and went up the walk to the cabin, eager to hear how Ruby's evening with Pete had gone and share what Andrea had told me about his vulnerability. Ruby liked to flirt and play around, and it had been a long time since she'd been serious about anyone but Colin Fowler. But Pete had struck me as a very nice guy. She needed to know—if she didn't already—that he was nursing a wounded heart.

Chapter Twelve

MCQUAID

Friday Evening

"Chisholm Road." In the passenger seat, McQuaid hunched over the GPS on his phone. "His name is Lester McGown. Mantel's stepbrother. Lives in a single-wide west of New Braunfels, on Chisholm Road."

"You're sure that's where Mantel's got Sally?" Blackie asked, cranking up the windshield wipers another notch.

They were driving south on I-35 toward New Braunfels, flying like a bat out of hell through the thick, rainy twilight. Sunset was still over an hour away but clouds hung like a leaden curtain over the highway and everybody was driving with full lights.

After he'd left the house, McQuaid had stopped at the PSPD office to pick up Blackie and the Taser. "I don't like this," Sheila had said when she heard that Mantel had taken Sally. "It could turn ugly. I'm going with you." She reached for her duty belt.

"No," Blackie replied firmly. "We agreed. We're not going out together on the same . . . situation." He gave her a quick smile. "And don't try to pull rank, Chief. You've got a baby on board—remember?"

She glared at him. But Blackie wasn't budging, and after a moment she said, "Okay, then. Who's your backup?"

McQuaid spoke up. "I'm in contact with Harry Royce, with the Rangers. He'll give us whatever we need." He wasn't telling the full story, though, and all three of them knew it. Urgently, he said, "Come on, Blackie. We need to get this show on the road."

They traded McQuaid's truck for Blackie's heavier, faster Dodge Charger. It had been his Adams County squad car. He'd bought it when he left his post as sheriff because its Hemi V8 engine was fast and powerful enough to easily catch up to anybody who thought he was faster and more powerful, and its all-wheel drive gave him a definite edge in back-country terrain. (Not that he needed these advantages now, since his work as a PI rarely involved chasing crooks across the back country. But it felt good to have it, just in case.) He'd had it repainted—the Charger was now all black, no longer black and white—but it still looked enough like a cop car to fool somebody who gave it a quick glance. Blackie said it made him feel like a sheriff again, even when he was just going to the grocery store.

"No, I'm not sure that's where they've got her," McQuaid replied to Blackie's question. He clicked out of GPS and went to Google Earth, zooming in tight. "But before somebody slapped a hand over her mouth, she managed to let me know that she was in a single-wide out in the country somewhere. When Harry emailed me the addresses this afternoon, he told me there's a single-wide at the McGown place on Chisholm. He sent a guy out there earlier today. Somebody's living there but nobody was home."

Mentioning Royce reminded McQuaid that he'd intended—as he'd said to Sheila—to let him know what was going down. Harry had said he'd be watching his son pitch in Little League that night, but if the lightning was flickering in West Austin the way it was flickering here, the game had probably been called and Harry was home, beer in hand, watching television.

But McQuaid didn't want to *talk* to him, actually. When Harry learned that Mantel had Sally, he would tell McQuaid to back off and let the Special Response Team take over, even though they wouldn't know where they were going and wouldn't have a plan to handle the action when they got there. There would be gunfire and dead people. Sally might be among them, and McQuaid knew he couldn't let that happen—not because he gave a personal damn about Sally, but for Brian's sake.

So instead of a phone conversation where he'd have to answer questions, he would text Royce a much abridged version of events, just to get it on the record, in case he had to explain himself afterward. And if Royce replied with a set of instructions and a barrage of do-this, do-that, he would ignore it. He was, after all, an indie. Royce wasn't paying him, and Royce couldn't fire him.

The text message sent, McQuaid clicked back to Google Earth. He was looking at the white roof of a mobile home, parked some fifty yards behind a small house and half hidden under a clump of trees. His stomach muscles clenched. Was that the single-wide where Mantel was holding Sally? The man was a brute with a short fuse and Sally had a quick, loud mouth and a way of pissing people off. She might irritate Mantel to the point where he figured her orneriness outweighed her usefulness as bait or decided that killing her was a nice down payment on what he owed McQuaid for sending him to Death Row.

Was she still undamaged, still alive? McQuaid was kicking himself for being stupid enough to let Mantel move in and snatch her. It couldn't be said that it was his *fault*, exactly, since he'd had no way of knowing that Sally was going to put herself in harm's way. But he should have thought ahead, should have tried to imagine what stupendously, spectacularly stupid thing Sally might conceivably do—like showing up unannounced at his house—and make damn sure she didn't do it.

Yes, he'd been careless. If he'd anticipated what she was going to do, they wouldn't be in this situation. And the whole damn thing was his fault, come to that. Every single one of the five dead people would be alive right now, if he had pulled that trigger just once. Jeez. Just *once*.

"How much farther?" Blackie was utterly relaxed and calm behind the wheel. The traffic was lighter than usual and he was staying in the far left lane, cruising smoothly past the slower vehicles. If the drivers glanced at the Charger's passing rack of LED lights, they would take it for a cop car for sure, or a low-flying UFO.

McQuaid refocused. "A couple of miles." He flicked back to the GPS. "Get off at the next exit—short ramp, move quick to the right and hang a right on 337. It's six point five miles to River Road. Right again, then another three point four miles to Chisholm." He pocketed his cell and flexed his hands, trying to relax his cramped fingers. He had traded his shoulder holster for an ankle holster for the Glock and he was wearing the Taser on his belt. He'd changed out of his street clothes, too, and into his nighttime surveillance outfit: a black T-shirt and black nylon zip-up jacket with black jeans.

Blackie took the off-ramp, cleared a motorcycle and a panel truck, and moved to the right as the wind from a squall line picked up a discarded newspaper and sailed it across the road. A spill of bright lights from the McDonald's on the corner splashed the wet pavement like colored paints. "Got a plan?" he asked, slowing for the turn onto 337.

McQuaid shook his head. "Making it up as we go along. One good thing, though. They won't be expecting us. We'll surprise them." *If* they were headed to the right place.

"We could get some backup, if you think we need it. I know the chief here." The dash light illuminated Blackie's relaxed expression. In all the years McQuaid had been acquainted with the man—how many? twenty? twenty-five?—and in some pretty hairy situations, he had never seen him lose his cool, a powerful asset in a working partner. McQuaid knew that under his jacket, Blackie was wearing his Smith & Wesson 5946 service pistol, loaded with a fifteen-round magazine. And in a locked gun box in the Charger trunk, he kept a twelve-gauge tactical shotgun.

"We could," McQuaid agreed. "On the other hand . . ."

He let his voice trail off. You never knew what kind of backup you'd get from the locals. A siren, a careless car-door slam, a loud voice, a nervous young cop with an itchy trigger-finger. And Sally, held hostage by a guy with a deep, serious grudge who was facing a death sentence, one way or another. This was going to be dicey, but until they understood more about what they were up against—who, where, when, how many—he figured they were better off dealing with it themselves.

"Yeah," Blackie said. "At this point, surprise is our best weapon. They don't know we know where they are."

"*If* that's where they are." McQuaid spoke the words that had been ricocheting around in his head and they both lapsed into silence. Mantel hadn't called back with directions. They were banking that the single-wide Sally had mentioned was one of the two addresses Harry Royce had given them—the New Braunfels address. It wasn't the wrecking yard, McQuaid felt pretty sure. That one was in San Antonio. Anyway, New Braunfels was closer.

Chisholm Road was a narrow two-lane road that led downhill toward the river. The small frame houses were pushed far back from the road on overgrown, ill-kept lots haphazardly strewn with old tires and refrigerators, junked cars, even a derelict school bus. It was nearly full dark now, and there were no vehicles on the road, only a kid wearing an orange vest and reflectors on his pants cuffs, pedaling a bicycle through the persistent drizzle. There were no street-lights and the house numbers were badly marked. If it hadn't been for McQuaid's GPS, they would have driven past the address they were looking for, since a couple of the digits of the street number that had once been displayed on the mailbox had peeled off and the driveway entrance was nearly obscured by weeds and a dense sumac thicket.

"That's it," McQuaid said, jerking his head. "On the right."

Blackie slowed as they cruised past. The house in front was a white clapboard with a dark roof and a flock of pink plastic flamingos scattered across the grass. There were no vehicles, no lights showing. The single-wide trailer was fifty yards behind it, angled at the end of the gravel drive, under a clump of large live oak trees. There was one light burning in the living room window; the rest of the structure was dark. No vehicles there, either.

Blackie cut the lights and pulled off the road onto the right shoulder. The Charger was obscured from the house and the trailer by a thick patch of cedar. "What d'you think?" he asked.

"Doesn't look like Mantel is here," McQuaid said, his nerves jangling, so disappointed he could taste it in his mouth, like a bad hangover the next morning. He'd been expecting one, maybe two vehicles and at least two guys, and he was psyched to get Sally out. Where the hell was she, if she wasn't here?

"I'd say we try the place anyway. On foot." Blackie put up a hand and switched off the dome light so it wouldn't turn on when the doors were opened. "They may have stashed her here and gone off somewhere else."

McQuaid nodded. "I'll take the front entrance. You're under those trees on the right, covering me. Just in case."

"I'll go first." Blackie grinned cheerfully and patted his jacket pocket. "Don't knock until I'm set up where I've got a clear line on the door."

McQuaid watched as Blackie moved silently through the trees, then made his way up the long drive, past the silent house, to the single-wide. By the time he reached it, he'd already decided that they had either come to the wrong place or were too late. Mantel wasn't here.

Somebody else was, though. A table lamp was burning, and the drapes at the front window were pulled back just far enough that he could see a woman coming out of the kitchen with a drink in her hand. She pulled up her yellow T-shirt to scratch under her bra, then bent over to pick up a wineglass and a cigarette from an ashtray. Her movements were unhurried and unselfconscious, and she had the look of somebody who knew she was alone. The television was tuned to a game show, the blue-white flicker reflecting on the ceiling. The window was open and he could hear the flat, hard buzzer that signaled somebody's incorrect answer, followed by the disappointed sigh of the studio audience.

He glanced over at Blackie, who was crouching, tensed and alert, under the trees at the far right end of the trailer. He lifted his hand to the door and rapped, hard. The TV sound went off and there was silence.

"Who is it?" the woman asked warily. "What do you want?"

"Lookin' for Lester," McQuaid said, slow and friendly. "He told me to meet him here, him and Max. Sure hope I haven't missed them. Got held up on I-35. Big rig jackknifed in the rain. Major mess."

He waited, half expecting the woman to say that she'd never heard of Lester or Max. But she didn't. The door opened on the chain. "Sorry, they've already left," the woman said. There was a slight slur in her words.

Ah, McQuaid thought exultantly. He'd come to the right place. But he frowned. "Aw, hell," he said. "Did I miss them by much?"

"A little while," the woman said, and lifted the chain off the door. She was in her late thirties, he guessed. Her bleached hair hung loose around her shoulders and her heavy makeup—eye shadow, mascara, purple lipstick—obscured her attractiveness and made her look older, harder. She was barefoot and wore ankle-length black leggings so tight they looked like they were painted on. Her yellow T-shirt was stretched tight over her breasts and cut in a deep vee that showed a nice cleavage. The shirt said *Pinto's Sports Bar*, and McQuaid thought that must be where she worked. She wasn't wearing a wedding ring.

She took a sip of her drink and eyed him appreciatively, taking in his full height. She raised one shoulder and gave him an appraising smile, kittenish, flirtatious. "Don't think we've met. What did you say your name was?"

"Gillis." McQuaid returned her smile, giving her a slow, approving look up and down, his glance admiring, lingering deliberately on the cleavage. "Harvey Gillis." He raised his eyes to her mouth, to her face. "I'm sure I would remember it if we'd met."

The woman chuckled, deep in her throat. "Lester di'n't tell me he was 'xpectin' any more comp'ny tonight. And here I am, all by my lonesome." She stepped back invitingly. "You come on in, Harv, and let me fix you a drink. It's wet out there."

McQuaid glanced toward Blackie and saw that he had moved forward and was pressed against the trailer, a few paces to the right of the window, where he could hear what was said. Deciding that the risk was low, McQuaid stepped through the door. The room smelled heavily of smoke. There were a couple of half-empty pizza boxes on a low coffee table, a spilled potato salad container, a puddle of beer and several beer cans, wads of paper napkins, and a cell phone. Max and Lester had had a picnic. But the cell was in a pink case and bore a monogrammed name. Candy.

"Maybe Lester forgot about me," he said, and took a chance. "You're . . . Candy, right?"

She fluttered her eyelashes. "That's me. Candy. Real sweet. Lester tell you about me?"

"Just enough to whet the appetite." McQuaid grinned and took another chance. "Lester and Max—they picked up the girl, I understand. Where'd they head off to? I'll catch up to them."

Candy's expression darkened. "Max's girl? Man, you don't wanna mess with her." She blew out a stream of smoke. "Believe me, she is a pain in the old patootie. A *massive* pain."

"I wouldn't be surprised to hear that," McQuaid said truthfully. Maybe the abduction had brought out Juanita, who was more than a pain in the patootie. By herself, Sally could be destructive. When Juanita came out, she was dynamite.

"Yeah." Candy drained her wineglass and went on,

aggrieved now. "I had a headache and Cody—he's my boss—brought me home from Pinto's a little early. I was tired to the bone after waitin' tables and puttin' up with jerks all afternoon—and wearin' those damn three-inch heels, which absolutely *kill* my feet. I was lookin' forward to a nice hot bath and a bowl of soup and here's Lester." She made a low noise, almost a growl. "He went over to Houston last weekend and when he came back this afternoon he brought this big bear of a guy, this Max guy, home with him."

"Houston, huh?" McQuaid asked, interested. So Lester had been over in Houston when the two female witnesses were killed.

"Right. And Max is draggin' this crazy woman he picked up somewhere, and she's changed her friggin' mind and ain't havin' a friggin' thing to do with him."

McQuaid nodded. It sounded like Sally—or Juanita—wasn't taking kindly to being kidnapped.

Candy rolled her eyes. "Why in *hell* any man would want a chick who has such a smart mouth on her that he has to shut it up with duct tape is beyond me. She wasn't even very pretty."

Duct tape? That didn't sound good at all. And Sally wasn't just pretty, she was beautiful, at least when she was dressed up. McQuaid hesitated, then ventured uneasily, "Maybe it's not the same girl. Honey-blond, medium height, named Sally? Or she could be calling herself Juanita."

"Yeah, Juanita. That's her name. Juanita." Candy frowned as if she were still trying to figure out what had happened. "She *was* pretty, actually. Or she would be if she paid a little attention to herself. She was a little . . . well, kinda messed up, I guess you'd say."

"Messed up?" He felt his stomach muscles tighten.

"Like she was having a really bad hair day and her

makeup was all smeared, which I guess could be because of that tape on her mouth, which Lester seemed to think was funny. I didn't get a real good look at her, though. Lester's friend, that guy Max, he hustled her outta here pretty quick after I got home. And then they all three got in the car and left." Candy threw a disgusted glance at the pizza cartons and beer cans. "Leavin' me to clean up after their party, of course. I swear, I don't know why I put up with Lester. He is a class-A jerk."

The situation was becoming clearer. McQuaid was guessing that Candy had walked into the situation unexpectedly. That she didn't know that Mantel was Lester's stepbrother, or that he was an escaped convict, or that Sally was an unwilling guest at their party.

"Sorry it screwed up your evening," McQuaid said apologetically. "Lester should have thought of that before he brought Max and Juanita home with him."

"Damn straight." Candy squinted playfully into her glass. "Wow. Empty already. What'd'ya know about that?" As she lifted her arm, McQuaid saw the bruises—a wraparound purplish bruise on her upper right arm, with a clear thumb pad and finger pad impressions. She'd tried to cover them with a makeup concealer, but they were still quite obvious. And they told a story. She cocked her head. "You need a drink, Harv. Let me fix you one."

"Wish I could, but I need to catch up with Lester," McQuaid said. "Do you know where they went off to?"

There was a bottle of Scotch on the divider bar between the living room and the kitchen. She poured herself another drink, then ducked into the kitchen. Over the sound of the tap, she said, "You really don't want to go back out in that rain, Harvey. Take off your jacket and let me fix you a nice one. Lester won't likely be back until late. You're more'n welcome to wait."

While she was in the kitchen, McQuaid picked up the pink cell phone and pocketed it quickly. "I'd like to, Candy," he said ruefully, as she came back to the living room. "I really would. But Lester might not be too happy about that, you know? I'd sure hate to make trouble for you." He looked down at her bruised arm, then up to meet her eyes. She flinched and put her hand over the bruise, as if to cover it up. "Anyway," he went on, "I promised Lester I'd connect up with them. Any idea where they went when they left here?" He reached for the only other possibility he could think of. "San Antonio, maybe? Joe's place? Joe Romeo?"

"You got it." Candy stuck out her lower lip in a pout. "Joe is a damn jerk, too, y'know, Harv? I've never liked him, even though he's Lester's cousin. Just like Lester." She was still covering her arm. "I am about at the end of my rope with that guy. I work like a damn dog, bring my paycheck home, and he pulls stunts like this. Like that girl, I mean." She sniffled and swiped the back of her hand across her eyes, smudging her mascara.

"Like you said, though, she was with the other guy," McQuaid replied comfortingly. "With Max. And Max can be a little pushy sometimes. Likes to have his way. I bet Juanita was his idea, and Lester was just along for the ride." He smiled and took a step back. "Listen, Candy, I really hate to go. But with this rain and all, I'd better be on my way. Am I pretty far behind them?"

She sighed regretfully. "Twenty minutes maybe. They phoned ahead and Joe said they should come to the wrecking yard. Max is on his way to Matamoros, and Joe's fixing him up with a vehicle."

Matamoros, huh? "That's Joe," McQuaid said. "He may be a jerk to women but he's always glad to help a friend in need." He frowned. "Say, what's Lester driving these days?"

"He's still got that old green Camaro," Candy said. "It doesn't run too good, though." Another roll of her eyes. "My Kia is in the shop, or he would've taken that."

McQuaid nodded. "Did Max say whether he's planning to take Juanita with him to Mexico?"

"He was talking about it," Candy said. "But she was giving him such a hard time, maybe he'll think twice. I would, if I was him. I mean, if I was a man, I sure wouldn't want a woman who wasn't willing." She gave him a hopeful look. "You *sure* you won't have a drink with me, Harvey, honey?" She lifted her glass again. "Jes' a quick one, for the road?"

"Thanks, no," McQuaid said, feeling suddenly sorry for her. He put out a hand and touched her face, wiping the mascara smear off with his thumb. And then, on an impulse, he bent and brushed his lips against her cheek. "You hang in there, Candy. You're a good woman—you hear? You don't want to stick around waiting for this thing with Lester to work out. You need to find yourself a man who will be nice to you."

She pulled back, staring at him, then dissolved into tears. McQuaid didn't wait to see what happened next.

Back in the Charger, putting the key in the ignition, Blackie spoke admiringly. "I didn't hear the whole conversation, Harvey, honey, but I gotta say that you have one smooth line. 'Find yourself a man who will be nice to you.'" He chuckled. "Is that how you managed to snag China?"

"Go to hell," McQuaid growled. He pulled out his phone and turned on the GPS. "We need to get on the stick. They're about twenty minutes ahead of us. Max is picking up a car at a wrecking yard in San Antonio, with the idea of heading for Matamoros. Lester's girlfriend said he was talking about taking Sally to Mexico with him." He winced at the thought of the dark bruises on Candy's arm—bruises she had tried to conceal—and her comment that Sally was kind of "messed up." What had Max and Lester done to Sally? What were they doing *now*? She was the bait, wasn't she? Why hadn't Mantel called him to yank his string?

"So, where are we headed?" Blackie asked, pulling back onto the road. "I couldn't hear what Lester's girlfriend was saying. Have you doped out where Mantel has gone?"

"Head back to I-35," McQuaid said, pulling the address out of the email Harry Royce had sent him. "South to San Antonio. Romeo's Wrecking Yard, off Anderson Loop."

"Romeo's Wrecking Yard." Blackie chuckled drily. "Man, you sure know some terrific places to spend a Friday night. Great company, too. A Death Row escapee, his step-brother, a junkyard owner, and your wacky ex-wife." He shook his head.

"File a complaint with the management." McQuaid paused, calculating the odds. "Listen, you think we oughta revisit the question of backup? If we do, I don't think there's any point in trying to get Royce's team down there. That kind of operation would take hours to coordinate, and we don't have that kind of time. With those guys, it would probably end up being a bloody mess, too."

"Right," Blackie said thoughtfully. "Actually, given that it's a hostage situation, it could turn into a pretty big deal. I wonder who we know that's local." He pushed his mouth in and out for a moment. "Hey. Remember Jocko? He used to be in SAPD Fraud—worked with us when we did that forgery investigation in San Antonio a couple of years ago. *Muchos cojones*, that guy. And what about Carlos Cisneros?

They're both in Homicide now. Carlos is another tough hombre. Smart, too."

"Possibilities," McQuaid said, remembering both men and thinking that he liked four to three odds a lot better than two to three. He thought about the weaponry in the back of the Charger and added, "I'll let them know the situation. It would be good if they brought along some crowd control." He slid a half-serious glance at Blackie. "Say, how about asking Sheila? Sounded like she'd be glad to help us out. You could phone her, get her to meet us, and—"

"Hell, *no*," Blackie said vehemently, and slapped the palm of his hand against the wheel. "As long as my wife is behind the desk, I'm okay with her job. But the thought of her out on a live situation like this one is enough to make me crazy."

"Oh, yeah?" McQuaid raised his eyebrows. "To hear her tell it, you're a hundred percent in support of her work on the force."

"I'm a hundred percent in support of her work as *chief* of the force," Blackie said grimly. "Especially now that she's having this baby. You've held down that chief's job and you know what it's like—ninety-five percent administrative. She's not likely to get shot up as long as she's riding the desk." He made a gritty noise. "Anyway, this is Bexar County. If we're inviting anybody to this party, it oughta be somebody local. They'll want full credit."

McQuaid nodded. "Got it. Let's see who we can dig up." He went back to his phone.

Chapter Thirteen

In the Mediterranean area, olive oil was an important fuel for the lamps that provided the most reliable lighting for interiors that were dark even during the day. The most common olive oil lamps were shallow pottery dishes in which a cotton wick (a twist of twine, a woven strip) was held above the surface of the oil, often by a clay nob at the side of the dish or at one end. Because olive oil was cheap and abundant, the lamps could be used for daylong illumination, and several could be assembled to raise the level of light in a single room.

Olive oil is generally a safe fuel because of its low volatility. But as you know if you've tried to cook with it over a high flame, it has a lower smoke point than other vegetable oils. Frying or cooking over high heat is not recommended. An oil or grease fire is no joke, so it's always good to be careful.

China Bayles
"Virgin Territory"
Pecan Springs Enterprise

Ruby already knew all about Pete's broken heart, as it turned out. Pete had told her the whole sad story, in between barbecue and curly fries at the Feed Lot in Luckenbach and dances at the Luckenbach Dance Hall, where the Almost Patsy Cline Band was playing sentimental Western swing to an appreciative crowd.

"They were engaged," Ruby said, twisting a carroty strand of hair around her finger. "Pete had known her for years. They were planning to get married at the end of summer, after the olive harvest, when he could take some time off."

Her voice trailed away. She was sitting cross-legged on the bed in her ratty old sleeping shirt, an oversize blue-and-white tee that she's worn for our sleepovers almost as long as I've known her. On the front it says *Dallas* in blue letters, over a blue football. On the back it says *This Girl Loves Them Cowboys*.

"And then?" I prompted.

Ruby took a breath. "And then she ran into this guy she'd known in college, fell madly in love with him, and broke her engagement to Pete—without a word of warning. He said it was like a bolt from the blue." She smacked a fist against the flat of her hand to illustrate. "Just *wham.*"

"Gosh, that's too bad," I said sympathetically. "Everybody says that Pete is just your basic Mr. Nice Guy. Sounds like he got a raw deal." I pulled off my shirt and hung it in the tiny closet, next to the plaid blouse I was planning to wear tomorrow. I turned and gave Ruby a stern look. "And here's the thing, Ruby. You are under orders from Andrea, who told me to tell you not to break Pete's heart. Chet's a little worried about it, too."

"Break his heart!" Ruby straightened her shoulders,

indignant. "Of *course* I'm not going to break his heart. What makes you think I'd do a thing like that, China?"

I kicked off my sneakers and shucked out of my khakis and hung them up, too. "Maybe because you don't have a very good track record with cowboys?" I suggested, digging my nightie out of the duffel bag at the foot of my bed. "Your T-shirt notwithstanding."

"But Pete isn't a cowboy!" Ruby sounded defensive. "He's responsible for the olive groves. He's an expert in the management of olive trees and the making of olive oil. And anyway—"

"Okay, okay," I said. I dropped the nightie on the bed, picked up my toothbrush and toothpaste and headed for the little bathroom. "I wasn't dissing Pete. So he isn't a cowboy. I'm mistaken. I apologize."

"Good," she said tartly. "Does it hurt?"

"Not yet. Maybe later. But the fact remains that you have moved from one man to another—most of them cowboys— since Colin died. Hark has tried to settle you down, but you—"

"Hark is very sweet and I like him a lot." Ruby got off the bed and followed me to the bathroom door. In her sleep shirt, her face scrubbed and her hair a disorderly mass of carroty curls, she looked like an innocent sixteen. "But I have never claimed to be in love with him or with any of the others. And I don't think I can be accused of breaking anybody's heart— let alone Hark's. We've been having a good time together, that's all." She paused, leaning against the doorjamb. Her voice thinned. "Colin Fowler was the love of my life, China. For a long time, I thought nobody could measure up to him. But he's been gone for three years. It's time I got over it."

"What have I been telling you, Ruby?" I said. "Right. It's time you got over it."

"Right. So now—" She threw up her hands.

My toothbrush in my hand, my mouth all foamy with toothpaste, I straightened up and met her eyes in the small mirror over the sink. "So now what?"

"So Pete . . ." She swallowed. "So Pete's a whole different story, China. Really, I mean."

I stared at her, still foamy-mouthed. I was beginning to get the picture. "Coming out here this weekend." I bent over and spit in the sink, then wiped my mouth with the towel and turned around to face her. "It wasn't about me at all," I said accusingly. "It wasn't about Maddie or Eliza's will and that legal stuff. It was about you. And Pete. You *and* Pete."

"Well," she said. She lifted a shoulder and let it fall. "Well . . ."

"And the workshop? That was just an excuse! Admit it, Ruby. You cooked the whole thing up as an excuse to come here and see Pete and get him to go out with you. Isn't that it?"

She ducked her head. "Well, I guess, yes, sort of. I mean, I heard . . ." She took a breath and began to spill the story. "A couple of weeks ago, Maddie let me know that the girl Pete was engaged to had broken up with him. To tell the truth, I've been interested in the guy ever since he came to work here a couple of years ago." She brushed a bit of lint off her sleep shirt. "In fact, I fell for him right away. I thought he was really smart—about the trees, I mean, and making olive oil, and helping Maddie keep things going here at the Last Chance. He knows how to get things done and he just *does* them, without a lot of fuss or calling attention to himself. And he always seems so much in charge, but he's never pushy about it or—" She stopped, smiling a little. "He's just . . . well, great, you know? And you're right."

The smile faded and her voice fell. "You said it. He's your basic Mr. Nice Guy."

"So?" I pulled my nightie over my head and wiggled it down around my hips. "You've never told him you're interested?"

She shook her head. "I couldn't, before. While he was still engaged, I mean. I knew he was involved with that girl, and he's such a true-blue guy. I figured I'd only embarrass him and make a great big fool of myself. So I just sort of admired him from afar. Quietly. Anonymously. Until to-night." She clasped her hands and her voice became dreamy. "Tonight, I got to admire him up close. And I was right. He's everything I thought. And more. Lots more."

"So what do you think?" I was watching her face. "Is Mr. Basic Nice Guy interested in *you*?"

The smile faded again. "I . . . I don't know, China. I usually know when a guy is interested, but not this time. We laughed and sang along with the band and danced all the slow dances, every one of them—he's got great moves. He dances like he loves dancing. With me." She took a breath. "He kissed me good night, and I don't think he goes around kissing . . . well, everybody. But I don't know if he's interested." She turned away, but not before I saw the look in her eyes, a look I hadn't seen since Colin died. "Actually, I got the feeling he wasn't. Seriously, I mean."

"It may be just too soon," I said, trying to be comforting. "If this girl really broke his heart, he may not be ready to lay it all on the line again so soon. He was counting on getting married in a few months and now that's gone, *poof*. He may not trust himself to make another choice just yet. Or trust you." Which brought us back to where we'd started, but with the shoe on the other foot. I gave her a careful, scrutinizing look. "Are you prepared to have *your* heart broken?"

Ruby is always quick with words, but she didn't answer me for the space of several long breaths. And then, very quietly, she said, "Yes." She closed her eyes. "Yes. If that's what it takes. Yes. Yes."

"Omigod, Ruby," I said, not quite believing it. "*Really?*"

"Really." She opened her eyes. "We're going out again tomorrow night. But Pete wants it to be a crowd scene— like maybe he's making sure we're not alone. Anyway, he said to tell you that you're invited. And Chet. He's asking Andrea and Jason, too."

"Understandable," I said. "He probably wants to see how you get along with his friends. Anyway, Chet and Andrea will want to check this out, make sure Pete isn't lining up for another big disappointment." I looked at her, frowning a little. "This could get complicated, couldn't it? I mean, you have a house and a shop in Pecan Springs, and Pete has a job out here. If this goes anywhere, it's going to be hard for you to get together."

"I know." She narrowed her eyes, considering what I'd said. "But the best things in life are usually the hard things, don't you think?"

I had to agree. I remember how hard it had been for me to say yes to McQuaid because I was afraid of losing my independence, my personal autonomy, my control over my life. Now I knew how silly that was. McQuaid was the best thing that had happened to me, ever. If Pete was good for Ruby and Ruby was good for Pete, they would work it out, no matter what compromises it took to make it happen.

At the thought of McQuaid, my insides knotted up. Tomorrow, he was offering himself as bait to lure Mantel out into the open where he could be captured. I hoped he knew what he was doing. I hoped he'd be *safe*. I swallowed the thought and managed a smile.

"Well, gosh," I said, "this calls for a celebration." Barefoot, I padded over to the compact refrigerator where I had stowed the bottle of white wine Andrea had given me. I took two glasses out of the cupboard, found a corkscrew, and did the honors.

"To you and Pete," I said, handing Ruby her glass. I held up mine in a toast. "Here's hoping that both of you get what each of you wants most."

"Here's hoping," she agreed fervently, and clinked her glass to mine.

The wine was very nice. One toast deserved another, we decided, and another after that, while we talked about life and love and how amazingly difficult it is to find a relationship flexible and strong enough to survive whatever the universe throws at it. We found ourselves talking about the couples we knew—and I told her about Boyd wanting to marry Maddie, which surprised her.

"Boyd and Maddie," she said wonderingly. "Maddie and Chet I understood, and thought it was a pretty good idea. But Boyd and Maddie? After all he's put her through over her inheritance? Why would she even consider it? It doesn't make any sense."

I gave her my theory: Boyd hoped that marrying Maddie would clinch his possession of the Last Chance *and* the West Texas oil property, and Maddie hoped that marrying Boyd would allow her to keep her olive orchards.

"It still doesn't make sense," Ruby lamented. "Marriage is about love. It's not about land and money and—"

"Ruby," I said, "over the course of human history, how many marriages have been made for land and money? The majority of them, I'll bet."

She sighed. "It *still* doesn't make sense."

It didn't, I had to admit. So we had another glass of wine, thinking that might help us understand the situation a little better. Which took us to the bottom of that particular bottle.

Which was no doubt why I was sleeping so soundly an hour or so later, when Ruby leaned over me, shaking me by the shoulder.

"China, wake up," she said, shaking me again, and harder. "Wake up, China! I'm smelling smoke."

"Smoke?" I said groggily. "You're having a nightmare. Go back to bed."

"No, no, I mean it, China. Something's burning. We need to—There!" She stopped, holding up her hand. "Did you hear that?"

I did. It was the sound of breaking glass. A window. But not our window—must be next door. And now I could smell smoke, too, and a lot of it.

I was already out of bed and skinnying into the clean jeans and T-shirt I'd laid out for Saturday and pulling on my sneakers, not bothering to lace them up. I glanced at the clock. Midnight. On the other side of the room, Ruby was tugging on her leggings under her Cowboys sleep shirt.

"Hurry!" I cried, and we both ran out onto the front porch.

The smell of smoke was stronger outside, harsh and acrid, and an eerie orange light glinted off the trembling leaves of the cottonwood trees. I heard a rumble of thunder from somewhere close by, and a vivid pulse of lightning skittered from cloud to cloud just to the south. The coming storm squall was pushing an erratic breeze. We could hear a muted roar, punctuated by a loud crackling.

We ran to the end of the porch. That's when we saw the

flames, flickering around the back of Sofia's log cabin and licking hungrily up under the eaves. Flames and sparks fountained against the black sky, and a nearby cedar tree suddenly exploded like a firebomb. The patchy showers that afternoon had dampened the foliage, but not nearly enough, and the wind was shoving the plume of fire up the tree-and brush-clad hill that rose sharply behind the row of cabins. The long drought had baked the thickets of elbow bush and yaupon holly and Texas mountain laurel to a dry, easily flammable tinder. If the fire wasn't contained, the whole hillside would be an inferno in a matter of moments.

"Ruby, call 911!" I vaulted over the railing and off the porch, thinking of Sofia. Was she still in the cabin? "Get EMS, too. This doesn't look good."

"Can't call from here," Ruby said. "No cell phone signal! I'll have to drive down to the ranch house and use the land-line." She turned and ran indoors for the keys to Big Red Mama.

By the time she was out and starting the van, I was on Sofia's front porch, pounding at her door. "Sofia!" I screamed. "Sofia, open the door!"

But there was no answer, and even when I put my shoulder to it, the door refused to budge. I stepped to the window beside it. Through the glass I could see that sections of the cabin's back wall—the kitchen corner, midway down the wall, beside the bathroom door, and the corner nearest Sofia's bed—were ablaze. In the corner nearest her bed, the licking flames had plumed upward into the rafters, and the fire illuminated the heavy smoke that billowed across the single room. I tried to push up the window sash, but it was locked. I reached down, snatched up the nearest flowerpot, and threw it through the widow, then felt inside for the lock, turned it, and pushed up the sash. I waited for an instant, fearing a sudden explosion of high-energy flame as oxygen from the open window fed the hungry fire. But it didn't happen. Not yet.

"Sofia!" I called and got a lungful of smoke. Coughing, I brushed the glass off the sill and dove headfirst through the window. I landed awkwardly on my shoulder, knocking over a bookshelf and pulling down a crashing cascade of books and Mexican pottery. As I scrambled to my hands and knees, I could see Sofia, clad in a thin white nightgown, lying unmoving, half on, half off her narrow bed.

I crawled quickly to her. The smoke hung like a hot, sooty blanket just over my head, tendrils curling downward, colored orange by the flickering, fitful flame. The air was thick and so acrid that it stung my eyes, but as long as I stayed on my hands and knees I could breathe, more or less. I grabbed Sofia and pulled her off the bed to the floor. Her eyes were closed and her head was lolling, but this wasn't the place to try resuscitation. Crawling, I dragged her with me to the door, thinking only about getting us both safely out of there, dimly grateful that this was a small house and we didn't have far to go. While the log construction was old and dry, the logs themselves were thick. The place would burn, but not as fast as a stud-wall building. I reached up to release the lock and pull the door open, then scrambled to my feet, grabbed Sofia under both arms, and hauled her down the porch steps and twenty feet down the path in front of the house, a safe distance from the fire.

McQuaid and I had taken a course in CPR the year before, and I knelt on the ground beside her and began the rhythmic compression I had learned. I was tentative about it, since Sofia was elderly and her rib cage was fragile, but I kept at it, counting, pushing, pushing, counting. My shoulder—the one I had fallen on when I went through the window—was throbbing, and my eyes were gritty from the smoke. I seemed to have been working on her forever, but it couldn't have been more than a few moments before she gasped, coughed, and began to gulp in air. I sat up straight and dropped my arms. She was breathing erratically, but she was breathing on her own. After another moment, her eyes opened and she tried to speak. But her voice was so smoke-roughened and hoarse that I couldn't make out the words.

"Just be quiet," I said, smoothing the white hair back from her forehead. I could hear a truck in the distance. "Ruby has called EMS. You'll be all right, Sofia."

"No!" Frantically, she pushed against me, raising herself on one elbow just high enough to see the cabin. I glanced over my shoulder. I could see the flames in the open front window now, and black smoke was pouring out. She coughed, cleared her throat, and managed, "The box! Go in and get it, China, before it burns! Please!"

"Shh," I said, and made her lie back down. "Just rest now, Sofia. Just be quiet. Everything will be fine."

"No, no, no!" she cried, struggling to sit up. "No, Maddie needs it! The papers—" She coughed. "Please," she managed, her voice breaking up. "Oh, *please* get the box."

Get a box out of that burning cabin? The fire was so hot I could almost feel my hair crisping. What box was she talking about, anyway? What was so important that she was asking me to risk my life to get it?

And then I remembered. She must be thinking of the heirloom olive-wood box that she had shown me that afternoon. The box from Spain, that held Eliza's important documents. Deeds, perhaps. Legal documents. Letters.

At that moment, Big Red Mama slid to a hard-braked stop in front of the cabin, a battered black pickup truck right behind her. The truck was pulling a white tanker rig—the 1,600-gallon water tanker trailer that Maddie had pointed out to me earlier that day, the one they used for irrigation and fighting brush fires. I thought of the burning hillside behind the cabin and felt a rush of relief. Out here, you couldn't stand around and wait for the volunteer fire department, which could be twenty minutes or a half hour away, or more. You had to be ready to take on the job yourself.

Pete was behind the wheel of the pickup, with Jerry on the seat beside him. He shoved it into low gear, turned sharply across the roadside ditch, and roared up the rise between the cabins, bouncing over rocks and smashing a couple of small cedar trees. He was headed toward the back of the cabin, I thought, to pour water on the back wall, where the fire seemed to have started. Or maybe he'd decided that the burning cabin—almost completely engulfed now—was beyond saving and that he should put his efforts into containing the wildfire racing up the hillside. I didn't know how far 1,600 gallons of water would go against that kind of fire, but it would be a start.

Ruby and Maddie had jumped out of Mama and were running frantically up the rock-lined path toward us.

"Sofia!" Maddie cried, falling to her knees beside the old woman and gathering her into her arms. "Are you all right? What happened? How did it start?" She buried her face against Sofia's shoulder and began to cry. "Never mind, dear. You're safe. That's all that matters. You're safe."

"You're okay, China?" Ruby put her hand on my shoulder. "You're not burned or anything?"

"Just a little smoky." I got to my feet and bent over, trying to cough the smoke out of my lungs.

"And Sofia's all right? She's breathing?"

"Yes," I said. "I had to do CPR for a few moments, but she came around." I coughed again. "Is EMS on the way?"

"EMS and the volunteer fire department," Ruby said. "Chet and Jason are on their way, too. They're bringing a tractor with a front-end scraper blade, to build a fire line and keep the blaze from spreading." She looked anxiously toward our cabin. "It's a good thing the roof is metal. Shingles would probably go up in a hurry."

From behind the cabin, Pete was yelling, "Jerry, forget the cabin. You get on the pumper while I take the hose up the hill. There's a lot of heavy fuel up there. It could go over the crest and into the orchard on the other side."

I turned back to Sofia, now cradled in Maddie's arms. Maddie was wearing a pajama top over her jeans and her hair was a mass of tangles. She looked up at me, her eyes wide, her face illuminated by the flames.

"She keeps muttering something about a box," she said. "Do you know what she's talking about?"

"This afternoon, she showed me an olive-wood box that belonged to Eliza," I replied. "She wants me to go in there and get it. Do you know what might be in it?"

"I don't have a clue," she said. "But whatever it is, it's not worth risking your life, China."

I nodded, and thought of something. "Maddie, was Boyd with you this evening?"

"Boyd?" She gave me a bewildered look. "No. I haven't seen him all day. Why—" Sofia moaned and she pulled her attention back to the old lady.

I turned to look at the cabin, trying to get a fix on the situation. I had been involved in only one serious fire in my life, a trailer fire on Limekiln Road, not far from my house. I had arrived too late to help the woman who had died inside.

But I'd been on the scene—in fact, I had been standing right in front of the door—when the flashover happened. That's what I was told later, anyway. Inside the structure, the flames and hot gasses had gotten hot enough to ignite everything in the whole place, all at once. The powerful explosion blew out the front window and tumbled me tail over teakettle down the hill. Was that likely to happen here?

I didn't think so. The front door hung open and thick black smoke was pouring out of the open window. The risk of flashover seemed low, and the last time I'd seen that box, it wasn't far from the door. I took a step toward the porch and the old woman opened her eyes.

"Get the box," she said, and began coughing. "The *box*!" she moaned. "Please, please."

Still holding Sofia, Maddie reached for my hand. "No, China," she cried urgently, and Ruby said, "Don't be an idiot, China. Don't go in there!"

I pulled away from both of them. It would take me no more than ten seconds to get in and grab the box, ten seconds to get out. That is, assuming that the damn thing was still on the table beside Sofia's chair. If it wasn't . . . well, if it wasn't, there wasn't any possibility of searching for it.

I looked up at the cabin again. The fire was blazing along both side walls toward the front and the metal roof was buckling along the edges from the heat. But the roof and the walls were still intact—for now. If I was going back in there, I couldn't hesitate. It was now or never.

I sucked in a lungful of air, pulled up my T-shirt to cover my mouth and nose, and went in with a rapid crouch. My eyes burned from the acrid smoke that was billowing just over my head. I could hear the snap, crackle, and pop of flames burning through the old, dry timbers of the cabin. I could barely see where I was going, but when I bumped into

Sofia's chair, I thought I knew where I was. After another moment or two of groping through the smoke, I found the table and put a hand on the box. I grabbed it, clutched it against my chest, and turned toward the door. I was only two quick strides away from safety when it happened.

There was a sudden ear-splitting explosion. The hair on my head crackled, and I felt a scorching, searing heat through the back of my T-shirt. The force of the blast shoved me off my feet and tossed me through the open door and headfirst down the steps, still clinging to the box. I landed, hard, beside Sofia and Maddie, cracking my head against one of the river rocks that lined the path.

I felt a blinding pain and saw a brilliant cascade of neon stars. And then there was only an infinite blackness.

Chapter Fourteen

MCQUAID

Friday Night

As Blackie drove through the dark, rainy night, Mc-Quaid finished his phone calls. He had connected with both of the guys at the SAPD. They understood the situation immediately and were eager to help, especially when they heard that if there were arrests to be made, they'd be the ones making them. Then he pulled up Google Maps on his cell and clicked from the map view to the street view of Romeo's Wrecking Yard. He wanted to get a sense of where they were going and what they would be facing when they got there.

Romeo's was located in far south San Antonio, off I-35 at Cassin and over to Loop 353, the New Laredo Highway, which was lined with junkyards, automobile parts stores, equipment rentals, and stretches of empty, weedy lots. The street view on his phone showed him that the wrecking yard itself was concealed behind a head-high, white-painted corrugated sheet-metal fence, designed to block the unsightly acres of junked cars from the eyes of passing citizens. The fence stretched for almost a hundred yards along the highway, with *Affordable Transmissions and Engines* painted on it in two-foot-high red letters. A narrow steel utility building, its green paint speckled by irregular patches of rust, bore the sign *Romeo's Wrecking Yard. Auto Parts, Recycling, Foreign and Domestic.* The structure wasn't huge, just big enough to garage a couple of large trucks. In the street view, McQuaid could see a single door in the front, with what looked like narrow glass sliding windows on each side. He frowned. The building was the only one visible, but there could be more than one, hidden behind that tall fence.

He clicked from the street view to Google Earth, then zoomed in close. He was looking straight down at the wrecking yard, and from what he could see, the long single-story metal building was the only one on the lot. So that's where they had to be holding Sally. But behind the building were the junked autos and trucks: ten double rows of a couple dozen cars parked diagonally in each row—say, fifty vehicles times ten. Five hundred cars and trucks, more or less, in what appeared to be a more or less permanent configuration, although of course you never knew how long ago Google's spy-in-the-sky satellite had flown overhead and captured this view. There appeared, as well, to be several buses and quite a few heaps of used tires, piled up here and there. In one corner of the yard was the crusher, which could flatten a half-dozen autos without working up a sweat. In the picture McQuaid was looking at, he could see a man standing beside the crusher, ready to operate it, and another man coming toward him, rolling a tire. He shivered, remembering that he had read recently that if you were sitting at an outdoor café, writing in your notebook and one of the current generation of spy satellites was parked overhead, it could make you out, easily. The next generation—the one

SUSAN WITTIG ALBERT

that was already in the works—would be able to read the page in your notebook. It was pretty damn scary.

He backed out, to a wider view. There were what looked like light standards at the back corners of the salvage yard, so far away that the lot itself would be dim and heavily flocked with dark shadows. He and Blackie had flashlights, but using them was problematic in a situation like this. If a shooter saw a flashlight approaching in the dark, he would fire to the right of it—his right, about belly-level. He'd hit his target 90 percent of the time, because 90 percent of the population is right-handed.

Shaking his head, McQuaid took another look at the rows of junked cars. If Mantel and his friends were tired of listening to Sally or Juanita—or both—bitch at them about the accommodations, they could tape her mouth, tie her up, and stash her in one of those five-hundred-plus junkers. He hoped that wouldn't happen. It would be like looking for a needle in a haystack.

"Got any ideas?" Blackie asked in a conversational tone. "How do you want to handle them?" They had come off I-35 at the Cassin Lane cutoff to Loop 353.

McQuaid pocketed his phone. "Still working on it," he said briefly. He sat back in the passenger seat, eyes fixed on the highway unrolling ahead of them at the margins of the Charger's headlights. In his mind, he was scrolling rapidly through a half dozen scenarios that might allow them to get Sally away from Mantel without getting her killed—and another three or four that might allow them to take out Mantel (and Lester and Romeo, if necessary) without getting killed themselves.

But although Google had given him a static, fairly clear preview of what they were about to get into, there were too many unknowns in this dynamic situation. Those windows in front would be useful in one scenario, for instance. But he couldn't tell how many windows and doors there were in the back and the other side of that metal building. He also couldn't tell whether the junkyard was guarded only by junkyard dogs (bad enough) or by a guy with a gun. Or by a guy with both a gun and a squad of junkyard dogs, who might be on patrol on the perimeter. And whether there were just three bad guys—Mantel, Lester, and Romeo—inside that metal building, or a whole cast of bad guys: Romeo's and Lester's friends and associates, recruited from the nearby streets and hangouts. For all he knew, Sally was being held hostage by a gang of five or ten. Or a dozen. In which case, he and Blackie would be pretty damned sorry they hadn't called in Royce and his Special Response Team, who would storm the place in fine SWAT-team style and shoot everything that moved.

At the same time that McQuaid was working dispassionately through the options, calculating odds and weighing outcomes, he was feeling a deep-down passionate gratitude (and even a measure of self-congratulation) that the woman Mantel was holding was his *ex*-wife and not his wife or daughter. He had certainly slipped up when he failed to anticipate the possibility of Sally's showing up in Pecan Springs, where Mantel could snatch her. But that only showed that he had known what he was doing when he insisted on sending China and Caitie out of harm's way for the weekend. His wife, whom he loved with a fiery intensity that sometimes frightened him, was out at the Last Chance Ranch, enjoying a quiet, uneventful evening with Ruby and a few friends. Things might be going up in flames here, metaphorically speaking, but China was safe and out of danger. He had to figure out how to get Sally out of Mantel's clutches, but he could do that without investing a lot of emotion in the puzzle. If China were in jeopardy, he would be going crazy.

And after a while he gave the whole thing up, for now, anyway. It was pointless to try to construct a plan until they got where they were going and he saw the actual layout and could figure out where Sally was being held, and by how many, and what kind of firepower they had. But right now he had two aces up his sleeve—or rather, two cell phones in his pocket: one of them his, the other the pink phone he had picked up while Candy was pouring herself another Scotch and water.

And two ideas.

"The major advantage we've got," he said aloud, "is time."

"How do you figure that?" Blackie asked. He slowed and downshifted for the right turn off Cassin, onto 353. At the corner was a big salvage yard, a building materials warehouse, and a truck storage lot. It was mostly light industrial, storage yards, auto repair shops, and big empty fields here. There was no traffic and the area was dark, with only a few security lights burning. Romeo's was a couple of miles to the north, on the other side of Leon Creek.

"So far as Mantel knows, he's dealing just with me—and I'm still back at the house in Pecan Springs, waiting for his call. He doesn't have any idea that I've already got a fix on his location or that there are two of us as close as a couple of miles. When he calls, he'll figure I'm at least an hour away."

Blackie frowned. "You're not concerned that Lester's girlfriend will phone him and tell him that his good buddy Harvey showed up at the trailer, looking for him? They might figure that was you."

"She could try." McQuaid reached into his jacket pocket

and pulled out the pink cell phone. "But if she does, she won't be using this."

"Uh-oh." Blackie glanced at it. "Class-B misdemeanor theft." He grinned. "Could get you a two-thousand dollar fine and a hundred eighty days in the hoosegow."

"I borrowed it," McQuaid said. "She'll get it back tomorrow or the next day. In the meantime, I thought I might use it to make a call." He paused. "Or send a text."

"Oh, yeah?" Blackie was interested. "Who to?"

"Lester," McQuaid said. He turned on the phone and found Lester's number at the top of Candy's favorites list. "Not just now, though. I'm still working out the sequence. First, we have to find out if they actually are at Romeo's. Second, we'd better be sure our backup is going to show. And third, we need to hear from Mantel. He's using Sally's phone to contact me. He should be calling any time now." *In fact*, McQuaid thought uneasily, *he should have called before now.*

As if Blackie had read his mind, he asked, "If he doesn't?"

McQuaid considered. "We'll have to call him. But the longer he waits, the closer we are and the stronger our hand. Time's on our side."

Blackie bent forward, trying to catch the street numbers on the mailboxes along the road. "Romeo's should be coming up pretty quick now."

McQuaid looked down at his GPS. "This should be it. Next building on the right."

Blackie slowed and cut the dash lights and they both looked to the right. A wooden sign announced *Romeo's Wrecking Yard.* A streetlight shone wanly at the curb and a single security light over the front door of a narrow metal building was mirrored in a collection of puddles in the asphalted parking area. On each side of the front door was a narrow sliding glass window, with light shining through, but barely. The windows appeared to be streaked with grime. There was no door visible on the south side of the building and McQuaid couldn't see the back, but on the north side, close to the rear, there was another security light over a door. No windows that McQuaid could see on either side. A green Chevy Camaro detailed with scrolled red and gold flames was parked out in front, an anonymous-looking dark blue Volvo beside it. A black pickup truck with *Romeo's Wrecking Yard* painted on the door was pulled up alongside the building. Three vehicles.

"The Camaro is Lester's car, according to Candy," McQuaid said as they cruised past. "The Volvo could be the car Romeo is giving Max, so he can drive it to Mexico. Looks like the truck belongs to Romeo himself. I'm guessing that there's just the three of them inside. Or four. And Sally."

"So we know they're here," Blackie said. "But they don't know *we're* here. Have you figured out how you want to play it?"

"Getting closer," McQuaid said. At that moment, his cell phone buzzed. "McQuaid," he said into it.

"If you want your wife alive," Mantel said in his gritty voice, "you'll have to drive down to San Antonio to get her. South side of town. Take I-35 straight through, then head west on Cassin to Loop 353, the Laredo Highway. Right on 353, about two miles, to Romeo's salvage yard. You've got one hour."

McQuaid looked over at Blackie and gave him a thumbs-up. "An hour!" he squawked, putting a panicky yelp into his voice. "Hey, man, give me a break! San Antonio is a good forty-five minutes from here, and the south side is maybe a half hour more. And if I run into traffic—"

"I don't give a good goddamn about the traffic," Mantel broke in. "You get your ass down here and take this broad off my hands, or I'm gonna kill her, swear to God. She's—"

There was a commotion. "Mike!" Sally cried. "Mike, is that you? Oh, please, hurry! Hur—"

"Shit!" a male voice exclaimed. "Damn it, Max, the bitch *bit* me."

Mantel laughed. "That's what you get for clapping your hand over her mouth, Lester. Feisty broad, ain't she? Better tape her trap shut again." He spoke into the phone. "We're getting damn tired of your wife. She don't know when to quit." His voice hardened. "You come on *now*, McQuaid. When you get here, come to the door on the north side and ring the buzzer. And don't even think of pulling any fancy tricks. Come with a crowd and your woman will be dead. Come by yourself, and I'll turn her over to you so we can get our business done. Our *unfinished* business." There was a pause. In a lower, darker voice, he said, "Hey, man. You know what I'm talking about, don't you? We've got a score to settle, you and me."

McQuaid clenched his fist, straightened his fingers. He was flashing back to the time before, remembering his hand holding the gun rock-steady, aimed at Mantel, his finger on the trigger, ready to pull. He was remembering how it felt to choose. *He had made a choice—and now five people were dead. Five who would be alive if he had made a dif-*ferent *choice.*

"You get what I'm saying?" Mantel repeated impatiently. "If you don't, say so and I'll spell it out for you."

"I get it," McQuaid said roughly. "I'll be there in an hour." He clicked off. "He wants me to think that this is going to be about the two of us. He'll hand Sally over and then there'll be a one-on-one shootout. But I have the idea that's not what he's setting up. He's telling me to come to the rear door and ring the buzzer."

Blackie nodded. "He probably plans to station a shooter—Lester, maybe, or Romeo—in one of those junked autos with a clear view of that door. Ring the buzzer and you're a dead man."

"Lester, probably. But they figure they've got an hour before they spring their trap. They have no idea we're already here." McQuaid checked the rearview mirror. No traffic behind or ahead. "Pull over and let me out, Blackie. I'm going to make sure those yahoos don't try to leave the premises while we're not looking—or if they do, that they don't get far."

Blackie pulled over to the curb. "How do you aim to do that?"

McQuaid dug in his pocket and showed him. "Just the kind of thing your friendly neighborhood vandal would bring to the party."

"Should work," Blackie said approvingly. "Want help?"

"You stay here and keep the motor running."

"I'll do it. You keep clear of the junkyard dogs."

McQuaid planned to. But if there was a dog at the junkyard, it wasn't in the vicinity. He got out of the car and swiftly walked the twenty yards back to the metal building where the two cars and the truck were parked. Squatting in the shadow of the truck, it took him fewer than twenty seconds to make a quick thrust into the left front tire with his pocket knife. Then he moved around to the front of the building and took care of Lester's Camaro and the Volvo with the same hard, swift strokes. And then, crouching low, he went to the window to the left of the door and peered in, hoping to see Sally—or failing that, identify where the others were.

But the window had never been washed, and the light

inside was dim. All he could see was a shadowy grouping
of several people-sized shapes and an occasional movement.
Listening hard, he could make out the raspy sound of laugh-
ter and a voice or two but no words, and then the sudden
metallic blare of a diesel train whistle a block away blotted
out even that. He took a good look at the window itself while
he was at it. It was a single-paned slider, locked but not
barred. It shouldn't give them any trouble.

Three minutes after he left the Charger, he was back
again.

"Get a look inside?" Blackie asked as he got in.

"Yep. Couldn't see how many, but I don't think it's more
than the three of them—and Sally. Of course, Lester or Mantel may have invited a couple more. They could be expecting
them to show up in the next hour." That would make sense,
McQuaid thought. It was all the more reason to get this show
on the stage *now*. He pointed ahead. "See the corner where
the board fence ends? Laramie Street. That's where our
backup is supposed to meet us. Turn right there."

Unpaved, Laramie wasn't much more than a wide dirt
alley. There was an empty, block-sized field on the left; on
the right, Romeo's. Here and around the back, the head-high
sheet-metal fence was replaced by a six-foot chain-link with
a couple of strands of barbed wire strung along the top,
obviously installed with the idea of making it difficult for
thieves to get into the yard and strip parts from the automo-
biles before the salvage yard owners got around to doing
that job themselves. But it wasn't impossible to get over it,
McQuaid thought, eyeing the fence. All they needed was a
bolt cutter and they were in. He wouldn't be surprised to see
a dog or two on patrol, though. That's what most yards used
to protect the premises.

"What did Jocko say they'd be driving?" Blackie asked

as the Charger's lights picked out a black van parked off the road, a half block from the corner at the end of the chain-link fence.

"The department's black Ford van," McQuaid replied. "Looks like they beat us here."

Blackie flicked his lights twice and pulled in behind the Ford. As he did, the doors opened and two guys in plain clothes—two reassuringly *large* guys—got out and came toward them. Blackie cut his lights and buzzed down the window.

"Hey, Jocko," he said. "Climb in, man. Let's talk about how this is going down."

Jocko was a burly, sandy-haired man in his thirties with a red brush of a mustache and shoulders like a wrestler. He was dressed for night work in a black canvas jacket and jeans, with a black cap that said *Spurs* in dark gray letters. Carlos was a square-chinned, gray-haired man dressed in a military-style dark blue nylon jacket over a brown shirt, with jeans and black canvas shoes. The shoulders of their jackets were rain-spotted, as if they'd been out and about. Both of them wore side arms under their jackets, and both had an air of personal competence and authority.

As they got into the Charger, McQuaid felt immediately better. Yep—four to three was a lot better odds than two to three. And these weren't guys you'd want to mess with. What's more, they were local badges, which meant that he and Blackie weren't going to be hauled in for operating on somebody else's turf. He reached across the Charger's seat and shook hands with Jocko and Carlos.

"Thanks for coming out tonight," he said. Blackie echoed him.

It had been a while since they'd all been together and they spent a minute or two catching up, renewing their friendship, getting reconnected. Male bonding, China would have said. But not long, because they were there for a reason and McQuaid was anxious to get the job started and get it done right. He had briefed both of them on the phone, and they had checked in with their boss in Homicide before they came.

"You boys *sure* you got a fix on Max Mantel?" Carlos asked, raising one thin black eyebrow. "When I got your call, I checked with the boss and he phoned Harry Royce, up in Austin. Royce was watching his kid pitch a Little League game, but he'd been on the line with Houston. He told the boss that the Rangers' Special Response Team is closing in on Mantel as we speak. In fact, he said that they have him cornered in a lumber warehouse not far from the Ship Channel. They expect to have him in custody shortly."

"Barring complications," Jocko put in. For a big man, he had a high, squeaky voice that sounded like it might be coming from a fourteen-year-old kid with braces. "Royce told Roper—that's our boss—that Mantel doesn't aim to go back to Huntsville." He grinned mirthlessly. "Which wouldn't hurt my feelings none. Since he's been out, there've been five people dead, including a cop, a DA, and a couple of witnesses."

Five people. Five.

McQuaid shook his head. "Royce's guys only *think* they have Mantel cornered. I talked to him on the phone less than ten minutes ago. He's in that building over there." He jerked a thumb in the direction of the metal building. "It belongs to Joe Romeo, who owns this salvage yard. Far as we know, he's got just two guys with him—Romeo and a stepbrother, Lester McGown. They're holding a woman hostage. My ex-wife."

"Jeez," Jocko squeaked sympathetically. "Your ex? How in the hell did Mantel happen to snatch *her*? Man, that's rotten."

But Carlos understood. "Now I got it," he said, pointing an index finger at McQuaid. "You're the cop who put him away, aren't you? He snatched her to bait you. You show up to get her, he aims to take you down."

McQuaid gave him a brief smile. "That's what he's got in mind, yes. I'd just as soon that didn't happen."

Blackie turned to look at the pair. "So you guys talked to your boss before you came out here, right? He's okay with our little expedition?" He grinned. "I know what it's like to work in a department. We wouldn't want to get you in any trouble with the powers that be."

"Right," Carlos said. "Roper's okay with it."

"Roper's okay with it because he thinks it's a wild-goose chase," Jocko put in, pulling a cigarette out of a crumpled package and lighting it. "He thinks the action is happening in Houston, so he told us we could waste our own time any way we wanted."

Carlos chuckled. "If he thought Mantel was here in San Antonio, he'd have the whole freakin' department out."

Jocko buzzed the window beside him down a couple of inches to let the smoke out. "But if we bring Mantel in, it'll mean merit points down the line."

McQuaid nodded. As former police officers, both he and Blackie had had plenty of experience in that part of the job. As PIs, they were commissioned security officers—what in other states were called bounty hunters—and could make a legal arrest anywhere in the state of Texas, including right here, if they had to. But they were in Bexar County, this was an active crime scene involving a hostage, and it was smart to involve the local police. It also saved time—and maybe some hazard—since if this operation was successful, Carlos and Jocko would make the actual arrests and take possession of the three prisoners. According to Royce, Romeo was clean, with no priors until today. But Lester already had two misdemeanor possessions and one felony armed robbery—and he was likely involved with the murders in Houston. And for Mantel, this was a last chance, *his* last chance. He was a dead man walking, a convicted murderer with an execution date. He planned to kill McQuaid for revenge and take Sally with him as a guarantee of a safe escape across the border. If that proved impossible, he would a helluva lot rather be executed here at Romeo's than live the interminable hours until his execution. Yes. It was definitely good to have cops on the scene.

"So let me give you what we've got," McQuaid said, and began the briefing. It didn't take long.

"The vehicles," Jocko said, tossing his cigarette out of the window. "Can they get to them?"

"Tires slashed," Blackie said. He raised his hands. "But don't look at me. Your friendly neighborhood vandal did it." He pointed to McQuaid, and Jocko laughed, an almost comic, high-pitched whinny.

"They may not be in any shape to get to the vehicles," McQuaid said, "if you brought the crowd control." In his phone call, McQuaid had asked them to bring an M79, a single-shot weapon that can launch non-lethal tear gas cartridges. "Fire a half-dozen CS rounds through those front windows, and they shouldn't have anything on their minds but scrambling out of that building and into the fresh air." CS gas—tear gas—was one of the most effective riot control agents available.

"We brought a couple M79s," Jocko said. "Plus all the CS we're likely to need. And the masks you asked for."

"Twice as nice," Blackie said approvingly. "Get the job done in half the time."

"Not knowing exactly what you had in mind for the

party," Carlos said, "Jocko and me took a quick tour around the back fence before you guys arrived. We didn't see nobody, no dogs, no nothing."

"Good to know," McQuaid said.

"Yeah," Jocko said. "No dogs is good. These salvage yards usually got dogs. Mean ones."

"The lot is a long, fenced rectangle," Carlos went on, "with the sheet-metal fence along the highway and chain-link on the other three sides. The building has a twelve-foot overhead door on the back—that would be the west side. But apart from that, the only two exit doors are the one at the front of the building, facing the street, and the one in the left rear, on the north. No windows but the two on either side of the front door."

"Sounds like something we can manage," Blackie said. "What's your plan, exactly, McQuaid?"

McQuaid laid it out and they agreed on the timing and the signals. "They won't be looking for me for another—" McQuaid looked at his watch. "Another forty-five minutes. We'll go now. Jocko and Carlos, you take the front and fire the M79s through the two narrow windows beside the door. Fire two rounds each, rapidly. Hang on maybe ten seconds, fire two more rounds. The interior appears to be high-ceilinged and open, and you'll want to fill it with gas. Blackie and I will take the rear doors, both the single door on the north and the overhead door at the back. That's where they'll likely emerge, since you're firing from the front of the building. We'll signal when they start coming out, and you can move in to apprehend. But stay covered. They may come out firing."

"If they're able," Carlos said. "They won't be, if they get enough CS. It's pretty potent."

"What about the hostage?" Jocko asked, frowning. "No attempt at negotiation?"

"If we try that," Blackie said, "we'll lose the surprise. If you lay down enough tear gas in there, fast enough, you'll disable them to the point where they won't be thinking about the hostage. If she's bound hand and foot, she may not be able to exit and may get gassed. But it'll be a temporary discomfort."

"One more thing," McQuaid said grimly. "However this goes down, let's not give Mantel what he wants—suicide by cop. Let's send him back to Huntsville."

"Aww," said Jocko.

Carlos elbowed him. "We got it," he said.

"Guess that pretty well covers it," McQuaid said, and opened his door. "Let's roll."

"Hot dog," Carlos said.

Chapter Fifteen

The olive tree is a slow-growing, disease-resistant tree with an average life span of some five hundred years—one of the longest-lived species of trees on the planet. The most ancient may be the gnarly-trunked Al Badawi tree, in the Bethlehem district of the West Bank, which experts say may be five thousand years old. A runner-up at some four thousand years: the still-productive Olive Tree of Vouves, on the island of Crete, which has been declared a national monument. Olive branches symbolize victory, and branches from this tree were used to weave wreaths for the winners of the 2004 Athens Olympics and the 2008 Beijing Olympics.

Olive wood is hard, heavy, and strong, with a fine texture, attractive streaks of brown and yellow, and a high polish. It is among the densest of woods and hence is extremely fire-resistant. Precious and costly, it is used to make small items: jewelry, bowls and cutting boards, and decorative objects and boxes.

China Bayles
"Virgin Territory"
Pecan Springs Enterprise

The Kendall County fire marshal told me later that it wasn't a flashover that singed my hair, scorched my shirt, and flung me out the front door like a rag doll. It was the exploding propane gas tank that sat against the outside back wall of the cabin, behind the small corner kitchen. The fire got too close and too hot. The tank blew up like a bomb, shooting flame and fiery shrapnel in all directions and sending me flying through the air and out onto the front walk. I landed next to Sofia and cracked my head smartly against a rock.

The few minutes after that were filled with fiery Fourth of July sparklers and patches of thick, roaring blackness. The next thing I knew, Ruby was cradling me in her arms, her cheek against my singed hair, crooning anxiously, "There, there, China, you'll be all right. Come on, sweetie, wake up. Wake up, please!"

"I'm awake," I mumbled, and pushed myself up, trying to sit. "Ooh," I said, as the world cartwheeled around me. I felt as if I were riding on a carnival Tilt-A-Whirl. My head hurt and my T-shirt seemed to be plastered to my shoulders with hot glue. "What happened?"

"There was an explosion," Ruby said. "It blew you out of the cabin and you hit your head on a rock."

"Roll over onto your stomach, China." It was Maddie's calm voice. She was kneeling beside me. "The EMS will be here in a few minutes. We need to see how badly you're burned."

"Yes, nurse," I muttered. But when I was lying on my stomach, the world stopped tilting and whirling and I could pay attention to the pain in my shoulders. I winced as Ruby ripped my scorched T-shirt to get a look at the damage.

"It's not as bad as I thought," she said. "It looks like the skin is beginning to blister a little. And your bra—I can see its imprint across your back. It looks like you got sunburned through your shirt." I could feel her fingers unhooking my bra.

"Aloe vera," I said, through thick lips.

"Hello, Vera?" Ruby asked, worried. "There's nobody named Vera here." She leaned closer, scrutinizing me. "China, are you *okay*?"

That made me snicker. Almost.

"No, *aloe*," I said, trying to speak more clearly. "I think I remember seeing a big pot of aloe vera beside the porch steps. Best thing in the world for burns—if it hasn't been fried by the heat."

"Oh, sure!" Ruby jumped up. A moment later, she was back with a couple of thick leaves of aloe in her hands. "It would be better if I could peel them with a knife," she said.

"Snap them where they're thickest and pull the green skin back an inch or so," I said. "And then squeeze, as if you were squeezing a tube of toothpaste. It'll be gooey. Just slather it on." In a moment, I could feel the cooling aloe as Ruby smeared the clear, jellylike sap liberally on my shoulders and back.

"Oh, Ruby, that's wonderful," I said. "Thank you."

"Do you think this aloe vera will work on your hair?" Ruby asked, still slathering. "It sort of got scorched, too."

I reached up and felt the back of my head—and came away with a handful of brittle and frizzed strands. "Oh, God," I moaned. "I'll be bald!"

"No, it's only a patch or two that's scorched," Maddie said comfortingly. "If you get a good cut, you'll be fine."

I heard the wailing of a siren in the distance—several

sirens. "At last!" Ruby said excitedly. "The fire department. And the EMS!"

Suddenly reminded of the situation, I sat up, clutching my unfastened bra and the unburned front remnant of my T-shirt against my breast. Behind me, I heard a loud, splintery crash as the roof fell in. I turned to see flames streaking upward against the dark sky. Fiery fragments rained down around us, trailing arcing plumes of smoke like a fireworks display. The cabin was completely engulfed now, a total loss, with nothing left for the fire department to save. But the men would be busy. The threat now was the fire racing through the dry brush and trees on the hillside, which could leap over the crest and into the olive orchard on the other side. The olive trees were fire-resistant, Maddie had said. They might not be destroyed, but they could be badly damaged.

Beside me on the walk, Sofia heard the crash, too, and moaned.

"How is she, Maddie?" I asked. "Is she breathing okay?" Smoke inhalation can be terribly serious. I was glad that EMS would soon be on the scene.

The old woman was covered by a striped woolen blanket Ruby had brought from our cabin and Maddie was gripping her hand. "She's breathing, yes," Maddie said, "although if it weren't for you, she wouldn't be. And she keeps trying to say 'thank you' for risking your life to rescue her box." She adjusted the blanket. "I still wish you hadn't done it, China," she added. "I can't imagine what she could be keeping in it that could be *that* important."

"The box," I said, suddenly remembering my trip into the burning cabin. "Did I manage to—"

"Yes, you did," Ruby said, as the EMS team ran up the walk toward us. Reassuringly, she added, "The box is safe.

I took it into our cabin when I went to get the blanket for Sofia." She looked toward the lane. "Here comes Chet and Jason with their tractor," she said, sounding relieved. "Andrea's right behind them, in the truck." She breathed a sigh of relief. "Lots of help. Everything will soon be under control."

The next few moments were busy, in an orderly way. The EMS paramedics transferred Sofia onto a gurney, loaded her into their ambulance, and one of them began administering oxygen. Maddie climbed into the vehicle with her. Andrea ran up the walk to see how I was and told me that she was going to the hospital as well—she would follow the ambulance in her truck. She promised to call the answering machine at the ranch house with frequent updates on Sofia's condition.

She looked up at the burning cabin, her eyes wide and frightened. "How in the world did it *happen*?" she asked. "Sofia was afraid of fire. She was always so careful—never left a candle burning, never left a fire in the fireplace unattended."

"I don't know," I said. "It's something we'll have to find out."

Then it was my turn, and one of the paramedics came back up the walk to look me over. "Not too bad," he said, examining my bare back. "Good thing you got that aloe on there so fast." He peered at the large bump and slight cut on the side of my head, where I'd whacked it against the rock, then tested my reflexes and turned on his little light and peered into my eyes. I thought I passed inspection, but he wasn't letting me off the hook.

"You were lucky about that burn," he said. "It isn't too bad, but you got a little concussed when you hit that rock. It'd be a good idea for you to let an ER doctor check you out tonight. There's room in the ambulance, or you can go in your friend's truck."

"I don't think that's necessary," I said. "I've had worse sunburns. And my head is fine, really it is. I'm sure I can take care of myself here just as well." I gave him what I hoped was a candid and engaging smile. "If I start feeling woozy, my friend Ruby can drive me to the ER."

I was lying. My head wasn't exactly fine. There was a reason I hadn't tried to stand up yet, and I had a headache the size of Dallas. But I was afraid that if I let them book me into the hospital, it would be noon the next day, or maybe even later, before I could bail myself out. If I checked into the hospital, I would have to call McQuaid and tell him. He would insist on coming to sit beside me and hold my hand and worry. What's more, there was something I needed to do here. Here and *now*, preferably before the night got another hour older.

"That is *not* a good plan, Ms. Bayles," the paramedic said severely. "I advise you to come with us and see a doctor. Tonight."

Polite but stubborn, I held my ground. And since I was over twenty-one and in evident command of my faculties, the paramedic finally agreed that I could stay where I was— *if* I signed a waiver saying that I had refused medical treatment and agreed to assume responsibility for all proximate and contingent legal, financial, and moral consequences, including my own personal death. In other words, I was giving up the right of my nearest and dearest to sue the paramedic, his employer, or the hospital if I keeled over the minute the ambulance drove around the corner and out of sight. I scribbled my signature on the waiver and traded it for a tube of white burn ointment, which the guy allowed might be almost as good as the aloe vera Ruby had smeared on my burns.

The paramedic climbed into the ambulance and they took off, lights flashing and siren wailing, with Andrea following close behind. Ruby broke off a couple more leaves of aloe vera and slathered another thick layer of the jellied sap on my burns. She fetched a clean Mickey Mouse T-shirt out of her suitcase in our cabin and helped me pull it over my head. I was braless and jiggly. But at least I wasn't facing the volunteer fire department—not to mention Pete, Jerry, Jason, and Chet—naked from the waist up.

Ruby looked at me closely. "Does your head hurt?" she asked worriedly.

I had been more than ready to lie to the paramedic, but I hate to lie to Ruby. "Well, maybe a little," I said, rubbing the goose egg over my ear.

"I think you ought to go back to our place and go to bed." Ruby looked at the heap of flaming rubble that had once been Sofia's beautiful cabin. "There's nothing we can do to help the fire crew, you know."

That was true enough. The county fire marshal's truck had just pulled up, with two more pickup trucks behind him. Volunteers wearing bright yellow firefighters' gear, helmets, and heavy gloves were running up the steep hill to get to work. Pete's tanker was empty, but the firefighters had driven their brush truck up the hill as far as they could go, then pulled their hoses out and were spraying down the flaming underbrush. Equipped with shovels, axes, and rakes, the crew was working both sides of the blaze, and Jerry was running a chain saw somewhere close to the top of the hill. Chet and Jason were piloting a tractor with a scraper blade, creating a wide firebreak around the perimeter of the fire. It wouldn't be long before the blaze was completely contained, but the firefighters would likely stay until past dawn, digging out hotspots and watching the wind to make sure that flying embers didn't hopscotch into an unburned area and ignite a new blaze.

Ruby was right. There was nothing we could do to help the fire crew. There was something I urgently needed to do, though, so I took the hand Ruby held out and let her pull me to my feet.

"Come on," she said. "Let's get you back to the cabin. I'll get you some aspirin for that headache and we'll have another glass of wine. What you need is sleep."

I stood for a moment until the Tilt-A-Whirl stopped spinning and I could walk without staggering like a drunk. Finally, I said, "I'll be glad to go back to the cabin, but there's something we have to do first."

I might have slurred a word or two, because Ruby put a hand on my arm and bent forward to peer at me. Sounding concerned, she said, "You don't look all that good, China. I think you should—"

"Come on," I growled, and shook off her arm. I trudged around the burning ruins of the cabin, heading toward the back. My head was pounding, I could feel the pain of the burn on my shoulders, and every other step was a stumble. But I knew where I was going and I was determined to get there.

And I did, with Ruby striding along beside me, pleading with me to listen to her. If anybody had been around to see us, we must have looked like a comic pair. Ruby was wearing her ratty, knee-length Dallas Cowboys sleep shirt, leggings, and flip-flops, her hair a tangle of carroty curls dusted with ash; I sported a Mickey Mouse tee, my face and arms were streaked with black soot, and my hair looked as if I had dressed it with a blow torch. And I jiggled.

"But where are we going?" Ruby cried, her flip-flops slapping the ground.

"Not far." I rounded the back corner of what had been Sofia's home and stopped. "Right here."

"Here?" she asked. "But why? Really, China, I don't—"

"I want to see where the fire started." I bent over to examine the corner of the old cabin.

Like our cabin and all the others, Sofia's home hadn't been built directly on the sloping ground. Instead, it sat like a heavy log box on top of wooden beams that rested on square concrete piers—a common kind of construction in Texas, called pier and beam. Because the land sloped toward the lane, the piers under the front of the house were about three feet high while the piers at the back were only eighteen inches or so. Under the cabin, there had been a crawl space where the plumbing and electrical connections were installed. There was no skirting around the foundation. It was all open. Or rather, it had been, before the fire. Ruby had told me earlier that the logs were from the original construction. They must have been well over a century old and very dry, and they had burned fast. Sections of the log walls were still standing, especially in the front of the house, but the old wooden floors had burned completely through to the ground. All that was left was flaming rubble, studded by the concrete piers. An erratic wind was blowing, but it couldn't dispel the heavy, acrid smell that hung over the burned cabin, and I could hear the sharp pops and crackles of flames and the occasional sigh of a timber falling to ashes.

As I stood there at the back corner of the house, I was remembering that when I had gone through the front window to look for Sofia, I had seen that the back wall was ablaze—but not entirely, and not evenly. Now, as I tried to picture it in my mind, it seemed to me that the fire had been brighter and more intense in the right rear corner of the large single room, near Sofia's bed, where I had seen the flames streaking up the wall into the rafters. I remembered seeing another area of flames in the center of the back wall, beside the door to the lean-to bathroom. But it seemed smaller, and so did the fire in the back left corner, the kitchen corner.

Of course, the room had been filled with smoke, so maybe my vision had been obscured. And I had been intent on getting Sofia out of there, so I hadn't paid a lot of attention to anything else. But the uneven nature of the blaze was curious, I thought now, and it was puzzling me. It wouldn't be at all unusual for a fire to start in the kitchen—a stove burner that Sofia had forgotten to turn off, or the electric percolator carelessly left on—and spread to the rest of the house. The kitchen was probably the source of most household fires.

But how could a fire start in the kitchen, leapfrog sideways along the wall, and then leapfrog again, into the opposite corner? And as I remembered it, the fire had seemed to have a head start—to have been burning longer and brighter and hotter—in that right rear corner, *not* in the kitchen. Something wasn't right here, and I needed to find out what it was. That might not be possible, though. If Pete and Jerry had hosed down the back wall in an effort to save the house, they might have destroyed what I was looking for—whatever *that* was.

The night was pitch black, but there was a glow from the fire on the hillside and from the flames that still burned in the interior of the cabin, and I could see fairly clearly. There was enough left of the wall to tell at least part of the story, and what I saw on the outside pretty clearly mirrored what I had seen on the inside when I entered the burning house. At this moment, I was standing just outside the point where the fire had been most intense, in the corner nearest Sofia's bed. The bathroom, a small square structure built against the back of the cabin, had not completely burned. When I stepped around it to look at the kitchen corner, I saw that it was pretty heavily burned now, and I noticed the mangled remains of what might have been a mid-sized propane tank. Between these three burned sections, however, the logs at the base of the walls were intact and unburned, at least three or four feet high.

I went back to the outside corner of the cabin, nearest what once had been the bed. The night sky was black and the area was lit only by the flames on the hillside. I was bent over, looking, when the corner was suddenly brightly illuminated and I heard a man say, "How about we shine a little light on that?"

I straightened up, blinking. The man holding the flashlight was thin and weather-beaten, with piercing blue eyes and a close-trimmed gray beard. He wore khaki pants tucked into fire boots, a blue short-sleeved uniform shirt, a red cap that said *Kendall County Fire Department*, and a silver badge on his breast pocket. I couldn't read the badge or the insignia on his sleeve, but I could guess who he was. I was right.

"Tom Sullivan, fire investigator." He set down the large metal toolbox he was carrying and held out his hand—the hand that wasn't holding the big, businesslike torch. "Who are you?"

"China Bayles," I said, shaking his hand. Ruby was at my heels. "And this is Ruby Wilcox. We're from Pecan Springs."

"We're not exactly dressed for company." With an apologetic grin, Ruby offered her hand.

"Nobody is when there's a fire in the middle of the night." His tone was firm and not entirely friendly. "What's your business here?"

"We're guests at the ranch," I said. "I'm here to do a workshop tomorrow."

I understood Sullivan's firm tone. I had been involved in a couple of arson investigations in my earlier incarnation as a criminal defense attorney and I had done my share of research on the subject. Some arsonists like to stick around and bask in the glow of their flaming handiwork, so if you hang around the scene of a fire—which was exactly what Ruby and I were doing—you're liable to find your name on the fire investigator's suspect list. And since it now appeared to me that there could be three separate ignition points in this cabin fire, I was pretty sure that what we were looking at was arson, and I was glad to see somebody who knew what he was looking at. Or looking *for*.

"We're staying in that cabin," Ruby explained, pointing over her shoulder. "We smelled the smoke and got up. China pulled Sofia out of the burning house while I drove down to the ranch house to call 911." She put a hand on the back of my head. "That's how her hair got all singed," she added helpfully.

Sullivan took out a small notebook. "B-a-l-e-s?" he asked. A radio at his belt crackled. He listened a moment, unhooked it, said "Roger. I'm on-scene. Check you in ten. Out." He looked at me. "B-a-l-e-s. Right?"

"No, B-a-y-l-e-s," I said, and watched him scribble. "China. As in the country. Yes, that's my real name," I added, when he looked up and raised an eyebrow at me.

"You entered the structure when it was burning?"

"I did," I said, and waited for the *how* and *what* questions I knew were coming. I wasn't disappointed.

"How'd you get in?" His pencil was poised now. He was scrutinizing me. "What did you do once you were in there?"

"The front door was locked," I replied. "I broke in

through the front window, crawled to the bed—the smoke was pretty heavy—and pulled the lady—Sofia—out the front door. It was a quick trip. Quick as I could make it."

"Sofia's been taken to the hospital," Ruby put in. She gave me a proud glance. "China is quite a hero. Heroine," she corrected herself hastily. "She went back into the burning building a second time, to get a box that Sofia was worried about. Would you like to see her burns?"

"That won't be necessary." Sullivan was still scribbling. "You were the woman who got blown out when the propane tank exploded?"

"That's me," I said. "So it was propane?"

He nodded. "Standard household hundred-and-twenty-five gallon tank. The fire weakened the fittings, ignited the gas, and it went off like a bomb. I didn't see it, but there would have been shrapnel flying everywhere. Lucky you weren't badly injured." He flipped the page in his notebook. "When you went in the first time, where was the fire? What exactly did you see?"

While Sullivan took notes, I told him about seeing the intense fire in the right rear corner, in the area by the bathroom door, and in the kitchen corner. "Seemed a little strange to me," I added, "so Ruby and I came back here to have a look."

"Yeah, strange." He looked from me to Ruby. "Before the fire—did you hear anything? Somebody walking, a vehicle, a dog barking?"

"Before the fire," I said ruefully, "we were *asleep*. Sound asleep, I'm afraid."

"We had a nice bottle of wine before we went to bed," Ruby added, in explanation. "The fire woke us up about midnight."

"How about earlier in the evening, before you went to

bed. Any unusual traffic on this lane? Strange cars, trucks, motorcycles, anything?"

"We were both out, in different places," Ruby said. "I got back first, about nine thirty. China got back about ten."

I frowned. "Yes, that's right. I got back about ten. But—"

Sullivan looked at me. "Yes, but what?"

"Nothing," I said hesitantly. "But I'll keep thinking about it."

"Okay." He gave me a close look, then pocketed his notebook and took out an expandable metal pointer. "Let's see what we've got here." He aimed his torch on the ground just inside the pier that had supported that corner of the cabin. "Ah," he said, letting out his breath, long and slow. And then: "Aha." He probed delicately with his pointer, and I saw that he was poking at a pile of partially burned rags.

"Jeans," he said. He wrinkled his nose. "Smell anything?"

"I don't have a very good smeller," I said.

"I do," Ruby put in. She was leaning over us, looking intently at the half-burned jeans. "I smell lighter fluid." She hesitated. "And something else." Another hesitation. "This is weird. I think I smell . . . crayons? And maybe putty?"

"You're smelling rancid olive oil," Sullivan said. "*Really* rancid olive oil. And lighter fluid."

"So somebody soaked the jeans in olive oil," I said, "and added lighter fluid to get the fire started."

"That's what it looks like," Sullivan replied. "I'll take a look, but I'll bet we'll find the same kind of fuel setup beside the bathroom and at the kitchen corner. Three points of ignition."

I nodded. "That would square with what I saw when I came through the window."

"But how was it started?" Ruby asked. "With a match?"

"I'll have a better idea once I pull this stuff out and do a forensic analysis," Sullivan said. "The arsonist might have used candles. The average candle burns at a rate of about thirty to forty-five minutes per inch."

"So a four-inch candle could burn for, say, two hours," I said thoughtfully. "Give or take."

"That's about right," Sullivan replied. "He—or she— could have set the candles, with the oil-soaked jeans wrapped around the base, and added a few squirts of lighter fluid to ensure that when they burned down, the olive oil would ignite. That would give plenty of time for a getaway. Once ignited, the oily denim would sustain flame for quite a while, long enough to set fire to the dry flooring just above it. Once that caught, the walls would be next." He withdrew his pointer. "I don't want to disturb this material until I can start working on it, but I'm betting we'll find traces of candle wax."

"But why olive oil?" I asked. "Surely there are more effective fuels. And the candle—it might have blown out. There are all kinds of ways this could have gone wrong. It doesn't seem very . . ." I hesitated. "Very well thought-out."

"Maybe it was a spur-of-the-moment thing," Ruby put in. "Maybe this person only had a small can of lighter fluid, but a lot of olive oil and some old rags. So he used—"

She stopped, biting her lip, and I knew what she was thinking. Pete and Jerry and Maddie—yes, Maddie, too— had easy access to hundreds of gallons of olive oil. And so did Chet, I thought uneasily, remembering the bottles of rancid oil in the backseat of his Jeep. And then, with a jolt, I remembered where *else* I had seen similar bottles.

"Right." Sullivan stood up, brushing his hands. "Could be somebody working on the spur of the moment with available supplies. As far as the olive oil is concerned, that's probably what was handy. Plenty of olives growing around here. And the stuff *is* flammable, as you know if you've ever had it catch fire in a skillet. In fact, it's fairly long-burning, which is what you want if you're aiming to start a structure fire."

Ruby and I exchanged grim looks. "What's next?" I asked.

"I'm declaring this a crime scene." He opened his tool kit and took out a roll of yellow crime-scene tape. "You can go back to your cabin now and get some sleep. But first, give me your contact information." He handed Ruby his notebook and pencil.

We took care of that, then Ruby touched my arm. "Come on, China. I'll grab some more of those aloe leaves for your shoulders. Maybe I'll put a few in the fridge, too. Cool aloe might feel really good."

I looked up the hillside. Jason was driving the tractor and I could see Chet silhouetted against the flames about a hundred yards away. He was wielding a chain saw, taking out larger trees in front of the tractor. I looked at Ruby and pointed at Chet, mouthing, *I have to talk to him.*

She frowned. "You look awful, China. You need to get off your feet. Really."

"I will," I said. "In a few minutes. You go on."

"I'll go with you."

"No," I said, and turned to hike up the hill.

It was tough climbing. Troubled by what I was thinking and no longer distracted by the conversation with Sullivan, I could feel my head throbbing and the skin on my shoulders and back was tight and hot. I had to pick my way through charred underbrush and around the still-burning cedar stumps. The ground was hot and this wasn't the best terrain for sneakers, but I kept on going. I had to.

I was halfway up the hill when Chet looked up and saw me. He turned off his chain saw, pulled out a handkerchief and wiped his face, then put up his hand, telling me to stay where I was. He began making his way downhill. A few moments later, he was gripping my arm.

"What are you doing up here, damn it?" His voice was rough. "I heard you got knocked out in that propane blast. I wanted to get down to see how you were, but we've been pretty busy up here."

"I'm okay," I said. It was a lie but there were more important things. "You have to come down to the cabin with me. There's a guy here from the county fire department. We need to talk to him."

"Tom Sullivan?"

"Uh-huh. You know him?"

"Sure. Everybody knows Tom. He's the county fire investigator. Every time there's a fire, he's on scene. What's this about?"

"Just come on," I said, and started back down the hill.

Sullivan had finished looping the crime-scene tape around the back of the cabin and was about to go to the front when we stopped him.

"Hey, Chet," he said. "Looks like you guys are getting things under control up there." He glanced from one of us to the other. "So what's on your minds?"

"Earlier, you asked me if I had seen any strange vehicles," I said. "The answer is still no. But Chet and I did see a vehicle behaving . . . well, strangely. I think it might be something you need to know."

Sullivan took his notebook out again, flipped to a clean page, and glanced at Chet. "Okay, shoot."

"You're thinking of those lights we saw on the road?" Chet asked, and I nodded, not wanting to prompt or lead his answers. He frowned. "Well, it happened like this. China and I are old friends from our law school days. We—"

"You're a lawyer?" Sullivan looked at me. "I should have known."

"Ex," I said, unsmiling. "Go on, Chet."

"We had dinner with Jason and Andrea, at their place," Chet said. "We were driving back across the Guadalupe, across the old Last Chance ford." He cocked an eyebrow. "You know that road, Tom? Nobody uses it but people who live on the Butler ranch. On both sides of the river."

"I know the road," Sullivan replied evenly. "What time?"

"Maybe nine thirty, twenty to ten." Chet looked at me, and I nodded, agreeing. "We were climbing the little rise on this side of the river when we saw Boyd's Dodge RAM coming toward us."

"Boyd Butler?"

"Right. I figured he was spending the evening at the Last Chance." Chet ducked his head. "With Maddie."

"He wasn't," I said quietly. "I asked her. She hadn't seen him."

Chet turned to look at me, surprised. "He *wasn't* with her?"

I shook my head.

"So he could have been *here*," Sullivan said. "Here, at this cabin."

"Yes," Chet said. "I mean, this lane intersects with the old road."

Sullivan was making rapid notes. "And how did you know it was Boyd's truck?"

"It's got a burned-out light in the light bar. It's the only truck around here with a light bar like that. You can pick it out heading toward you a quarter mile away." Chet paused, frowning. "The weird thing was, though, that it didn't keep coming. As soon as we saw him—or he saw us—Boyd swung off the road. Turned his lights off, too. I knew where he was, but I didn't stop to see what he was doing. Figured it was his business, whatever he was up to." He rubbed his hand on his cheek, where the fire had reddened it. "Also figured he didn't want to be bothered. Maybe didn't want to be seen."

I could see where this was going, and my criminal-defense-attorney self stepped up to the bar. "Actually," I said carefully, "we didn't have any way to know it was *Boyd* behind the wheel. Chet recognized the truck, but we never saw the driver."

"Thank you for that correction, Counselor." Chet rolled his eyes. "That's why they called her Hot Shot in law school," he said to Sullivan. "She always has to have the last word."

"She's making an important point," Sullivan said thoughtfully.

Chet considered that for a moment. "We saw Boyd driving that truck at Jason's place just before supper. And he *never* lets anybody else put a hand on the wheel. His Dodge is a religion with him." He gave me a so-there look, as if we were keeping score.

"One more thing," I said quietly. "At Jason's place, when we pulled up behind Butler's truck, I noticed a crate with some bottles—five or six, maybe—in the back. Olive oil bottles, with a big black X marked on the labels."

Chet was staring at me. "I saw those bottles, too. But what does that have to do with—"

Sullivan closed his notebook. "Olive oil may have been one of the accelerants used in this fire." Thunder rolled in the distance and a flicker of lightning lit his face. "Sorry to take you away from the fire, Chet, but I need you to show me where that truck pulled off the road. Can you do that?"

"Sure," Chet said. He blinked, then slowly turned his attention from me to Sullivan. "Tom, you're not saying that—" He broke off. "Jeez. I guess you are. But what . . . I mean, why would he . . ." He whistled softly. "It doesn't make any sense. I mean, Boyd and *arson*?"

"Let's talk about it later," Sullivan said, reaching for the radio on his belt. "I need to take a look at the place where that truck pulled out. If we've got another scene to work, I may have to get some backup out here. I don't want to lose any evidence to rain." As he was keying the radio, he turned to me. "It would be good if you came along, if you're up to it. Another pair of eyes would be good. I'll get you guys a flashlight."

Twelve or fifteen minutes later, at the pull-out area, Chet and I were climbing out of Sullivan's van and making our way through the dark, each of us armed with a flashlight. In the lead, Chet used his light to pick out the parallel tracks of truck tires in the sandy soil. The tire prints were clear: a heavy pickup with dual rear wheels. We followed the trail to the point where the truck had stopped behind a yaupon holly thicket. There, it had backed up and turned, then pulled forward again in a tight semicircle through the brush, joining the road about twenty yards away from the point where the truck had pulled off.

I knelt down and peered at the tire prints. They were nondistinctive, except for one thing. "The left front tire has a hunk of tread missing." I straightened up and pointed at the imprint in the dirt, where the two-inch gouge could be clearly seen. "You could check Butler's Dodge. Maybe you'll find a match." I was glad to see it. Without some kind of corroborating evidence, all Sullivan had was our claim that we had seen a truck with a missing light on the bar. If the case went to trial, that might not be enough. And even with that—

And then I noticed something else. A cigarette, crushed and bent, lying where it might have been tossed out of the driver's window. "Hey, look!" I said. With luck, Boyd's DNA would be on it. That would clinch it.

"Don't touch," Sullivan cautioned. He took out his cell phone and shot several photos, then turned and took several shots of the tire print with the distinctive chip in the tread. "We need to get a cast of this," he muttered, as the thunder rumbled again, closer this time. "Before we get a washout."

He unhooked his radio from his belt, called his dispatcher, and put in a request for another investigator, somebody named Murray. Then he went back to his van and got an evidence bag and a large sheet of plastic. He bagged and labeled the cigarette and we covered the tire prints to protect them from the weather.

That done, he turned to Chet. "Do you mind hanging out here until Murray shows up to make a cast of that tire print? I need to get back up to the cabin before it rains. And get a deputy to drive over to Butler's place and take a quick look at the truck."

"Sure, I can stay here," Chet said. He stuck his hands in his pockets. "Jeez," he said, shaking his head. "I just don't believe it. I keep coming back to why. Why would Boyd set a fire at Sofia's cabin? Why, why, *why*?"

A half hour later, Ruby and I found the answer to Chet's insistent question.

We were almost too tired for sleep, but Ruby, with her

customary foresight, had tucked a care package into her suitcase: a bottle of aspirin, her favorite sleepy-time tea (a blend of chamomile, passion flower, lemongrass, orange blossoms, rose petals, and hawthorn), and a container of really scrumptious home-baked rosemary shortbread cookies.

It was nearly three a.m. I had taken a couple of aspirin and we were lying on our beds, sipping and munching and trying to make sense of what had just happened. I was lying on my stomach, propped on my elbows, since Ruby had liberally slathered aloe gel on my shoulders.

We were also talking about how to handle the workshop that was scheduled for that afternoon, just hours away now. But my hair was singed, my shoulders were burned, and I was afraid I wouldn't be entirely coherent. I hated to say it, but I had to suggest that we cancel the workshop.

"We're all going to be exhausted," I said, "Pete and Jerry especially. They'll probably have to keep an eye on that fire area, to make sure the embers are all out, so they won't be available to help. And with Sofia gone, there'll be nobody to manage the kitchen for lunch."

"I agree," Ruby said. "On top of all that, Maddie will likely stay at the hospital until Sofia can come home." She sat up. "I am making an executive decision. Starting at—" She peered at the clock. "Starting at eight a.m., Andrea and I will telephone everybody who registered. We'll tell them that we've had a fire here and we have to reschedule. I'm sure they'll understand."

"Bless you," I said, and reached for another cookie. That's when I noticed the box—Sofia's olive-wood box—on the table beside my bed. One corner was splintered and the top was scratched, but it was still beautiful. Curious, I sat up on the edge of the bed and pulled the box onto my lap.

"Gosh, I forgot all about that," Ruby said, and came over to sit beside me. "Wonder what's in it." She wrinkled her nose. "I hope it's important enough to justify risking your life to rescue it."

Lifting the lid, I saw that the box was crammed with papers, documents, and photographs. I pulled out a few, glanced at them, and set them aside. Nothing looked very promising until the box was almost empty. That's when I found it: the reason Sofia wanted so desperately to have this material preserved. I opened an envelope and took out an official-looking document. Unfolding it, I scanned it, then took a deep breath and read it again, more carefully, entry by entry.

And then—wordlessly—I handed it to Ruby.

"What's this, China?" She opened it, frowning. "Why, it's a birth certificate. A baby born in Houston. A baby girl named Madeline." She turned to look at me, wide-eyed. "Madeline . . . Madeline—that must be our Maddie!"

"There's no father listed," I said. That space was blank. "But look at the mother's name, Ruby."

Ruby looked back down at the paper. "It's . . . it's Eliza! But this is *wrong*, China. Maddie's mother and father were killed in a car wreck. They were friends of Sofia's. That's how Maddie ended up here, at the Last Chance Ranch." She was silent for a moment. Then, biting her lip, she raised her eyes to mine. "But what if—"

"Yes," I said. "But what if that wasn't true? What if that was a fabrication? A made-up story designed to conceal the fact that Eliza bore a baby out of wedlock—her Spanish lover's child—and didn't feel she could raise her daughter alone?"

"More likely, she felt she couldn't bring her illegitimate

baby to her father's ranch," Ruby said softly. "He would have been brutal to her about it."

I stared at her. "Even though Sofia was *his* illegitimate daughter?"

Ruby nodded.

"So she felt she had no choice but to give Maddie up for adoption," I said softly. "And maybe Sofia helped out by arranging for the baby to be adopted by friends."

"That's entirely possible," Ruby said. "They might even have been relatives."

"But then they were killed in a car accident. Little Madeline was scarred, but survived. So she ended up here at the Last Chance, after all."

"Where Eliza and Sofia raised her as their daughter," Ruby concluded. "But why all the secrecy? By that time, old Mr. Butler was dead and his disapproval couldn't have meant anything. Why didn't Eliza just come right out and say, 'This is my little girl. I'm her mother.'"

"People have their reasons," I said. "She might have thought it would be confusing for Maddie, or maybe she didn't want to admit that she'd lied."

"Now, *that's* a possibility," Ruby said emphatically. "Eliza was a very positive person who never liked to own up to an error. My mother used to say that only God knew all of Eliza's mistakes, since she never could admit them to anybody else." She paused, reflecting. "And maybe she felt it really didn't matter. She and Sofia, together, gave Maddie everything she needed. *Both* of them were her mothers, in all the ways that counted."

"But not in the eyes of the law." I took a breath. "You know, Ruby, this throws a big monkey wrench into Boyd's lawsuit over the inheritance. Chet told me that Tinker Tyson, the probate judge, made a point of saying that if Maddie had been Eliza's daughter, there would have been no dispute over the new will."

"Yes!" Ruby cried triumphantly. "Now we know that Maddie *is* Eliza's daughter. All she has to do is take this birth certificate to the probate judge and he'll be forced to reverse his ruling. The Last Chance will belong to her, and Boyd will be out of luck." She frowned. "Unless Maddie agrees to marry him."

"Boyd is out of luck already," I said flatly. "He's not going to be marrying anybody for a good long time—that is, if Tom Sullivan is able to find the evidence to prove that he's the one who set the arson fire that destroyed Sofia's cabin."

"Boyd!" Ruby exclaimed.

I told her about the evidence we had found at the place where Chet and I had seen the truck pull off the road. "If the forensic evidence is strong enough, Boyd could be charged with arson and attempted murder. He could get up to ninety-nine years—and that's if Sofia lives."

"If she dies?" Ruby asked quietly.

I tightened my jaw. "It'll be arson and murder. The prosecution can go for the death penalty."

Ruby let out a long breath. "How . . . awful."

"It's an awful crime," I said grimly.

But Chet's question still echoed in my mind. Why, why, *why*? So what if Sofia could prove that Maddie was Eliza's daughter and could inherit her mother's property? Boyd had already staked his claim to marriage with her. He was a good-looking, persuasive guy. He must feel confident that he could get what he wanted by going that route. So why would he—

And then I understood. I looked down at the birth certificate again. Eliza Butler and Boyd's father, Howard Butler, had been brother and sister. Which meant that Eliza's daughter, Maddie, and Boyd were first cousins.

Which meant . . .

"Yes, of course," I said aloud.

"Of course what?" Ruby asked.

"Sofia was right when she said that Boyd and Maddie *cannot* marry," I said. "Texas is one of the twenty-five states that prohibit first-cousin marriage."

"Oh, my gosh," Ruby whispered. "You're right, China! Boyd is *doubly* out of luck!"

I folded up the birth certificate. No wonder Boyd felt so desperate that he was willing to risk everything in order to get rid of Sofia and destroy the documentary evidence of Maddie's relationship to Eliza—and to himself. A fire could accomplish both goals *and* look like an accidental house fire at the same time.

But Sofia hadn't died in the fire, because Ruby had smelled the smoke and I had been able to get into the cabin in time to pull her out. Sofia could testify that she had told Boyd about the birth certificate that evening—had perhaps even shown it to him. Which would put him at the scene of the crime, with a compelling motive. If the worst happened and she died, both Chet and I could testify that we had seen him leaving the area. There was a good chance that Sullivan's investigation would turn up some forensic evidence at the scene of the crime, too. For instance, his DNA might be found on those jeans that had been used to start the fire.

Ruby got up and began to pace back and forth between our beds. "Honestly, China, when I asked you to come out here this weekend, I had no idea that we were going to run into all *this*. I thought we would just relax and you would do an interesting workshop and I—"

"And you would get to spend some time with Pete," I said. "And embark on an exciting new romance."

She stopped pacing. "Well, yes, sort of." She smiled ruefully. "I guess."

I reached out and patted her hand. "Next time, sweetie, why don't you break out your crystal ball and look into our future? If we had known all *this* was going to happen, we might have found a different weekend for the workshop."

I stopped. If we hadn't been sleeping here tonight, if Ruby hadn't been awakened by the smell of smoke, and if I hadn't gotten into the cabin just in the nick of time, Sofia would have died in the fire. The birth certificate would have been destroyed, Maddie would never have known that she was Eliza's daughter, and she and her first cousin might have ended up married. The thought of all this made me shiver, and once I started, I couldn't stop. I wrapped my arms around myself and held on tight.

Ruby looked at me, frowning. "Is your head hurting?"

"A little," I admitted. I closed my eyes and thought about it for a moment. "I guess it's hurting somewhat more than a little. You think it would be okay if I took another aspirin or two?"

"I think you're so tired you're about to collapse," she said. "Lie down on your stomach again, sweetie, and I'll put some more aloe on your shoulders."

"Yes, Mom," I said meekly, and followed orders as Ruby set to work.

I felt better with my eyes closed. After a few moments, I said, "I hate to ask this, but I'm feeling so rocky—do you suppose we could go back to Pecan Springs tomorrow?" I opened one eye and peered at the clock. It was three thirty a.m. "Today, I mean. I know you've got a date with Pete this evening, but things are so uncertain here that he'll probably cancel anyway. Maybe he can come to Pecan Springs next weekend, instead. You could come over to our house for dinner."

"Yes, we're going home," Ruby said emphatically. "I think it would be a good idea for your doctor to check you out. We'll leave after I've taken care of the cancellations. And talked to Pete."

"Thank you," I mumbled. "I feel better already."

A few moments later, I was drifting off to sleep, thinking of McQuaid and hoping that Mantel had been captured somewhere around Houston and that my husband's Friday night had been quieter—and quite a bit less explosive—than mine.

Chapter Sixteen

MCQUAID

Friday Night

McQuaid was surprised at how well the plan worked. It went down just the way they laid it out, as if they'd rehearsed it a dozen times.

They left their vehicles parked on Laramie, and he and the others—Blackie, Jocko, and Carlos—climbed the chain-link fence and picked their way through the rows of auto salvage to the metal building where Sally was being held. While McQuaid and Blackie stationed themselves where they could monitor the back door, Jocko and Carlos went around to the front. After a moment, McQuaid heard the sudden crash of breaking glass, then the *thump-thump* of the M79s. From the inside came several surprised yells, Sally's screams, and—as the tear gas filled the structure—some high-velocity cursing.

"Police!" Carlos yelled through the broken front window. "Out the back door, no weapons, hands over your head. *Now!*"

Jocko stayed out front, lobbing more CS into the building and keeping an eye on the front door in case somebody thought he had a better idea. Carlos ran around to the north side and skidded in beside McQuaid. After a couple of minutes the rear door was flung open, and a dark-haired man in a dirty red T-shirt stumbled out, coughing, hands clasped over his head. It was Romeo. In thirty seconds, Carlos had him cuffed and secured to a junked auto. One down, two to go.

The next one out was Lester McGown, blinded by the tear gas and weeping. He tripped and fell before he got more than a couple of yards beyond the door and lay facedown as Carlos cuffed him. Two down, one to go. Mantel was still in the building—with Sally.

Then, wearing tear-gas masks and carrying weapons, McQuaid and Jocko broke in through the front door, armed. By this time, Mantel couldn't see, but he fired off a couple of wild shots anyway. McQuaid raised his gun, thinking *Five dead who would be alive if I'd made a different choice,* and caught Mantel as he hunched over a jammed gun.

But when he fired, he made the same damn choice again and fired at the gun in Mantel's hand. A split second later, Jocko brought the man down with a bullet to the thigh. McQuaid snatched up Sally, bound and still screaming, flung her over his shoulder, and pushed out through the rear door.

The mop-up took much longer than the takedown. Blackie called 911 for Mantel, who was bleeding badly, while Carlos called his boss to report that he and Jocko had taken custody of Max Mantel and request a crime-scene team. Incredulous, Roper at first refused to believe him, but when Carlos sent him a cell-phone photo of the fugitive, propped up against a wrecked SUV, he had to accept the fact. Jocko happily held a gun on the two cuffed prisoners while McQuaid found a hose and helped Sally wash her face. Then he called Harry Royce and told him they had taken Mantel.

Royce didn't believe it, either, especially since he thought Mantel was cornered in a lumber warehouse in Houston. "You and who else?" he demanded.

"Blackie Blackwell and a couple of badges from San Antonio Homicide," McQuaid said. "You didn't get my text?"

"I got it." Royce sounded disgruntled. "It was so weird that I figured you were off on another of your wild goose chases."

"We were." McQuaid raised his voice as an ambulance pulled into the salvage yard, siren blaring and lights flashing. "Bagged us some geese, too. Mantel's been shot—probably a shattered femur. The San Antonio cops will maintain custody at the hospital, but you'll probably want to send somebody to ferry him back to Huntsville." A squad car slid to a stop with one last, loud burp of the siren. "Lester McGown and Joe Romeo were with him when we picked him up," McQuaid added. "They're on their way to SAPD headquarters on South Santa Rosa. Houston will want to send somebody to question them. They may have been involved with the killings over there—McGown, anyway."

Royce was sputtering.

McQuaid grinned. "That's what's wrong with us indies. We never know when to quit." He paused. "By the way, SAPD will be tacking on several more charges. The most significant: kidnapping. Mantel and McGown picked up a hostage."

"A hostage?" Royce asked, startled. "Who? How did you—"

"My ex-wife," McQuaid said. "I toyed with the idea of letting Mantel keep her. I was kinda hoping maybe he'd take her to Mexico with him and lose her down there somewhere.

But she's my kid's mother, and I was afraid maybe Brian would hold it against me."

Royce gobbled something about wanting to debrief him and McQuaid said, "Yeah, sure. Later. It's been a long day. I'm going home." He clicked off the call and went to watch the EMS bundle Mantel onto the gurney and shove him into the ambulance.

He didn't feel like celebrating. There were still five dead. And this one was alive.

Chapter Seventeen

It was the middle of Saturday afternoon when Ruby pulled into the driveway of our house on Limekiln Road and turned off the ignition. "How are you feeling?" she asked me.

"Not bad," I said evasively. Actually, my shoulders hurt, the goose egg on the side of my head was aching, and my head was itchy where my hair had been singed. I was a mess. I was glad that McQuaid wasn't here—at least, I didn't see his truck.

I frowned. Whose was that beat-up red Ford Fiesta parked in the drive? It looked familiar, but—

"Come on, sweetie," Ruby said. "I'll help you get settled."

"Sally," I said, staring at the car. "That's Sally's car." I could hear my voice rising. "What the devil is *she* doing here?" I have a short fuse where McQuaid's first wife is concerned, especially after all we've been through with her. And today, of all days, I wasn't in the mood.

"Oh, damn," Ruby said softly. She pressed her lips together

and reached for my hand. "Listen, China, you don't have to deal with her today. Why don't you come home with me? You can get in the bathtub while I fix us both a nice Bloody Mary and then we can just relax for the rest of the day."

"No. Thank you, but no." I sighed and reached for the door handle. "I might as well get this over with. I just don't understand why she's here. And why, if *she's* here, McQuaid isn't. She's his problem, really, not mine."

Which wasn't exactly true, since Sally had definitely proved to be my problem in the past. I opened the door and got out, then pulled my duffel bag out of the backseat, along with the sack containing the bottles of Last Chance wine and olive oil I'd been given.

Ruby turned off her engine. "Well, then, I'll come in and help you—"

"Bless you," I said. "I really appreciate it, but there's no point in both of us getting tied into knots." Ruby doesn't like Sally any better than I do. "I'll simply ignore her. My clothes smell like smoke and I smell worse. I'm planning to jump in the shower and do an olive oil treatment on my hair before McQuaid gets home. Sally can fend for herself."

"Okay, dear," Ruby said, and turned the key in the ignition. "I'm going to drop in at the shops to touch base with Cass. I'll see you Monday. But you call me if you need me, you hear?"

"I will," I said. "And don't forget to let Pete know that McQuaid and I are expecting you to bring him to dinner as soon as you're both available."

She gave me one of her great Ruby smiles and drove off. A few minutes later, I was standing in my kitchen, which I had left all neat and tidy. But it wasn't tidy now.

I gasped and my eyes widened. There was a blue duffel bag and a woman's purse on the floor. Two of the chairs had been tipped over, and cans and boxes were scattered across the pantry floor. On the counter, the knife rack had been knocked over and the knives were lying every which way. In the sink, my grandmother's favorite saucer was broken in a gazillion pieces. My flour canister had been knocked over, the lid had come off, and flour was scattered across the floor. Large dark prints of a man's boot and smaller basset-paw prints and even smaller cat-paw prints tracked through the white flour and around the table and—now white—tracked through the door and into the hall. Winchester was huddled in his basket. There was no sign of Caitie's cat.

I dropped my gear and stood, still trying to take it all in. Was that Sally's duffel? Her purse? I bent over, pulled out a wallet, and flipped it open. Yes, bad-penny Sally had turned up again—and this time, she had made a total mess of my nice, clean kitchen.

Furious, I raised my voice. "Sally? Sally, what the *hell* is going on here?"

The only answer was a plaintive whine, and Winchester clambered out of his basket. His paws and his nose and the tips of his ears were white with flour.

"Oh, Winnie," I crooned, "you poor doggie!" and hurried to give him some fresh water. "Tell me what happened," I said, as he slurped thirstily. But of course he couldn't. All he could do was wag his tail to tell me how grateful he was that a grownup with some sense had *finally* showed up to take charge of things.

"Sally?" I called again, but there was still no answer. I followed the floury footprints into the dining room, where with a sudden heart-stopping stab of fear I saw a bloody handprint on the wall, and my butcher knife on the floor, and more white footprints—a man's work boots, they looked like—leading to the French doors, and a white tennis shoe on the floor. A *woman's* tennis shoe.

"Sally!" I cried. I flung the doors open and ran out onto the brick patio—just in time to see McQuaid's truck pulling up the driveway.

FIRST things first.

It turned out that McQuaid was as badly in need of a shower and change of clothes as I was, so we took care of that little bit of personal business first. Together. Which might have led to a nice little interlude in the bedroom if my shoulders hadn't been blistered.

"Sunburn," I said, to avoid a lengthy explanation.

"Poor you," McQuaid said. "Well, then, later. When you're feeling better." He kissed me again.

Then we went downstairs to the kitchen, where we did a quick cleanup of the mess on the floor. Then McQuaid made us a couple of sandwiches and heated some leftover vegetable soup while I poured us each a glass of Last Chance wine.

While we worked, McQuaid told me his story: how Sally had been ambushed and kidnapped right here in my kitchen; what he had learned from Candy at McGown's single-wide trailer in New Braunfels; and how events had unfolded at Romeo's Wrecking Yard in San Antonio—all to the accompaniment of my astonished gasps and little cries. Finally, the story was done. Almost.

"Where is Sally now?" I asked, pouring us both another glass of wine. "And why was she trying to find a hideout in the first place?"

"She's with my folks in Seguin." He sounded disgusted. "It turns out that she was on the lam from a bill collector—

279

you know Sally. Or rather, Juanita. She says it was Juanita who bought all those clothes. Anyway, this guy was giving her a really hard time. She was trying to get away from him."

"What's she going to do now?"

"I hope I was able to talk some sense into her," McQuaid said wearily. "But with Sally, you never know. There are limits to how far debt collectors can go, and sometimes they cross the line. It sounded to me like this one was harassing her. I told her to go home and call the hotline at the Office of Consumer Credit Collection. They'll tell her how to handle it."

I looked around the kitchen. "But how did she end up *here*?"

He made a face. "When she couldn't reach me, she tried to get Brian to let her stay with him for a while. Brian told her that wouldn't work out, and suggested that she come here. That's what she did—without asking."

"And Mantel came here looking for you?"

"Not exactly. He was looking for my wife." McQuaid turned his wineglass in his fingers. "He wanted bait—to lure me. He thought Sally was you."

I stared at him. "But I thought *you* were—"

"You're right. I thought I would be the bait. Didn't work out that way." McQuaid was still looking pretty smug, though. "However, it *did* all work out in the end. Mantel is under guard at the hospital and as soon as he's released, they'll be taking him back to Huntsville. McGown and Romeo are being questioned by Houston Homicide and will be charged in the murders there as soon as the DA's office sees the evidence." He chuckled. "While all this was going down, all I could think of was how glad I was that Caitie was with the folks and that you were safe out there on that ranch, where nothing bad could happen to you."

"Ah," I said thoughtfully, and rubbed the back of my hair, still damp from the shower.

"I was meaning to ask you," McQuaid said. "What did you do to your hair? It looks . . . different."

I raised an eyebrow. "Are you sure you want to know?"

"Well, of course," he said.

But then, when I had told him, all he could do was shake his head. "So it wasn't sunburn."

"No," I said. "I did a stupid thing. But I'm glad I did it. Now, Maddie knows the truth about her birth mother. And there'll be no question about her inheritance."

He shook his head again. "I will never understand," he muttered, "how you and Ruby manage to get yourselves into such *trouble*."

"Listen to the pot calling the kettle black," I retorted.

He eyed me. "Any idea what's going to happen with the arson investigation?"

"Too soon to tell. It'll probably be a week or so before Tom Sullivan comes up with enough forensic evidence to make a case." I got up to refill our soup bowls. "Maybe Pete—he's Ruby's new heartthrob—will have some news for us when he comes for dinner."

McQuaid looked down. "Speaking of news," he said, "I dropped in at Brian's when I was in Austin yesterday. And . . ." He paused.

"And?" I prompted. "I hope he likes his new roommate."

"I'm pretty sure he does," McQuaid said quietly. He lifted his eyes to mine. "Her name is Casey."

"Ah," I said. "That *is* news."

McQuaid reached for my hand. "There's more," he said, and told me.

I sat there for a moment, taking it in. And then I said,

"We'll have to have them for dinner. How about next weekend? I'll email Brian and invite them."

McQuaid cocked his head. "I'm glad you're okay with it. I have to confess that it took me a bit to get used to the idea."

I thought of everything that had happened over the past couple of days, about the many ways that love could go wrong, and how good it felt when love was *right*. I smiled.

"Of course I'm okay," I said. "Brian just needs to know that his folks love him and back him all the way, whatever his choices. He can work out the rest on his own."

McQuaid picked up my hand and kissed it. Then he glanced at his watch. "Omigod, look at the time! I'm supposed to be at the park, helping Blackie with the Lion's Club barbecue!"

Life goes on.

It was two weeks before we could get the gang out to our house for a Saturday night supper under the live oak trees in the backyard. Caitie covered the picnic table with a yellow cloth, filled a red ceramic pitcher with wildflowers and put it in the middle of the table, then set eight places with our favorite plastic picnic plates and yellow paper napkins. Ruby brought an old-fashioned potato salad. Caitie proudly deviled a dozen of her girls' largest and most beautiful eggs. I made a pot of baked beans and baked a rosemary focaccia, my favorite herb flatbread. McQuaid grilled three chickens (*not* Caitie's girls, of course). Cass brought dessert: a sumptuous apple-pecan crisp made with olive oil. Pete brought several bottles of Last Chance wine and a very nice bottle of Last Chance olive oil.

And Brian brought Casey.

I had to agree with McQuaid: she was a very pretty girl, her dark hair sleekly cornrowed, her chocolate skin flawless, her large brown eyes expressive. She was athletic—she and Brian set up the volleyball net in the yard and she proceeded to whip the daylights out of him. And she was doing well, she told me, in her pre-med studies.

"I want to be a GP, not a specialist," she said, in her soft Louisiana accent. "I'm going back home and working with my people."

Brian looked smitten, and confided to me that he'd been nervous about bringing her to the picnic and was relieved that everybody was so welcoming.

"Of course we are," I said. "Your friends are our friends, always."

"Thanks, Mom," he said, and my heart warmed.

As it turned out, Pete did have news, and plenty of it. Sofia had recovered and, after several days in the hospital, was back at the Last Chance, where Maddie had moved her into the ranch house and given her Eliza's bedroom. Sofia had reported to the sheriff that Boyd had come to visit her the night of the fire. She'd told him that Maddie was Eliza's daughter and that marriage between them was impossible. To prove it, she had showed him Maddie's birth certificate. Furious, he had stormed out of the cabin. That was the last she had seen of him.

With this information, the sheriff named Boyd a suspect in the arson investigation, and when the results of the forensic analysis revealed his DNA on the jeans used to start the fire, he was charged with attempted murder and arson. He was in jail, with a bail hearing scheduled for the next week.

"And Maddie?" I asked. "What's happening with her appeal to the probate judge's ruling?"

Pete chuckled. "Tinker Tyson took one look at the birth

certificate you rescued from the fire and reversed himself. Maddie is now the undisputed owner of the Last Chance Olive Ranch."

"Do you suppose," Ruby wondered, "that Maddie and Chet will get together at last?"

With a laugh, Pete cocked his head. "Chet's already made his move. I wouldn't be surprised to hear an announcement any day now."

That was all I needed to know. I lifted my glass.

"Here's to the Last Chance." I caught McQuaid's eye and smiled. "To those who take chances." I glanced around the table. "And to family and good friends."

"To family and good friends," we all said, and raised our glasses.

Recipes

From haute cuisine to robust peasant suppers, olive oil is an essential ingredient in all kinds of recipes. But it's important to obtain the best and freshest oil you can find. Experts tell us that olive oil should be used within two years of its pressing; after that, the healthful nutrients are damaged, the flavor deteriorates, and the oil becomes more acidic. Extra virgin olive oil can last longer because it has a lower acidity to start with. If you can, buy your olive oil fresh from a grower or a specialty retailer with a high turnover, and choose a bottle from the darkest corner of the shelf. In your kitchen, store it on a cool, dry, dark shelf, away from the heat of your stove, and retire it to other uses when it's no longer at its flavorful best.

Chunky Gazpacho

Gazpacho is a soup (usually with a tomato base) made of raw vegetables and herbs and served cold. It originated in the southern Spanish region of Andalusia. It is widely eaten in Spain and Portugal. As a summer soup, it is refreshing and cool.

   1 large can (28 ounces) stewed tomatoes, undrained
   1 green bell pepper, seeded and chopped
   1 cup chopped cucumber, peeled and seeded

Recipes

½ cup chopped red onion
½ cup chopped celery
¼ cup sliced pimento-stuffed green olives
¼ cup fresh arugula, chopped
¼ cup fresh parsley, finely chopped
¼ cup fresh basil, finely chopped
3 cloves garlic, minced
3 tablespoons extra virgin olive oil
2 tablespoons balsamic vinegar
1 tablespoon lemon juice
1 teaspoon soy sauce (or more to taste)
salt and pepper

In a glass bowl, combine tomatoes with the rest of the ingredients. Stir well, breaking up tomatoes. Cover and refrigerate for at least 24 hours and as long as 3 days. Season to taste with salt and pepper. Serve cold. Serves 4.

Sofia's Lemon and Olive Oil Dressing

1 tablespoon salt
3 garlic cloves, minced
½ cup fresh lemon juice
½ cup extra virgin olive oil

Using a mortar and pestle (or the back of a heavy spoon and a small, sturdy bowl), make a paste of the salt and minced garlic. In a 1-cup lidded container, blend lemon juice and olive oil. Add the salt and garlic mixture and put on the lid. Shake well. Use as a dressing for fresh greens, sprinkling optional grated Parmesan or lemon zest on top of salad before tossing.

286

Recipes

Marinated Olives

1½ cups black olives
1½ cups green olives
1 cup olive oil
¼ cup fresh lemon juice
¼ cup orange juice
4 large garlic cloves, thinly sliced
2 tablespoons dried rosemary
3 tablespoons chopped fresh parsley
1 tablespoon grated lemon peel
1 tablespoon grated orange peel
½ teaspoon dried crushed red pepper

Mix all ingredients in a large bowl with a cover. Refrigerate for at least 1 day and up to a week, stirring occasionally. Let stand for 1 hour at room temperature before serving.

Cornish Game Hens with Mushroom-and-Herb Stuffing

2 Cornish game hens
Salt and pepper
2 tablespoons extra virgin olive oil

STUFFING
1 cup wild rice
2 tablespoons butter
10 fresh chanterelle (or your favorite) mushrooms, sliced

4 cloves garlic, finely chopped
¼ cup green onions, chopped
2 tablespoons dried rosemary, finely chopped
2 teaspoons dried thyme

Preheat oven to 375 degrees F. Sprinkle the Cornish hens inside and out with salt and pepper and set aside. Cook the rice according to the directions on the package. Heat butter in a medium skillet. Add the mushrooms, garlic, and green onions and sauté for 5 minutes or so. Add the rosemary and thyme and mix well. Add the mushroom-onion-herb mixture to the rice and blend. Season with salt and pepper to taste. Stuff each hen with the rice-and-mushroom mixture and tie the legs together with string. Brush the birds with olive oil. Bake until the internal temperature reaches 165 degrees F (40–45 minutes), basting occasionally. Let the hens sit for 5–10 minutes before cutting the string and serving.

Andrea's Lemon Olive Oil Cake

Yes, you *can* use olive oil in a cake! This rustic cake is light and lemony—and extra lovely with a bit of lemon verbena. If you don't have that herb in your garden, try one of the other lemon herbs: lemon thyme, lemon balm, or lemon basil. For the oil, you can use either extra virgin, regular, or light olive oil. Extra virgin yields a stronger flavor.

1 cup flour
2 teaspoons lemon zest

2 teaspoons finely chopped fresh lemon verbena
   leaves (can be omitted)
4 large eggs, separated
¾ cup sugar (divided into ½ cup and ¼ cup
   portions)
¾ cup olive oil
1½ tablespoons lemon juice
½ teaspoon salt

FOR GLAZE
2–3 tablespoons lemon juice
2 cups sifted powdered sugar
thin lemon slices for garnish

Preheat oven to 350 degrees F. Spray a 9-inch springform
pan with cooking spray. (If you don't have a springform
pan, a 9x13-inch glass oven dish will do.) In a small bowl,
mix flour, lemon zest, and lemon verbena and set aside.
With an electric mixer, in a large bowl, beat together egg
yolks and ½ cup sugar until thick and pale, about 3 minutes. Add olive oil and lemon juice, beating until just combined (mixture may appear slightly curdled). Using a
spatula, fold in flour mixture until just combined. In a
separate large bowl, beat egg whites with ½ teaspoon salt
until foamy, then gradually add ¼ cup sugar. Continue to
beat until egg whites just hold soft peaks, about 3 minutes.
Gently fold egg whites into the egg yolk mixture, one-third
at a time. Pour batter into prepared pan. Bake until golden
and a toothpick inserted into the center comes out clean,
30–35 minutes. Let cool for 10 minutes, then remove the
sides of the springform pan. Cool completely, then remove
bottom of pan and transfer to a serving plate. For glaze,

mix lemon juice and powdered sugar. Pour over cooled cake. Garnish with twisted lemon slices. This cake keeps well for several days.

China's Rosemary Focaccia

Focaccia is a flat Italian peasant bread, rather like a very thick pizza crust. For toppings, you can use onions, cheese, meat, or chopped veggies.

    1 (¼ ounce) package active dry yeast
    ¾ cup warm water
    3 cups all-purpose flour
    1 teaspoon salt
    6 tablespoons olive oil
    coarse salt
    2 tablespoons finely minced fresh rosemary

In a large bowl, dissolve the yeast in ½ cup of the warm water, and let sit 10 minutes until bubbly. Add flour, salt, and warm remaining water. Mix thoroughly with a wooden spoon and then your hands. Transfer to a floured work surface and knead until smooth (3–4 minutes). Place in an oiled bowl, cover with a damp towel, and let rise until doubled, about 1½ hours.

Preheat the oven to 425 degrees F. Punch dough down and place on an oiled baking sheet, forming into a rectangle about 9x13 inches. Press your fingertips into the surface to create dimples, then drizzle with the oil and sprinkle with coarse salt and rosemary. Bake about 20 minutes or until golden. Serves four—okay to double.

Recipes

Cass's Apple-Pecan Crisp

Olive oil—especially a mild-flavored variety—can be substituted for butter or margarine in most recipes for baked foods. It goes well with fruit, especially citrus, and chocolate. Here is a basic substitution guide:

- ¼ cup plus 2 tablespoons of olive oil for ½ cup of butter or margarine
- ½ cup of olive oil for ⅔ cup of butter
- ¾ cup plus 1 tablespoon of olive oil for 1 cup of butter

CRISP TOPPING
- 1 cup flour
- ½ cup rolled oats
- ⅓ cup brown sugar
- ½ teaspoon cinnamon
- ½ teaspoon nutmeg
- ¼ teaspoon ground cloves
- ¼ teaspoon salt
- ⅓ cup olive oil
- ½ cup chopped pecans (if you wish, substitute walnuts or almonds)

Combine the flour, oats, brown sugar, cinnamon, nutmeg, cloves, and salt in a bowl. Add the olive oil and stir with a fork until the mixture is crumbly. Stir in the chopped pecans.

APPLE FILLING
2½ pounds apples (about 6)
4 tablespoons lemon juice
1 tablespoon flour
2 teaspoons cinnamon
1 teaspoon allspice
1 teaspoon ground ginger
½ cup brown sugar

Preheat oven to 350 degrees F. Peel and core the apples. Slice thin. Combine in a bowl with the lemon juice, flour, cinnamon, allspice, ginger, and brown sugar. Spread the apple mixture in an oiled 12-inch baking dish and crumble the topping mixture on top. Pat it down gently. (The filling will shrink during baking.) Bake until topping is golden and filling bubbles, about 50 minutes. Serve hot or cold.

Ready to find
your next great read?

Let us help.

Visit prh.com/nextread